OSHO

THE LUMINOUS REBEL

Life Story of a Maverick Mystic

OSHO

THE LUMINOUS REBEL

Life Story of a Maverick Mystic

Vasant Joshi, PhD

wisdom
tree

First published 2010
Reprinted 2011, 2012, 2013

ISBN 978-81-8328-154-6

Published by
Wisdom Tree
4779/23, Ansari Road
Darya Ganj, New Delhi-2
Ph.: 23247966/67/68
wisdomtreebooks@gmail.com

Printed in India

I bow at the feet of
my beloved
master Osho
with a deep rejoicing gratitude for
his blessings and for showing
me the way.

CONTENTS

PREFACE

Lama Karmapa, late head of the Kargyupta, (or Red Hat) Sect of Tibetan Buddhism says, 'Osho is the greatest incarnation after Buddha in India. He is a living Buddha.'

Indeed, Osho offers both a seer's enlightened vision and a brilliantly constructive blueprint for a new humankind and a new world.

Osho is not a person, Osho is a phenomenon. One cannot comprehend his being and hence it is not possible to describe him in words. Osho is like the sun—radiant, powerful, luminous and nourishing. Such as we can see everything in the light spread by the sun we cannot see the sun through our eyes; similarly, one can see the reality of life in the light of Osho but one cannot actually *see* him.

Osho is the 'awakened one', the 'enlightened one'—one who has seen 'that which is' through pure consciousness and not through any mental projection. He shows that misery is the creation of the mind, and that the mind *can* be transcended. Even though the story of his extraordinary life is beyond verbal description, what little we may know of it can awaken us to find the same source of joy and divinity, peace and creativity that lies within us.

Osho is a rebel, not a non-conformist. He is not the one who, like the reactionaries, goes from one extreme to another. He is always in a balanced state. Osho is not a rebel as defined in the dictionary in the sense of one who is 'fighting back', or 'fighting against'. Indeed, Osho's rebellion is of that nature, but 'fighting back' gives only half of the picture, it is incomplete. Osho not only fought against all that is wrong, he not only dismantled the old, the rotten, and the irrelevant, but he also brought a new perspective, a new light in which we can see ourselves and the world around us with greater clarity and understanding. He completed the other half of the rebellion; he created a new vision for the entire humanity so that it may live a better life. This is why Osho is a self-defining phenomenon—he is his own definition. While on the one hand his rebellion consists of destroying the schizophrenic state of humanity—the state of division and dichotomy created between matter and spirit, body and consciousness, and on the other hand he shared an all inclusive enlightened vision of life in its totality guided by awareness and understanding, love and meditation, Zorba and Buddha.

He has no map, no guide; every moment is new to him. Every moment he arrives at a new space, at new experience, arrives at his own truth and his own vision. Truly, his life and work are *leela*. A *leela* is where one cannot make any logical sense out of it, it is beyond logic and rationalism—it is spontaneous, existential, trans-rational Divine Play of Absolute Consciousness.

Osho is a rebel because he challenges the conventional ways and means of mankind by doing what is forbidden by the society, in his own way, in his own time, and at the place of his choosing. A rebel does not fear whether what he does is forbidden; because he does it in the interest of the future of mankind. In fact a rebel shows, as Osho has shown through the power of his vision, that, *he is the future* of mankind.

A rebel is always alone in his fight against the false, the life negative, and the hypocritical. Osho says, 'I am in the majority of one.' We cannot put him into any category. He declares: 'I am a category by myself.' All rebels are a category by themselves—Buddha, Socrates, Jesus, Kabir, Meera—all are mystics, unique in their rebellion and in their vision. Osho calls such rebels 'the very salt of the earth'.

Osho is basically a scientist of the soul. He is not a man of 'religion' but his very being is a reflection of *religiousness*. He does not recommend that we go in search of God, but rather through meditation, love, and awareness we can spread godliness all around us. Hence, his message is: be free from the clutches of the past, discover your own path and move on with courage and commitment.

'One man against the whole history of humanity,' as Osho describes himself, it follows fairly naturally that he will be the most misunderstood. He says, 'People have always misunderstood me—perhaps that is my destiny.' (*Sat Chit Anand*). And mostly the misunderstanding arises because most people only see one snapshot of what is really an adventure movie. They see a pool rather than a river of consciousness. As time goes by, and our understanding of the full implications of that river increases, what is most striking is the *process*.

Yes, the essential was always there, is always there. But the form was tailored to the needs of the moment: what would best help his listeners at that moment to move on, to move away from that 'whole history', in which he could see people trapped, towards what he describes as the possibility of a 'Golden Future'.

In the earlier days he is projected as another J. Krishnamurti—against masters, disciples, techniques and so on. But he is also recognised as a firebrand who berates the conventional wisdom of his time—whether it was Marx or Gandhi, materialism or socialism. However, it seems Osho discovers that the people who will understand him are trapped in the religions. So he takes up religion.

I have heard a funny story of Osho turning up to talk on Krishna in Mumbai (then Bombay) in the late sixties. The doorman asked in surprise if it were true he was talking on Krishna, because 'you were here two years ago talking against Krishna.'

Osho replied, 'Yes, but if I speak against Krishna, nobody comes, so I am speaking in favour of Krishna. And if you repeat this conversation, I will deny it!'

So rather than staying with doubt, as J. Krishnamurti did, Osho begins with trust first as the foundation of a really intelligent doubt. But he says of this period and opens his heart as follows:

'...But now I am simply speaking the truth that is mine, because now I can trust that you will understand, that you don't need some via media: Jesus, Mahavira, Buddha, Krishna. I can talk to you directly, immediately. I don't need to play a game with words.

'...The game that I had to play was a necessary evil; otherwise it would not have been possible to find you. Do you think you would have come to an atheist, an amoralist, a godless, irreligious person? If you ask yourself that question you will understand why I had to use religion and religious terminology. I was using it against myself just for you. It was for your sake that I have been doing that whole number, but now there is no need.'

—From Personality to Individuality

So he plays the role of a master, initiates disciples, sometimes on railway stations, makes a satire out of our conditioning around *sannyas*, accepts the name Bhagwan to infuriate all, and then one day simply says, 'The joke is over.'

Of course, Osho has always insisted that he has no followers, only fellow travellers, but following is so easy and cozy. Then it is not our responsibility...One can put the responsibility on someone else, God, Guru, Buddha, Jesus whatever. But slowly and inexorably Osho withdraws his support to our projections, like a bird luring its young from the nest. And that would be the acid test. Creating something that depended on Osho's presence was one thing. To create something that is self-regenerating, self-growing, without any outer help, relying only on each individual's inner sources? Who would have thought it possible that today his work expands 'beyond our minds' as he forecast?

And then one day, suddenly he leaves. It was time to stand alone. His view is not to be too concerned with what he says but rather what he indicates. He leaves us alone, absolutely alone, so that we don't take anybody's help, don't cling to any prophet, so that we don't think that Gautam Buddha or Jesus is going to save us. Left utterly alone we are bound to find our innermost centre. He makes it clear:

'There is no way, nowhere to go, no advisor, no teacher, no master. It seems hard, it seems harsh, but I am doing it because I love you, and the people who have not done it have not loved you at all. They loved themselves and they loved to have a big crowd around themselves—the bigger the crowd, the more they feel nourished in their egos.

'That's why I called even enlightenment the last game. The sooner you drop it, the better. Why not just simply be? Why unnecessarily hurry here and there? You are what existence wants you to be. Just relax.'

—Om Mani Padme Hum

I am immensely grateful to Osho's loving parents, relatives, friends and disciples for their help and cooperation in putting this life story together. I am also very grateful to my friends and fellow travellers, Jayesh, Amrito, Neelam, Anando and Chaitanya Keerti who spared their precious time for giving invaluable feedback reading the manuscript. I am, in particular, greatly indebted to Prem Amrito (Dr George Meredith), Osho's personal physician and one of his caretakers, for allowing me to include his observations, particularly, the details of Osho's health are entirely based on his account.

I have incorporated in this book the account of Osho's life which was covered in the earlier work, *The Awakened One: Life and Work of Bhagwan Shree Rajneesh*. The book was published by Harper and Row, San Francisco 1983.

It has indeed been a highly rewarding experience writing this story—it carried a feeling of both joy and blessing. The book is not really a biography of Osho. The intent was never to bring every piece of detail from Osho's incredible oceanic life—that would have been foolhardy. The effort was more like weaving a piece of cloth with threads from my heart. It never escaped from my mind the challenging reality that writing this story was more like…as so beautifully expressed by William Blake:

To see a World in a grain of Sand
And a Heaven in a Wild Flower
Hold Infinity in the palm of your hand
And Eternity in an Hour.

I express my gratitude to Shobit Arya, publisher of Wisdom Tree for taking personal interest in publishing this story. Also, I am grateful to Nandita Jaishankar and Ankita A. Talwar, for editing the text with such care.

Dr Vasant Joshi

August 2009

I Belong to Eternity...Osho

I am not part of any movement.

What I am doing is something eternal.

It has been going on since the first man appeared on the earth, and it will continue to the last man. It is not a movement, it is the very core of evolution...

I am part of the eternal evolution of man.

The search for truth is neither new nor old. The search for your own being has nothing to do with time. It is non-temporal.

I may be gone, but what I am doing is going to continue. Somebody else will be doing it. I was not here and somebody else was doing it. Nobody is a founder in it nobody is a leader in it. It is such a vast phenomenon that many enlightened people have appeared, helped and disappeared.

But their help has brought humanity a little higher, made humanity a little better, a little more human. They have left the world a little more beautiful than they had found it.

It is a great contentment to leave the world a little better. More than that is asking too much. The world is too big; a single human individual is too small. If he can leave just a few touches to the painting, which for millions of years has been made by evolution, that's enough. Just a few touches...a little more perfection, a little more clarity.

I am not part of any fashion, any movement. I belong to eternity, and I would like you also to belong to eternity, not to a passing phase.

—*Socrates Poisoned Again After 25 Centuries*

WHO IS OSHO?

An absence of vision seems to have gripped the globe's most prominent nations…It has become painfully and globally evident of late: a failure by heads of government, sometimes entire parties and democratic systems, to come to grip with those issues that the governed consider most urgent… Clearly, the world needs a new vision.

—*Time* magazine, 12 July 1993

To millions of his admirers, disciples and devotees across the world he was simply known as 'Osho'. In India, and later to the world, he was also known as 'Acharya Rajneesh' and as 'Bhagwan Shree Rajneesh'. As explained by Osho himself, the name, derived from William James' word 'oceanic'—that which dissolves into the ocean—goes a step ahead of its literal meaning. Whereas 'oceanic' describes the experience, 'Osho' describes the one who goes through the experience. Osho means one who has dissolved into the universal ocean of consciousness and has lost his separate entity in the same way a dew drop disappears into the ocean. 'Osho' has also been used historically in the Far East meaning 'The Blessed One, on Whom the Sky Showers Flowers'.

Twenty-five centuries after Gautam Buddha, Osho turned the wheel of dharma once again to raise human consciousness. It is not easy to write about him. He is like a vast space containing all dualities, all diversities and all contradictions. He radiates consciousness which brings light to those who are groping in the dark. He symbolises spirituality in its ultimate glory. For the strife-ridden humanity, Osho is increasingly seen as perhaps the only alternative for creating a peaceful and wholesome society. His vision and his work exemplify a great spiritual revolution, an incredible transformation in the lives of individuals who care to grow intellectually and find happiness. He offers clarity and confidence, love and compassion, understanding and awareness to the entire humanity which is today beleaguered with destruction, pain and suffering.

Osho's revolutionary message comes from his own realisation of truth. Hence, his words have an authenticity and sharpness that have the power to bring about a total transformation in anyone who is willing to open up to him. Osho is different from almost all other self-realised, enlightened masters. He is perhaps the first among them who has succeeded in making religion contemporary and applicable to everyone, at every moment.

Often described as a rebel, an iconoclast, an enlightened mystic, absurd, anarchist, prolific author, outrageous, anti-Christ, spiritual terrorist, an intellectual giant, Osho is all this and more, simply because he is not part of any tradition, school of philosophy, or religion. 'I am the beginning of a totally new religious consciousness,' he declares. 'Please don't connect me with past; it is not even worth remembering.' He is Buddha, Lao Tzu, Krishna, Jesus, Kabir, Gurdjieff and more all rolled in one.

Osho has remained controversial throughout his life, just like other enlightened mystics. They have been controversial because their way of life is the way of change and transformation, which a society resists. Society prefers the status quo; it is at ease with the familiar. Hence the words and deeds of an enlightened master are not acceptable. It is this non-acceptance of the enlightened master's knowledge that creates controversy.

Also, as Osho says: 'I have not come to teach, I have come to awaken.' A teacher can never create a controversy because he is comfortable with the status quo; he is willing to follow the beaten path. A teacher says and does whatever seems acceptable to society. He has nothing to offer of his own, nor a knowledge that comes out of his own experience. It is only a master, such as Osho, who can bring us out of our age-old conditioning. He is here to awaken us from our religious and social hypnosis. He makes us aware of our original reality, to the reality around us, and to the reality of our future evolution as an enlightened being. For this, he provokes us and creates a friction of energy so that humanity can come out of its unconscious state. With regard to Osho, the controversy is more intense because he speaks his truth against governments, religions and old beliefs publicly and without fear. He declares that he is 'a category in himself'.

Osho is an enlightened, fiery mystic who demolished age-old beliefs, traditions and teachings. 'I teach utter rebellion,' he declares, 'I am not here to compromise. I have decided to be utterly honest and truthful whatsoever the cost.' In his discourses, he speaks about the need for a 'new man', a 'new mankind' or a 'new humanity'. Osho emphasises the fact that because we are a divided humanity, we are also a wounded one. To him, the divisions of mankind in East and West, North or South are meaningless. The world for him was essentially one and all such divisions were based on human ignorance. He would like to see the East and the West merge together, enriching each other. Only there, he says, lies the possibility for a truly lasting peace and harmony. In his vision of a new man and a new humanity there is no room for divisions. He says, 'Only a whole person can be a holy person.' According to Osho:

'The new man will not be either/or; he will be both/and. The new man will be earthly and divine, worldly and other-worldly. The new man will accept his totality and he will live it without any inner division, he will not be split. His god will not be opposed to the devil, his morality will not be opposed to immorality; he will know no opposition. He will transcend duality, he will not be schizophrenic. With the new man there will come a new world, because the new man will perceive in a qualitatively different way and he will live a totally different life which has not been lived yet. He will be a mystic, a poet, a scientist, all together.'

Similarly, Osho also saw the need to synthesise science and consciousness. He wanted to see a world where science can work not for destruction but for enhancing the human consciousness. In fact, he proposed that consciousness must guide the scientific endeavour.

Osho's *sannyasins* are often branded as a 'cult' and Osho is ludicrously lumped together with cult leaders such as Revered Jim Jones and Koresh. This is far from truth. Jim Jones and Koresh, both Christians, were obsessed with glory in death, resurrection and second coming. They fanatically believed in biblical prophesies and used their fanaticism in recruiting and controlling their followers. Both Jim Jones and Koresh, were products of blind faith, greed and ambition. They perhaps were seeking attention and recognition at any cost. Osho did not see his *sannyasins* as followers but as friends and fellow travellers. His vision of *sannyas* is based on the individual's freedom to be, to explore, experiment and enquire. He asks them neither to believe or disbelieve, but only to search for the truth that would bring light and joy in their lives. For Osho, a *sannyasin* is full of reverence for life. A *sannyasin* is one who lives naturally, one who is open to life in all its manifestations. A *sannyasin* is not bothered whether God is or not, his effort is to bring what Osho calls 'godliness', into life—a quality of awareness and compassion, love and celebration. A *sannyasin* cares for this world so much that he would create paradise on earth rather than leave the earth in search of a fictitious paradise. Osho's message is loud and clear: 'I don't want my people to leave the world…it is time that people should be strong enough in their awareness so they can remain in the society without compromising. Although it is far more difficult, it is a great challenge to live in society and not be part of it, to live in society but not allow society to live in you. That is my special contribution to the religious experience and to the rebellious human beings.'

Osho does not propagate changing society or the world at large, because, for him there is no society, only individuals. 'What we need is a totally different kind of change—a change in the heart of the individual… Instead of thinking in terms of revolution and changing the society, its structure, we should think more of meditation and changing the individual...,' he says. Those who have come to Osho, therefore, are individuals; they are seekers in need of change and transformation. They are ready to face problems that society avoids. They have the courage to face the illnesses society has been teaching them to hide or repress. Meditation works as the way for transformation, and is the very foundation of Osho's vision. In his words:

'The world can achieve harmony if meditation is spread far and wide, and people are brought to consciousness within themselves. This will be a totally different dimension to work with—not revolution, but meditation, transformation. And it is not as difficult as people think. It is only a question of understanding the value of meditation. My effort is to make meditation a science so it is not something to do with religion. Then anybody can practise it—whether he is Hindu or a Christian or a Jew or a Mohammedan, it doesn't matter...Meditation has to become almost like a wildfire. Then there is some hope.'

Meditation, *sannyas*, the commune, Rajneeshpuram, the world tour—these have all been powerful dimensions of Osho's work. Born out of love and compassion, experiment and dynamism, these are existential truths meant to wake up humanity. What has happened around Osho is not a movement, and certainly not a 'new religious movement'. Osho has not given us a 'new religion', only a new religious consciousness. He denies being a leader of any movement or even a part of any movement. 'I am not part of any movement', says Osho. 'What I am doing is something eternal. It has been going on since the first man appeared on earth and it will continue to the last man. It is not a movement, it is the very core of evolution.'

He made it known to all that the energy field he created, with his *sannyasins* for raising human consciousness would become stronger after him. Seekers from around the world who visit this campus, without exception, are able to experience the truth of this.

Osho has a vision. And it is *critical* that we pay attention to his vision of compassion and peace, love and infinite creativity, instead of waiting for the governments, politicians and religious preachers to solve our problems. It is too early to make any appraisal of Osho's contribution to humanity. But he clearly states what he has done. 'People may understand today or tomorrow or day after tomorrow—that doesn't matter—but one day they will understand it. One thing I can say that, whatever I am saying is going to be the future philosophy, the future religion, of the whole humanity.'

Just a few weeks before leaving his body on 19 January 1990, Osho was asked what would happen to his work when he was gone.

'My trust in existence is absolute. If there is any truth in what I am saying, it will survive…The people who remain interested in my work will be simply carrying the torch, but not imposing anything on anyone…I will remain a source of inspiration to my people. And that's what most sannyasins will feel. I want them to grow on their own qualities like love, around which no church can be created; like awareness, which is nobody's monopoly; like celebration, rejoicing, and maintaining fresh, childlike eyes…I want my people to know themselves, not to be according to someone else. And the way is in.'

Excerpts from:

Dimensions Beyond the Known
Darshan Diaries: Zorba the Buddha
The Invitation
Light on the Path
The Path of the Mystic

1

THE FAMILY

Osho's father, Babulal (affectionately also called Dadda which means an elder brother), was born in Timarni, a small town in Madhya Pradesh, in 1908. Babulal's forefathers belonged to the Digambara sect of the Jain religion. They (Babulal's paternal side) were followers of a small sect called Taran Panth. The sect was founded in the sixteenth century by a saint named Taran Swami, who was a contemporary of the Indian saints Kabir and Nanak. Taran Swami, a Digambara Jain himself, came from the Parwar sect of Digambars (Parwar sect is primarily located in Madhya Pradesh). Taran Swami opposed idol worship which was widely prevalent among Digambara Jains. He preached worship of the formless. He criticised the emphasis Digambara Jains placed on materialism and exhorted them, instead, to turn towards spirituality taught by Mahavir, founder of the Jain religion. For his views, Taran Swami, had to face a lot of harassment by the society. However, a few Jains and non-Jains as well, accepted Taran Swami's teachings and took him as their guru. Dadda's forefathers were amongst them.

Taran Swami's teachings are recorded in fourteen books. It is said that Osho, who read his books, in childhood, was inspired by his teachings to some extent.

Osho's grandfather came from a large family that originally belonged to a small town called Basoda. Basoda was hit by plague and the entire population was exposed to the epidemic. The family also lost a few members in the plague. Many, including Dadda's father and uncle, escaped with their families to Timarni where the in-laws of Dadda's uncle lived. One of Dadda's aunts also lived in Timarni. She loaned Dadda's father a few rupees to help him buy cloth with which he started a small business of his own. He would go on his horse from village to village to sell cloth. Later, the same aunt arranged Dadda's father's marriage and also found him a rented house to live in.

As the family grew, their financial situation became even more strained. Dadda's father decided to leave Timarni and try his luck elsewhere. One day he loaded his cart with all their belongings and set out with the family to Kuchwada, a small town in Madhya Pradesh, where the parents of his wife lived. Between Timarni and Kuchwada lay the town of Gadarwara. Though the town was not very big, it was quite prosperous—it was the biggest grain-producing centre in the area, at that time. Dadda's father decided to try his business in this town, so in 1934 they settled down in Gadarwara (Osho was already three years old by then).

Dadda and his father worked hard to make their cloth business a success. Osho's grandfather enjoyed his business and maintained the human touch in his dealings. Osho has very fond memories of it:

'I remember my old grandfather. He was a cloth merchant and I and my whole family were puzzled because he enjoyed it so much. For hours together it was a game with the customers. If something was worth ten rupees, he would ask fifty rupees for it, and he knew this was absurd. And his customers knew it too; they knew that it must be near about ten rupees, and they would start from two rupees. Then a long haggling would follow—hours together. My father and my uncles would get angry...But he (grandfather) had his own customers. When they came, they would ask,

"Where is Dada, Where is grandfather? Because with him it is a game, a play, whether we lose one rupee or two, whether it is more or less, that is not the point!" They (customers) enjoyed it.'

Osho's life has been greatly influenced by people in the family. Both of Dadda's brothers, Amritlal and Shikharchand, the youngest, have been important in Osho's life. Amritlal's literary knowledge and activities made him an early model for Osho, who began to express himself through poetry. However, Osho was closer to his younger uncle, Shikharchand. Shikharchand became an active member of the Congress party and was inspired by its progressive thinking. He believed in the concept of socialism and was responsible for implementing them in Gadarwara. The ideas had an effect on young Osho too. With Shikharchand he organised several group meetings of young men and inspired them to follow socialistic ideas. Because of his active participation in political movements, Shikharchand could not continue his studies beyond high school. He later became a disciple of Osho, his own nephew.

But of the greatest influences in Osho's life was perhaps his father, Dadda. Osho often used his father's qualities as examples in his lectures. His father was a very lovable man. He was well known in Gadarwara for the smooth handling of his multiple roles as the head of his family, businessman and a responsible citizen of Gadarwara. His simplicity, kindness, wisdom and an endearing sense of humour came through so clearly that anyone who met him soon got impressed.

Dadda was interested in pursuing formal education himself, but had to give up studies after fourth grade in order to help his father in business. However, he strongly encouraged his two younger brothers to continue their schooling—even against the wishes of his father who wanted them to join the family business. Dadda secretly provided money to Amritlal so that he could finish high school and move to the city of Jabalpur for his college education. This lead to trouble in the family. In 1932, Amritlal took part in India's independence movement led by Mahatama Gandhi and was imprisoned. When Dadda's father and other family members heard about it, they were shocked—the very idea of some one in the family going to prison caused tremendous uproar and unhappiness. Osho's grandfather was very angry and blamed Dadda for it—if Dadda had not helped him, Amritlal would not be in prison, he claimed. But Dadda remained determined and continued encouraging others to pursue education. In fact, in spite of all the opposition, he helped his children earn degrees in medicine, engineering and science.

Dadda's two qualities were remarkable—one was his love and deep respect for nature. His routine included early morning walks alongside the river and later swimming in it for hours. Osho's earliest memories of his father are associated with those daily walks with him. He recounts:

'The first thing I remember about him is that he would wake me up at three o'clock in the morning. I was very young then, when three o'clock was a sleeping time…He would wake me at three o'clock and take me for a walk. That was his first gift to me—the brahma mahurta (the holy time, early before sunrise). In the beginning it bothered me a lot. I used to practically drag behind him…but gradually I began to see and feel the beauty of early morning hours. Gradually I came to realise that the moments of the early morning are not meant to be lost. Perhaps God is never so close to the earth at any other time as he is during these early morning moments.'

Another quality that made Dadda such a lovable man was his friendly attitude and generosity towards others. Osho fondly remembers his father's lavish spending on friends and guests, even though he was not a wealthy man himself. Every day he had guests for dinner, even if it meant borrowing money. His object in life seemed to be sharing. Dadda was also actively involved in helping needy people, financially or any way that he could. He had a progressive mind and was prepared to depart from social norms even at the risk of getting ostracised.

But above all, Dadda was a deeply spiritual man. According to Amritlal, Dadda was well respected for his religious mind. Dadda used to visit temples, observe fasts and read holy scriptures as well. But this was just a part of his quest for spirituality. Inwardly, his search continued for that which cannot be confined to a temple, book, or a ritual. He spent the last ten years of his life in meditating regularly from three to six o'clock in the morning. He often went so deep into meditation that Osho's mother would get worried and try to wake him up in time for Osho's morning discourse which used to happen at eight o'clock (Dadda lived his last years at the Osho Commune in Pune). On several occasions Dadda remained in deep meditation for hours together and missed the discourse.

As for Osho's mother, Saraswati, she was always seen as a kind hostess, respected for her loving hospitality and also for being a perfect match to her husband who tremendously enjoyed entertaining friends, relatives, and others. She was a simple person and left her body as an enlightened being on 17 May 1997.

During her lifetime, people would ask her questions about Osho and his life when he was young, and she would answer them openly and unassumingly. She expressed her feelings in the following words about the questions she was continually asked.

'I wonder why he (Osho) took birth in this simple family (of ours), because people go on asking so many meaningful questions, and Osho talks with such wisdom…and (here) we are full of amazement at why should he have taken birth in this family! If we had been more talented parents we could have described so many things about (his life)…would have complimented him in so many ways. But we cannot. We feel stunned when these questions come. People pour questions, but we do not feel capable of answering them.' [1]

Saraswati was an only child and hence very dear to her parents. They lived in Kuchwada, a small farming village, located in the beautiful valley of the Vindhya mountains in Madhya Pradesh. Her father was a decently wealthy person with a kind disposition. In addition to farming, he owned a small grocery store as well. In those days, child marriages were common in India and Osho's mother was married when she was a mere child. Osho recounts:

'When my mother got married, she was only seven years old. I was asking her again and again, "Tell me how you felt?" She said, "I didn't know what was happening. I was simply joyous that something was happening. I used

to run out to see what was happening, and they would pull me back inside the house. And they locked me in on the day when the real ceremony was going to happen, because I was so much interested in the bands and the music and the horses (As the tradition went, it is considered inauspicious for the bride to see the bridegroom before the nuptial rites were over). And the people were coming..." And I asked my father, "What did you feel?" He said, "I don't know—I just enjoyed the horse ride." (The bridegroom was brought on horseback to the bride's home in a procession with local bands providing the music).'

It was from the union of these two loving, simple and honest people that on 11 December 1931 Saraswati gave birth to a very beautiful, healthy boy, at her parents' home in Kuchwada.

Osho's mother recounts that she got an indication of her son being a great soul a few days before his birth. When she was in her sixth month, a cousin of her's came to take her to Kuchwada for delivery. Monsoon at the time was at its peak and the River Narmada, which runs between Timarni and Kuchwada, was flooding its banks. The boatman refused to take them across the rising river.

Helpless, Osho's mother and her cousin spent three days near the river waiting for the waters to recede. On the third day a tall and impressive looking monk passed by and saw them waiting. The monk told the still reluctant boatman that in the womb of the lady was a great soul waiting to be born. He assured the boatman that he and his passengers would remain safe because of this soul and hence he should take both of them across without any fear. The boatman put his faith in the monk and took them across the dangerously high river. The monk's words came true. Everyone crossed the river without any harm or difficulty.

Saraswati was extremely happy at the birth of her son. Her parents too were overjoyed, especially the new grandfather. The grace and beauty of the child convinced the grandfather that a king of some past life had taken birth in their family and so he spontaneously named him 'Raja', meaning 'king'.

Saraswati's father loved his grandson so much that he would not allow her to take him back to Timarni, where she lived with Dadda and his father's family in their struggling cloth business. As Osho describes it, 'My early childhood passed at the house of my maternal grandparents and I had great love for them…They were feeling very lonely, so they wanted to bring me up. Therefore, I stayed with them up to seven years of age. I had taken them as my mother and father. They were very rich and had all possible conveniences. Therefore, I was brought up like a prince. I came in touch with my father and mother only after the death of my maternal grandparents…I had loved only them, and received love only from them.'

Whenever Raja (Osho) was taken to Timarni to visit his father and his paternal family, it was a joyous occasion for them. Osho's youngest uncle, Shikharchand, recounted the wonderful experience when Raja was brought to Timarni for the first time. Shikharchand was the first one to receive and hold the six month old child. He greeted the beautiful baby with immense joy. Later he gave Raja a new name: Rajneesh Chandra Mohan. Until his enrollment in school, the boy was called Raja; after that he adopted his formal name as Rajneesh.

The birth of Osho was not an ordinary event. It was the birth of a holy soul who had walked on this earth before in search of the truth. His last birth was 700 years ago in the mountains where he had a school that attracted disciples from various traditions and paths from faraway lands.

The master (Osho in his previous birth) then had lived to be one hundred and six years old. Prior to his death he had entered into a twenty-one day fast to achieve enlightenment. But he had the option of taking one more birth before finally disappearing in the eternal. He looked at his family of disciples; there were many who were still on their way to understanding the Truth, needing help. He also saw great potential in bringing about a synthesis between East and West, body and soul, materialism and spiritualism. He saw the possibility of creating a new man—a man of the future who was totally unattached to the past. He, who had come so close to the ultimate achievement for which he had continuously worked hard for so many past lives, decided to come back again into a human body, out of pure love and compassion for his people. He promised his disciples that he would return and share his Truth with them and bring their consciousness to a state of awakening.

The fascinating account of Osho's previous birth came to light accidentally; Osho himself had not mentioned it. Years ago when his mother was visiting Mr Ramlal Pungalia, a disciple of Osho, in Pune, he asked her if she remembered anything peculiar about her son's childhood. She told him that immediately after his birth, Osho did not cry or take any milk for three days, which was very unlike other infants.

I raised the same question once again to Osho's mother during my interviews with her in October 1979, and asked if she recalled anything more than what she had related earlier to Mr Pungalia. She described the incident in the following words: 'Yes, he did not take milk for three days. I was very much worried, but did not know what to do. My mother was looking after him. She kept feeding him water and told me not to worry. On the fourth day, after my mother gave him a good bath, he started taking milk.' I asked her if during those three days the child showed signs of any discomfort? She replied, 'Not at all, his health remained normal all through those three days.'

Osho later explained this unusual circumstance, himself:

'This is true. Seven hundred years ago, in my previous life, there was a spiritual practice of twenty-one days, to be done before death. I was to give up my body after a total fast of twenty-one days, but I could not complete those twenty-one days...When only three days remained in that life, I was killed...and those three days were omitted. In this life, those three days were completed (by taking milk only on the fourth day).'

The killing, according to Osho, was not due to any enmity or hostility. 'I have told many times in various discussions,' says Osho, 'that just as Judas tried for a long time to kill Jesus, though Judas had no enmity with Jesus, the person who killed me had no enmity with me, though he was taken to be and was treated as an enemy.' Osho continues:

'That killing became valuable. At the time of death, those three days were left. After all my strenuous efforts for enlightenment during that life, I was able to achieve in this life, after a period of twenty-one years, that which would have been possible to achieve during those three days. For each of those three days in that life, I had to spend seven years in this life.'

The account of Osho's previous life opens up the whole issue of whether or not there is rebirth after death, or whether there is any basis in the theory of reincarnation. Osho's explanation of it is based on his personal experience. This makes it significant to those walking on the spiritual path and also to those who are working in the areas of parapsychology and altered states of consciousness.

How is a person reborn again into a new body? How is a Buddha reborn? How was Osho reborn? How did he measure the space of time between his last birth and this one to be of seven hundred years? These are some questions to which Osho has given elaborate answers. 'I have an insider's view,' says Osho. 'A Buddha has an insider's view. When a man like Buddha is born, he is born perfectly aware. When a man like Buddha is in the womb, he is aware.'

As per Osho, death normally occurs in a state of unconsciousness; a state in which the dying person is totally incapable of experiencing or witnessing the occurrence of death. Witnessing it is possible only if one has experienced deep meditation, where one can see his body separate from the consciousness. Osho explains how it is to die and be reborn in full awareness:

'If you can die in your current life fully aware, not becoming unconscious when you die—you see every phase of death, you hear every step and remain perfectly aware that the body is dying, the mind is disappearing—then suddenly you see that you are not in the body and consciousness has left the body. You can see the dead body lying there and you are floating around the body... If you can be aware while you are dying, this is one part of birth, one aspect. If in this one aspect you are aware, you will be aware *when you take conception. You will float around a couple making love and you will be perfectly aware. You will enter into the womb perfectly aware. The child is conceived aware of what is happening.*

'...For nine months in the mother's womb you will be aware. Not only will you be aware, but when a child like Buddha is in the womb of the mother, the quality of the mother changes. She becomes more aware too... the mother immediately feels a change in her consciousness.'

Speaking from his own experience, Osho agrees with saints such as Buddha and Mahavir that the two greatest forms of suffering are birth and death. Osho goes a step ahead and adds that the pain of birth is much more intense and fundamental than that of death. He continues, stating that, 'If you can trust me, I say that the pain (of being born again) is greater than death...And it should be so because birth makes death possible...Birth is the beginning of suffering, death is the end. Birth has to be more painful—it is! And after nine months of total rest, relaxation, no worry, nothing to do, it is a sudden shock to be thrown out, that never again will there be such a shock to the nervous system. Never again!'

Osho had to face difficulties in being born once again. The biggest obstacle was locating a suitable womb. 'For any person who reaches a certain stage of development,' he says, 'It is difficult to find suitable parents for another birth.' Osho explains that during the times of Mahavir and Buddha people generally had higher spiritual qualities and advanced souls could easily find suitable wombs. In the case of Osho, a prevalent decline in spiritual consciousness made it necessary for him to wait for the appropriate time to find the right womb. In Dadda and Saraswati he met ideal parents because of their spiritual qualities, loving nature and higher consciousness.

Osho waited for 700 years to find himself a suitable couple to be born with, he explains how he calculated the gap of 700 years. He distinguishes first, however, between the nature of time measurement when an advanced soul is in the body and when it is only consciousness:

'*This measurement begins only with the body. Outside the body, it makes no difference whether you have been for seven hundred years or seven thousand years. Only upon acquiring the body does the difference begin.*'

Hence, in order to figure out the gap between his last death and present birth, he used an indirect method: he calculated the time by observing those who were with him in his past life and who may have been reborn several times since then.

'*Suppose that a particular person was known to me during my lifetime seven hundred years ago. In the time there was a gap for me (when I had no body), he may have taken birth ten times. However, there are memories of his past ten births. From his memories only can I calculate how long I must have remained without a body.*'

Distinguishing between the time measured when one is in the body and when one is in the 'bodyless' state, Osho says:

'*It is near about like this: For a moment I go to sleep and see a dream. In the dream I see that years have passed, and after some moments you awaken me and say that I have been dozing…In a dream, an expanse of several years can be seen within a moment. The time scale of a dream life is different…If, after awakening from a dream, the dreamer had no way of knowing when he slept, then it would be difficult to determine the length of time of his sleep. That can be known only by a clock: for example, when I was previously awake it was twelve o'clock, and now that I have gotten up after sleeping it is only one minute past twelve. Otherwise, I can only know because you were here also (at the same time with me); there is no other way of knowing. So only in this way has it been determined that seven hundred years have passed.*'

Osho emphasises that, in terms of spiritual growth, it is essential for individuals to know about their past lives so that they can begin their search from where they left off before. It can save significant amounts of energy and time spent in pursuing the search for truth in the present life. He explains: 'Therefore, what little I have told you about my previous life is not because it has any value or that you may know something about me. I have told this only because it may make you reflect about yourself and set you in search of your past lives. The moment you know your past lives, there will be a spiritual revolution and evolution. Then you will start from where you had left off in you last life; otherwise, you will get lost in endless lives and reach nowhere. There will only be a repetition.'

Osho grew up just as any normal child would, and yet there was something very different, very unique that distinguished him from other children. One of his outstanding characteristics was his tendency, right from an early age, to experiment. His interest in people, his keen observation of human nature, his creativity and his own search for the 'real' were factors that contributed to his experiencing life directly and authentically.

His search gave him extraordinary insights into the world around him and into the human psyche. With each insight he came closer and closer to the ultimate realisation of 'That Which Is'.

Excerpts from:

Take It Easy vol. 1
Dimensions Beyond the Known
Yoga: The Alpha and the Omega: Discourses on
The Yoga Sutras of Patanjali, vol. 4
Vigyan Bhairav Tantra, vol. 1

End notes:

1. "O Samadhi Alleluia!", *Sannayas,* no.6

2

YOUTH: THE
YEARS OF ADVENTURE

Even as a child, Osho exhibited a thirst for truth. His search was influenced by numerous encounters with death. He first experienced the shock of death at the age of five when his younger sister Kusum died; Osho was very fond of her. He was so upset at her death that he refused food and insisted on behaving as a traditional Jain monk, wearing a loin cloth and carrying a begging bowl. His mother described the scene in the following words: 'He would ask us to sit in a row with food. Then, wearing monk-like clothes he would walk from one end to other begging food with a bowl in his hand.'

It was only after considerable persuasion that little Osho agreed to resume his normal, routine activities.

Many of the encounters Osho has had with death were part of his own experiments. Three of the most significant had been predicted by an astrologer, as well. Osho's grandfather had consulted a very renowned astrologer who, after referring to the astrological chart of Osho, predicted that the child would not survive beyond his seventh year. He did not consider it worthwhile, therefore, to further draw the chart for a person destined to such a short life. After the astrologer's death, his son continued to work on Osho's birth chart. The son too was puzzled and finally declared that the child would face death every seven years and that he would almost certainly die at the age of twenty-one. These predictions naturally worried Osho's parents and family. But, as Osho points out, the astrologers were right, in a way. Seven, fourteen, and twenty-one were the years in which Osho had deeper and deeper interactions with death.

Speaking of his first, most profound experience of death, Osho says:

'At the age of seven I survived, but I had a deep experience of death, not of my own but of my maternal grandfather's. I was so attached to him that his death appeared to be my very own. My grandfather lost his speech in the very first attack of death. For twenty-four hours we waited in the village for something to happen. However, there was no improvement. I remember a struggle on his part to speak something, but he could not. He wanted to tell something but could not tell it. Therefore we had to take him towards the town in a bullock cart. Slowly, one after the other, his senses started giving way. He did not die all at once, but slowly and painfully. First his speech stopped, then his hearing. Then he closed his eyes as well. In the bullock cart I was watching everything closely and there was a long distance of thirty-two kilometers to travel…Whatsoever was happening seemed beyond my understanding then. This was the first death I had witnessed and I did not even understand that he was dying…The slow loss of his senses and his final dying became very deeply engraved in my memory.'

It was as if Osho's whole world fell apart with the disappearance of his beloved grandfather. Osho continues to describe how he felt at his grandfather's death:

'When he died I felt that it would be a betrayal to eat. Now, I didn't want to live. It was childish, but through it something very deep happened. For three days I just lay. I would not come out of the bed. I said, "When he is *dead, I do not want to live." I survived but these three days became a death experience. I died in a way and I came to realise—now I can tell about it though at that time, it was just a vague experience—I came to feel that, death is impossible.'*

This death brought another profound change in Osho as an individual—the destruction of an intimate, deeply affectionate relationship brought with it the very freedom to be with one's self, totally—to be alone. As Osho puts it:

'Death stared at me before the thrust of life began. For me the possibility of anyone else becoming my centre was destroyed in the very first steps of my life. The first centre that was formed broke down...The "facticity" of aloneness took hold of me from the age of seven. Aloneness became my nature. His death freed me forever from all relationships. His death became for me the death of all attachments. Thereafter I could not establish any bonds with anyone. Whenever my relationship with anyone began to become intimate, death stared at me.'

This does not mean that death made him negative towards others, only that he stopped seeing others in the context of a binding relationship. From then on, death became the context of every living being with whom he came into close contact. He remained conscious from that point on that a person he might feel close to today, could easily be gone tomorrow. The very reality of death and the futility of seeking any permanent relationship brought him closer to the realisation that in becoming alone one also becomes really happy. This is how Osho explains it: 'As that first feeling of aloneness became deeper and deeper, something new began to happen in life. At first that aloneness had made me only unhappy, but slowly it began changing into happiness...Thereafter, I did not suffer any unhappiness.'

It became apparent to him that his aloneness is, in fact, a state of becoming centered in his own self; it is a state in which he no longer felt dependent on the other. It was actually this freedom from dependence that made him permanently happy. He states: 'There was no other way but to revert back to my own self. I was, so to speak, thrown back to my own self. Slowly that made me more and more happy. Afterwards I came to feel that this close observation of death at a tender age became a blessing in disguise for me.' The event had a profound effect on the young child's growth. Osho himself puts it into words. 'This event can be considered as the first which left a deep impact and influence on my mind. From that day onwards, every day, every moment, the awareness of life invariably became associated with the awareness of death. From then onwards, to be or not to be had the same value for me.'

After the death of his grandfather, Osho came to live with his parents and paternal family in Gadarwara. At that time, Gadarwara was a small town of about 20,000 people. The town is about a hundred kilometres from the city of Jabalpur. Its inhabitants are mainly Hindu grain and cloth merchants, and the town is surrounded by small farming villages.

Osho was admitted to the Gunj Primary School of Gadarwara at the age of seven. But even at this early age he found traditional schooling limited for his creative intelligence and rejected the whole system. In the beginning, for almost two years, it was with great difficulty that he had to be persuaded to go to school. In order to avoid going to school, he sometimes made up stories. Once he came home crying and said he would not go back to school because his teacher had given him a physical punishment. His mother got upset about it and asked Osho's youngest uncle, Shikharchand, to go and straighten out the teacher immediately. Shikharchand took young Osho with him and headed out for the school. On the way, however, Osho admitted to his uncle that he was pretending and that the teacher had not punished him. He simply did not enjoy going to school.

Osho could not relate to dull, meaningless education and uncreative teachers. He did not find anything worth learning, anything more than mere words, numbers or irrelevant details—nothing good enough to propel his inner search. This disinterested him completely in the normal course of schooling and in fact created great aversion in him towards the subjects taught in school. Osho gives voice to his strong feelings in this matter:

'From my very childhood, I was not interested in any subject that was taught in school—hence my poor history! I was always wondering why these stupid names have to be memorised. Why, for what sin, are we punished to remember names of some people, dates, exact dates, exact names? And all that these people have done is something ugly! The history is bunk! Why should we be punished? So I was never present in the history class. I was never interested in language, any language, either.

'My whole interest lay, from the very beginning, in learning how to transcend mind. Neither history, nor geography, mathematics or any languages can help. All these things are irrelevant. My whole being was moving into a totally different direction.'

Osho found it equally difficult to relate to any teacher because he did not find anyone who could understand his needs or who had experienced what he was searching for. Though this created a great deal of misunderstanding about him as he came to be seen as immodest and discourteous, for Osho it was a valuable feeling as this lack of a teacher-figure again threw Osho back to his centre—he once again found himself alone. 'I could not accept anyone as my teacher,' explains Osho, 'though I was always ready to be student—but I did not find anyone whom I might call "my master".' He was, furthermore, looking for someone who could untangle for him the phenomenon of death, which he had witnessed so intensely and closely.

'Everyone I found, was very much involved in and with life. A person who had not seen death could never become my teacher. I wanted to respect (them), but I could not. I could respect rivers, mountains and even stones, but not human beings…I met no teacher whom I could spontaneously respect, because I did not feel that there was anything anyone knew that was such an absolute truth that without it life could have no meaning…I never felt that I was a small child and that I should remain under someone's protection and guidance. Not that I did not go to anyone: I did go to many people, but I always returned empty-handed and felt that all which was imparted I already knew. There was nothing which could be learnt from them.'

This intensified his inner search. In Osho's own words, 'I was thrown back upon myself from another direction as well because I never believed or felt that truth could be learned from others. There was only one way to learn and that was to learn from myself only.'

But young Osho was not all lost at school. Right from the first grade, Osho became known for his beautiful handwriting and ability to paint. He began to read newspapers and magazines when he was in the second grade and became a member of the Gadarwara Public Library, the youngest person ever to be a member. While in elementary school, Osho displayed his talent in writing poetry, short stories, articles and also in photography. In the sixth grade itself, Osho edited a handwritten magazine, *Prayas*, meaning 'effort'.

One of the things that made young Osho popular was his extraordinary storytelling ability, especially his narrations of detective stories. Swami Ageha Saraswati, a childhood friend, fondly remembers the days in school when, after the assignment was over in the Art class, Osho would tell his fellow students sensational stories from detective novels.

Another thing that developed Osho's mind was his love for nature, and his fondness for the River Shakkar (meaning 'sugar') and its sweet waters that flow through Gadarwara. He found not only a friend in the river but also a teacher. His whole being was involved with the river and its surroundings in all its moods. Here is a very poetic description given by Osho of his involvement with the river:

'In my childhood I used to go early in the morning to the river. It is a small village. The river is very lazy, as if not flowing at all. And in the morning when the sun has not yet risen, you cannot make out whether it is flowing or not; it is so lazy and silent. And in the morning when nobody is there, the bathers have not yet come, it is tremendously silent. Even the birds are not singing so early, no sound, just a soundlessness pervades. And the smell of the mango trees hangs all over the river…I used to go there, to the farthest corner of the river, just to sit, just to be there. There was no need to do anything, just being there was enough. It was such a beautiful experience to be there. I would take a bath, would swim and when the sun came up I would go to the other shore, to the vast expanse of sand, and dry myself there under the sun, and lie there, and sometimes even go to sleep.'

When his mother asked what did he do the whole morning, Osho would say, 'Nothing.' Not satisfied, his mother persisted with her questions. Osho says:

'My mother would insist that I must have been doing something, so I would say, "Okay, I took a bath and I dried myself in the sun," and then she was satisfied. But I was not—because what happened there in the river cannot be expressed in words "I took a bath". This statement looks so poor and pale. Playing in the river, floating in the river, swimming in the river; it was such a deep experience that to say simply, "I took a bath," makes no sense; or to just say, "I went there, had a walk on the bank and sat there," conveys nothing.'

Osho was fortunate enough to find a person who was deeply in love with the river. This man gave young Osho his first lessons in swimming and put him in touch with the river. The way this master swimmer taught him swimming gave young Osho a very insightful experience into the secret of being total. This is how Osho describes it:

'In my childhood I was sent to a master swimmer. He was the best swimmer in town, and I have never come across a man who was so tremendously in love with water. Water was God to him; he worshipped it and the river was his home. Early, at three o'clock in the morning, you would find him in the river, and in the night you would find him sitting, meditating by the side of the river. His whole life consisted of being close to the river…When I was brought to him, I wanted to learn how to swim. He looked at me and felt something. He said, "But there is no way to learn swimming. I can just throw you in the water and then swimming will come of its own accord. There is no way to learn it. It cannot be taught. It is a knack, not knowledge." And that's what he did. He threw me in the water and he stood on the bank. Two or three times I went down and I felt that I was drowning. He was just standing there—he would not even try to help me! Of course, when your life is at stake, you do whatever you can. So I started throwing my hands about. It was haphazard, hectic, but the knack came. When life is at stake, you do whatever you can and whenever you do whatever you can do totally, things happen! I could swim! I was thrilled! "Next time," I said, "you need not throw me into it, I myself will jump." Now I know that there is a natural buoyancy of the body. It is not *a question of swimming—it is only a question of getting in tune with water. Once you are in tune with the water element, it protects you.'*[1]

Swami Ageha Saraswati relates more insightful experiences from his childhood between Osho and the river. 'It was a sheer joy to spend nights at the river with Osho. It was incredible and sometimes frightening too because none of us, his friends, were ever sure what he would do while roaming on the banks. He was totally unpredictable, or to put it differently, he was utterly spontaneous, but we followed him with complete trust and the thrill of adventure. We spent a good deal of our time swimming with Osho in the river. Even with the river dangerously running high, Osho would ask us to jump in and swim across. Not only that, he would even point out a specific spot, on the opposite shore, where we had to reach. We could never make it because the current and the flow of the river were so strong that we were swept miles away from the suggested spot. Osho on the other hand would never fail in reaching the exact place where we were supposed to meet.'

Osho also sought refuge in the river. Whenever he was extremely sad, he would come down to the river and sit in meditation there. His friends have pointed out two occasions in particular—when his boyhood companion Shashi died, and again, on 30 January 1948, when Mahatma Gandhi was assassinated. Hearing the news of Gandhi's death, Osho told his friends that he was too sad to even weep. That evening he and his friends came to the river and sat in meditation.

For Osho, the river and its surroundings was an ideal place to practise deep meditation. Once, when asked whether he ever did any *sadhana* (spiritual practice), Osho recounted a very interesting story. When the cinema was still new in Gadarwara, a show would typically last for four or five hours and sometimes even more because the movie projector would break down occasionally. Osho would leave home early in the evening telling the family that he was going to the movies. But, he would instead spend his time lying naked in the sand on the river bank. The family never questioned his late hours as they put that down to the situation at the cinema theatre. His association with the river, therefore, was an experiment in being in a state of complete and deep relaxation. It helped him experience the deeper levels of his consciousness.

Osho also used the river for insights about death. His uncles, friends and relatives mention how he would jump into the flooding river and swim across it, or how he would climb up a seventy foot-high bridge and jump from there into the swelling river. One of the most hair-raising experiments was Osho's diving straight into a whirlpool. For him falling into a whirlpool was 'one of the most beautiful experiences'. Osho describes the nature of a whirlpool and his experience with it:

'In rivers, particularly when they are flooded in the rains, many powerful and strong whirlpools are created. The water moves round and round like a screw. If you get caught in it, you will be forced, pulled towards the bottom and the deeper you go, the stronger the whirl becomes. The natural tendency of the ego is to fight with it, of course, because it looks like death and the ego is very much afraid of death. The ego tries to fight with the whirl but if you fight with it, in a flooded river or near a waterfall where many whirls exist, you are most certainly lost because the whirl is very strong. You cannot fight with it. And this is the phenomenon of the whirl: on the surface the whirl is big; the deeper you go, smaller and smaller it becomes—smaller but stronger. And at the bottom the whirl is so small you can simply get out of it with no fight. In fact, near the bottom, the whirl itself throws you out. But you have to wait for the bottom. If you are fighting on the surface, you are done for. You cannot survive. I have tried it with many whirls; the experience is lovely.'

This description illustrates Osho's insight into death. The more one fights with death, the more one is bound to be twisted and engulfed by it; but instead of resisting it, if one allows oneself to go deeper into it, meditatively, one is sure to come out with a tremendously thrilling experience. As one penetrates into its mysteries and reaches the bottom, one automatically comes out of it unharmed and free of its fear.

As a child, Osho's preoccupation with death was extraordinary. It was his common practice to follow people carrying a dead body to the cremation ground. When his parents asked him why he went to the cremation ground so often, to the funerals of strangers, he said, 'The man is not my concern. Death is a beautiful phenomenon and also one of the most mysterious ones. One should not miss it.' Going ahead Osho added, 'The moment I heard that somebody had died, I would be there, always watching, waiting, witnessing what was happening.' He would watch and listen to people philosophising over the death of the person and quoting from the scriptures. This greatly annoyed Osho. 'I started feeling that these people are trying to avoid the real thing. By engaging themselves in a discussion, they are avoiding the phenomenon that has happened. They are not looking at the dead man. And the thing is there! Death is there and you are discussing it! What fools!'

Swami Ageha Saraswati confirms that as a young boy Osho would often go alone, in the night, to the cremation ground and spend hours lying there.

Because of this extraordinary tendency of his, Osho's family got worried. Partly because it was an unnatural thing to do and partly because he had approached the age of fourteen—another seventh year of his life when his death had been predicted. This time, too, Osho managed to survive physically, though he had once again encountered death consciously. He told the family that if death was certain, as predicted by the astrologer, then it would be better if he was prepared for it. He wanted to meet death halfway; he wanted to encounter it consciously. The family was shocked and puzzled to hear this but did not interfere in his plans.

Osho was determined to carry out his plans. He went to the school principal and requested a seven-day leave. He told the principal that he was going to die. The principal could not believe his ears. Thinking that Osho was planning to commit suicide, he asked for an explanation. Osho told the principal about the astrologer's prediction regarding the possibility of his death in the fourteenth year. He also told the principal, 'I am going into retreat for seven days to wait for death, If death comes, it is good to meet it consciously so that it becomes an experience.' The principal was astounded, but granted permission. Osho then went to an old, isolated temple near his village. There was a priest who was in-charge of that temple. Osho instructed the priest not to disturb him and asked him to provide him with something to eat and drink once a day while he lay in the temple waiting for death. It was a beautiful experience for Osho. Actual death never came, of course, but Osho did almost everything possible 'to become dead'. He went through some strange and unusual feelings. Many things happened to him, but in Osho's words, 'The basic note was that when you feel you are going to die, you actually become more calm and silent.' Some of his experiences, during that episode, are quite fascinating. Osho narrates one particular episode related to the fear of death:

'I was lying there. On the third or fourth day a snake entered the temple. It was in view; I could see the snake. But there was no fear. Suddenly I felt very strange. The snake was coming nearer and nearer and I felt very strange. There was no fear. So I thought, death may be coming through this snake, so why be afraid? Wait! The snake crossed over me and went away. Fear had disappeared. If you accept death, there is no fear. If you cling to life, then every fear is there.'

Once death is accepted as a reality, its acceptance immediately creates a distance, a point from which one can observe the flow of events in life. This brings one above the pain, sorrow, worries and despair that usually accompany such events. Osho phrases his experience related to such a state of detachment:

'Many times flies (insects) would fly around me or creep over me, on my face. Sometimes I got irritated and would want to throw them off but then I used to argue with myself, what is the use? Sooner or later I am going to die and then no one will be there to protect the body. So let them have their way. The moment I decided to let them have their way, the irritation disappeared. They were still on the body but it was, as if, I was not concerned. They were, as if, moving or creeping on someone else's body. There was immediately a distance. If you accept death, a distance is created. Life moves far away with all its worries, irritations, everything.'

This is not to say that Osho believed in the astrologer's prediction. Nevertheless, it did give him an opportunity, an incentive to explore and understand death. Osho concludes: 'Physically some day I will die, of course. However this prediction of the astrologer helped me by making me aware of death early in life. I could meditate and accept that it was coming, almost continuously.'

Thus, in passing intensely and meditatively, through the experience of being dead, it became apparent to Osho that even though his body could die in terms of being unable to respond to any stimuli, his consciousness would remain fully aware. He reflects, 'I died in a way, but I came to understand that something deathless is also there. Once you accept death totally, you become aware of it.'

Whether it was swimming in the flooded River Shakkar or exploring other sources of adventure, Osho remained the natural leader of a rather formidable gang of boys. They loved and respected him immensely. He was not only their comrade-in-arms, but also their mentor and guide. They were amazed at the sharpness of his mind, his courage and creative spirit. Osho responded lovingly towards his friends and cared for them deeply. Not only did he himself experiment with new things, he encouraged his friends to do the same. Every day they did something new to avoid repetition. He constantly reminded them to fight against superstition and hypocrisy.

Osho and his gang became so well known in the town for their fearless escapades, it is said that even the local thieves and murderers avoided confrontation with them. Their activities took place, during the day, and on full moon nights they would have fun freeing the donkeys of the town and riding them until dawn broke. Streams of complaints from indignant townsfolk always hounded Osho's family. His father, on hearing his prankster son's stories, used to get rather perplexed as to what to do, since he felt that most of the victims had nothing more to complain about than their wounded egos. Generally, Dadda did not pay attention, but there is one occasion when in exasperation he locked his son in a room. He refused to let Osho out until he relented, but the punishment proved quite pointless because the son was happy in his own company. He remained locked for hours without making any sound or movement. When Dadda got worried because of all the silence around, Osho told him in a cool voice that there was nothing to worry about and that he was happy to stay there indefinitely. On a different occasion, a teacher punished Osho for coming late to class. He made him run around the school grounds. But the idea backfired as young Osho enjoyed the exercise and continued to come late so that he could have more of it. Finally the teacher gave up!

Osho's first rebellious act in school was in his seventh grade. The principal was a harsh disciplinarian who was especially strict about the observance of rules and regulations of the school. Osho's free spirit never followed any imposed discipline. He believed in spontaneous self-discipline. At his school everyone was required to wear a cloth cap; Osho was permitted, however, to wear a woolen one, the only woolen one in the entire students crowd. One day Osho walked into the principal's room and declared calmly that henceforth the compulsory cloth cap would no longer be worn at the school and if cap wearing wasn't made optional, the students would go on strike. The principal must have had the common sense to read the situation correctly because from that day on caps were no longer compulsory. Later, Osho led several other protests at the school against meaningless rules, harsh disciplines, and hypocritical behaviour of the teachers.

Osho's rebellion also manifested itself in the form of pranks, whose purpose most often than not was to expose hypocrites in society and deflate their egos. His tricks and teasing though were not malevolent, neither did he want to hurt; what he did was purely out of good-natured fun. On the surface his energy seemed to be directed at the person, but actually what he aimed at was the age-old conditioning and egocentric behaviour. The person was never his target; it was the set pattern he was attacking. What Osho did in the small setting of his hometown was similar to his jibes at the priests and the pope, pundits and politicians. Not insulting but educating. The nature and quality of Osho's sense of humour can be seen in an interesting story told by his friend Swami Ageha Saraswati. It is a perfect example of how he would enlist unsuspecting participants in his exploration of human behaviour. It was his nature to take delight in exposing what he later called the 'right victim'.

There was a physician in Gadarwara who had put up a signboard with his name and a long list of his academic degrees on it. When the doctor was in his clinic, Osho with his friends would read aloud his name and degrees from across the street. The gang had instructions from Osho that whenever any one of them passed the doctor's clinic, he would read out the signboard. The doctor began to get annoyed at this, but the boys did not stop. The doctor finally lost his temper one day and made complaints to the parents of the youngsters. The parents were at a loss on this matter. They saw nothing offensive about it except that it was a little odd perhaps, and in fact were rather amused by the whole thing. The story soon spread in the little town, as well much to the doctors chagrin. But eventually the doctor recognised the egocentricity his sign symbolised and quietly removed it.

Though Osho was never into politics, his young mind was quite aware of what was happening around him. At the time, India was labouring under British rule and Osho was against it. Another boyhood friend of his, Gulabbhai, shared memories of Osho, revealing young Osho's deep concern over the political and social injustices in India. Gulabbhai who was closely associated with Osho from 1940 to 1950, became his disciple, although he was nine years older to Osho. 'Living unnerved through insecurity and being fearless, were the outstanding qualities of Osho,' said Gulabbhai, 'and we always marvelled at the way he showed his courage in exposing the evils of the society. Even though Osho was younger than some of us, we looked up at him with awe and great respect. The kind of rebelliousness Osho is showing now on such a global scale, we were fortunate enough to witness on a smaller scale during our school days.'

According to Gulabbhai, Osho never had any interest in becoming politically involved—his main contribution to the society was to speak out boldly against oppression, injustice and hypocrisy. Even though he was strongly against the British rule, he never became a regular freedom fighter for the Congress party or any other political party—his was always an independent voice. For sometime, though,

Osho did take part in the freedom struggle actively, but it was short lived. In 1940, a representative of the Indian National Army (INA) led by Subhash Chandra Bose met with Osho and his uncle Shikharchand. He persuaded them to form a youth wing of INA with Osho as its captain. Osho was also a member of another nationalist movement, Rashtriya Swayamsevak Sangh (RSS) but did not stay in it for too long, either. He soon quit both INA and RSS because he could not accept any external discipline, ideology, or a system. His opinions about Mahatma Gandhi were also in the same line. Though he admired Gandhi for his sincerity and untiring efforts, Osho was never taken in by Gandhi's ideas and idiosyncrasies. He has voiced his opinion about Gandhi's policies clearly.

Experimentation was as much a part of Osho's life as his rebellion. Every day he did something new and different—the search continued on all levels. He experimented with sleep by arranging unusual hours for rising and going to bed; he tried fasting; eating at strange hours; he meditated standing in the river, in the woods, in the rain. He experimented with the occult and yogic breath control, with magic and telekinesis. He also experimented successfully with hypnosis. 'Often Osho would involve his friends in his experiments,' said another childhood friend of Osho, Swami Sukhraj Bharati. Sukhraj recounts that when they used to go boating Osho would push a non-swimmer in the river, being careful to keep him from drowning, but at the same time allowing him to struggle. Sometimes he would push the head of a swimmer deep in the water for a few seconds. When the person forced himself out, Osho would ask, 'How was it?' By this he meant, how intense was the experience, how was it to be under water without being able to breathe? Osho would then explain that it is only when one comes to a point of such tremendous intensity where one's survival is at stake that the real search for God begins.

One memorable experiment of the young master included walking on a cliff in the middle of the night. His friend Swami Ageha Saraswati recalls:

'He would take us for a walk along the river in the middle of a dark night. He would then ask us to climb on top of the high hills and walk on the edge

of the cliffs—it was a hair-raising experience. We were scared to death. Hundreds of feet below lay the deep valley. One slip and we could have gone crashing down to our deaths. Whenever he would take us on such adventures, we always knew, however, that his main intention was to get us to experiment with fearlessness; his main purpose was to make us more and more aware, alert and courageous.'

The experiments were mostly directed to experience the state of meditation. Osho has described the walking on the cliff experiment and the experiment of jumping into the river from the bridge as examples of passing through moments when one transcends the mind:

'In my childhood days I used to take my friends to the river. There was a small path by the side of the river. To walk on that edge was very dangerous; just one step taken in unconsciousness and you will fall straight into the river, and that was the place where the river was the deepest. Nobody used to go there, but that was my most loved spot. I would get all my friends also to walk with me on that narrow edge. Very few were ever ready to go with me, but those who went had really beautiful experiences. They would all report, "This is strange, how the mind stops!" I would sometimes take my friends to the railway bridge to jump into the river from it. It was dangerous...it was prohibited. There was always a policeman standing on guard at the bridge because from there people used to also commit suicides. We had to bribe the policeman (for allowing us to jump from the bridge). Slowly he also came to know that these are the same people; they don't die...and they are not interested in suicide. In fact, he started loving us and stopped accepting bribe. He said, "You can jump. I will not look at that side. Whenever you want you can come." The bridge was very high...Before you hit the river, there was a point (of time), in the middle, between the bridge and the river, when the mind would suddenly stop. Those were my first glimpses of meditation; that's how I became more and more interested in meditation. I became interested in trying to find out how these moments can be made available without going to the mountains, to the river or to any bridges; how one can allow oneself to move into these spaces without going anywhere, just by closing one's eyes. Once you have tasted it, it is not difficult.'

In all experiments the main ingredient was courage. Osho has, in fact, maintained all along that a seeker of the truth is one who is continuously experimenting and courage is necessary to experiment. 'Courage,' according to Osho, 'is the greatest quality in life, because without courage there is no freedom, and without freedom no truth...'

Osho himself worked hard on remaining alert and aware. When he was in high school, for instance, one of the teachers Osho loved and admired insisted that in answer to the daily roll call students should say 'Present, Sir,' and not 'Yes, Sir'. Commenting on this, Osho says: 'Now this was just whimsical. It doesn't matter whether you say, "Yes Sir" or you say "Present, Sir." But I started feeling that he had some point in it, and I began meditating on it. And whenever he would call my name, I would say, "Present, Sir," and I would not (just) say it—I would feel it too: I am simply present, aware, alert. And I had beautiful moments; just for half a minute, I would become so present that the class would disappear, that the teacher would disappear.'

Osho was equally alert to the conditioning imposed from outside. He says: 'I was born in a Jain family and naturally just as everybody else is conditioned, the conditioning was imposed on me, too. The conditioning is so subtle, once you are caught in it, you become incapable of thinking or seeing for yourself; anything that goes against your conditioning, you become deaf to it. But I was continuously watchful, continuously alert; hence, I was not caught by the conditioning.' But it was not before the same conditioning caused him some trouble.

Traditionally, Jains do not eat meals after sunset. Osho was also brought up in this tradition, but once it caused him awful misery. Osho recounts the following incident:

'Up to my eighteenth year, I had never eaten at night. Once I went with a few friends to see a fort, nestled far away in the jungles. The fort was such a beauty that the whole day was spent in admiring it. The others, who were Hindus, were not interested in preparing food during the day. I was the only Jain, and I could not insist, because the other thirty did not show any interest in it. So I kept quite. In the night they cooked food. After the whole day's wandering in the forest and in the ruins of that ancient castle,

I was tired and hungry. I had never known such hunger, in fact. But eighteen years of conditioning reminded me I could not eat at night. And then, they started preparing delicious food…They tried to persuade me to eat and said, "Nobody is here, and nobody will tell your family, or your parents about this; nobody will ever know." I resisted—but the more I resisted, the more I was tempted. Finally I gave in and started eating. The food was delicious. But the whole night I suffered hell. I vomited at least seven times. That eighteen years of conditioning was not an easy thing to get rid of. I could not digest the food; my whole body revolted. Until all the food was thrown out, I could not sleep…'

Osho exhibited the art to think rationally and then to put his thoughts into words effectively at a very early age. He gave speeches and participated in debates from sixth grade onwards. His love for words caught momentum in the ninth grade and there was no looking back from there. Swami Ageha Saraswati told me that Osho—even in those early days—was known for his ability to pick any side in a debate and defeat the opponent in the argument. In Osho's words:

'It was easy for me to speak out. I started speaking out my views before I became enlightened. Speaking came naturally to me even before I became enlightened. I never learnt any oratory, and have neither been to any school where oratory is taught. I have never even read a book on the art of speaking. From my very childhood, I was argumentative and everybody wanted me to keep silent…In the family, in school, in college, and then in the university too, everybody was always saying to me, "Don't speak at all!" But all that gave me great opportunity and made me more and more articulate. It became a natural thing for me to argue with neighbours, with the teachers, or to argue on the street—anywhere. Just finding a man was enough to get me to argue.'

His exceptional oratory expertise made him well sought after. He once gave a series of seven-day talks on religion and spirituality at a friend's house. Even as an adolescent he was occasionally invited to enter into open debate with well known scholars, priest and pundits. With his insightful observations and pointed questions he always made them uncomfortable. An illustration of this can be seen in a speech he gave when he spoke at Teacher's Day celebration on 5 September at

D. N. Jain High School in Jabalpur. Osho shocked the audience when he spoke the following words: 'Today is the most unfortunate day for teachers…This day is being observed just because S. Radhakrishnan was once a teacher and is now the president. The real honour for the teachers will be when the president would give up his presidency and become a teacher.'

His passionate search made him read books on every possible subject. Often he would read through the night. This would give him a headache but he would apply a pain-killing balm to his forehead and get back to his reading. Then at dawn he would go to the river and take a swim. Although as a young boy he played games such as field hockey, soccer and volleyball, but he was always more interested in reading. Many of the books at the Gadarwara Public Library still have cards that show only Osho's signature, meaning that he was the lone reader of those books. The books ranged from politics and philosophy to science, religion to detective novels. Not only did he himself read widely, but he insisted that has friends also read something other than the usual textbooks. The Indian Nobel Laureate in literature, Rabindranath Tagore, was one of his favourite authors.

In his early days itself, he was branded a communist, for he extensively read the works of Marx and Engels and other communist literature. Because of his voracious reading habit, he missed school frequently and was threatened with expulsion from school. His interest in communism during high school stemmed from his deep concern for the poor. With the help of his friends, he built a small library that contained mostly communist literature.

Despite his serious interest in communist thinking, Osho personally leaned towards socialism. He and his friends believed socialism was the answer to the economic plight of India. But it was in high school, that he started becoming critical of it. In fact, around 1950, his friend Gulabbhai reports, he began criticising eminent leaders of the Indian Socialist Party such as Jaya Prakash Narayan. Osho once even attended the national executive meeting of the Socialist Party as an observer, which was held at a hill resort, Panchmarhi. The meeting proved quite disappointing to him.

Their (Osho and his friends) adolescent concern for the poor extended to fantasies about becoming Robin Hood and his merry men. It is said that they planned to buy guns and obtain a license from the police to use them in order to force the rich to give to the poor. But the plan did not, of course, go through. Osho, according to his uncle Amritlal, even formed a group of young people who regularly discussed communist ideology and their opposition to religion. Amritlal had seen written on the walls of their meeting place: 'Religion is an opium.'

In this phase of life, Osho remained an atheist, openly critical of religious rituals and blind faith in the scriptures. (It must be emphasised here, however, that the meditations Osho practised were not part of any religious ritual, or prescribed by any religion. In Osho's view, meditation is essentially a secular phenomenon; it has nothing to do with following a religion.)

'Those who have known me from my childhood would never have believed that religion and I could ever go together. It was beyond their expectations because what they call or know as religion, I had always fought against. What they call worshipping was just so much nonsense for me. What they called a sannyasin was for me nothing but an escapist. What they called scriptures, to which they used to bow their heads in worship, were but ordinary books for me upon which I could rest my foot. Whatsoever they asserted as being beyond doubt, I dragged into uncertainty and suspicion. Their God, their soul, and their salvation were all matters of joke and fun for me.'

Osho's search remained exclusively spiritual. The spiritual quest continued to be the undercurrent in all his activities. It appears that his disillusionment with Marx and socialistic ideas gave him greater clarity about his own sense of direction and commitment. It became quite apparent to him that the roots of human misery and unhappiness were not hidden in any particular social or political system. Rather, their origin was somewhere else. Osho came to see that only a revolution in consciousness, not politics, can bring peace and happiness. Another longtime friend of Osho, Shyam Soni, recalls:

'Once, when we were in high school, on a full moon night, some of us were sitting on the banks of the river. It was around eleven o'clock, and

everything was so quiet and peaceful. Suddenly, Osho broke the silence and said that his role lay in the field of religion and nowhere else. His place was in religion. I liked and appreciated his feeling, but could not believe it, because in those days he was very much into communism. However, I did not have to wait for too long since I began to notice soon after that night how everything except religion had become totally insignificant to him.'

This transition in Osho from interest in communism and socialism to religion and spirituality took place between the years 1945 and 1950.

Despite his outside activities and his preoccupation with ideas, he remained very loving and respectful towards his family members. He did not, however, hesitate to express his views frankly when necessary and always remained firm in his decisions. The following incident between Osho and his father illustrates the point.

'In my childhood I loved keeping my hair as long as possible. My father's shop and residence were together and I used to move in and out through his shop. He felt very embarrassed when people asked him, "Who is this girl?" In India only women are allowed to sport long hair and naturally he felt embarrassed and angry that I was creating trouble every day because of this. Finally he became so angry that he took his scissors, caught hold of me and cut my hair. I said, "You can cut my hair but remember, I am not going to leave it at that." He said, "What do you mean?" I said, "You will see tomorrow." And I went just on the other side of the road, where all the hair-cutting salons were. I had a friend, an old opium addict. I loved the man, because sometimes he would cut half of somebody's mustache and say, "Wait, I have to go somewhere." And then he would be gone for hours, and the man would be caught because he could not leave with half the mustache…And he was such a nice man; he would say, "There is no need to worry. If you don't like it, don't pay me anything." I used to sit in his small salon discussing various things with him, because it was a joy…So I went to him, because he was the only man who could have done what I had in mind. I told him, "I am tired of this long hair. Simply shave my head completely clean." In India a child's head is completely shaved only if his father dies. For a moment he hesitated. He said, "Your father will be very angry, I am telling you!" I said, "You don't be worried. It is my responsibility. And you are the only man with guts; no other barber

*is going to cut my hair." So he said okay. He cleaned out all my hair and I
entered my father's shop. Looking at me, immediately his customers asked,
"What happened to this poor boy? His father has died?" Now it was even
more embarrassing for him to admit, "I am his father." He called me inside
the house and said, "This is too much." I said, "I warned you. Whenever
I do anything I do it totally. From now onwards if you interfere with me,
remember, I can move to the other extreme."*

*'People from the neighborhood started coming to enquire... and when they
saw my father they said, "What is the matter? You are alive? And I have
seen with my own eyes that your son is completely shaved." In school,
my teachers and the headmaster on seeing that my father must have died
were very sorry. They told me, "We are going to your house to express our
sadness and mourn. Your father was a good man." I allowed them to go,
and when they would see my father sitting there, they were caught in a very
strange situation. My father would ask them, "Why have you come? There
must be some reason." They said, "There was...but your son is so strange
that when we were saying to him, 'He was a good man' he did not even tell
us that you were still alive." That was the last time he interfered with me.
He knew perfectly well that it was going to be dangerous.'*

At the age of sixteen, Osho received yet another deep shock when his
girlfriend from childhood, Shashi, died of typhoid. She lived near the
same old temple where Osho had 'died' at fourteen. Her father was a
doctor. Shashi who was a couple of years younger to Osho was very
deeply in love with him. Whenever Osho came to meditate at the
temple, she would watch him from her garden or window. Often she
would follow him to the temple, which sometimes annoyed the young
man for he usually wanted to be left alone. Osho would ask one of his
friends to guard the temple door so that Shashi would not disturb him
during his meditation. Despite this, Shashi knew that Osho returned
her love. He affectionately called her Gudiya and lovingly accepted
the food she brought to him after his meditation was over. When
Shashi was on her deathbed, Osho was with her. Death was certain,
but so was Shashi's determination to return, to be with her beloved
and to take care of him. She promised him she would come back. He,
too, promised her that he would call her, bring her back.

One of Osho's closest friends said that, after Shashi's death, Osho became even more distant and detached. For many days he did not talk to anybody. 'I do not remember,' Osho says, 'whether I ever cultivated any friendship, though there were many who wanted to be my friends. Many people became my friends not because they enjoyed being friends with me but because it was not possible to make me an enemy. But I do not recall that I have ever gone to anyone of my own accord and offered friendship. It is not that I never welcomed friendship. If someone made me a friend, I wholeheartedly welcomed it. But even then I could not become a friend in the ordinary sense; I have always remained aloof.' This kept him free, in a way, to be himself.

'Neither with any of my teachers, nor with any fellow students, or anybody else, could I develop such a relationship as would drown me or break my being an island. Friends came and stayed with me. I met many people as well; had many friends. But from my side there was nothing that could make me dependent on them or which would cause me to remember them...I may live with everyone, but whether I am in a crowd or a society, with a friend or an intimate, I am still alone. Nothing touches me; I remain untouched.'

From a very early age Osho used every experience, every situation, as a stepping stone towards inner growth. His awareness kept him from missing any opportunity in his search of truth. Deaths of his beloveds—his sister, grandfather, and Shashi—gave him extraordinary chances to understand the limitations created by attachment with the other and, hence, to transcend the duality. He seized upon these chances and made himself really free to be by himself. Osho's own observation in this regard is important:

'Life gives many opportunities for being thrown back to oneself. But the more clever we are, the quicker we are in rescuing ourselves from such an opportunity. At such moments we move out from ourselves. If my wife dies, I am immediately in search of another whom I can marry. If my friend is lost, I begin to search for another. I cannot leave any gap. By filling that gap, the opportunity I would have had to revert back to my own self, is lost in a moment, along with its immense possibilities. If I had become interested in the other, I would have lost the opportunity to journey towards the Self...'

In experiencing his aloneness, Osho became more of an 'outsider', or a 'stranger'. He became rooted in a state of detachment in which even in the midst of activities and people, he remained alone. 'I became a universe unto myself,' says Osho.

It is not too difficult to see that in his childhood and adolescence, Osho lived a very eventful and independent life. Whatever he did, he took full interest in it and was honest about it. Significantly, however, he never identified himself with an act; he always maintained a distance between the act and himself. Throughout his adventures, and in each of his experiments, he never let himself be led astray by unawareness.

His actions were part of his continuous search of that which is eternal, the ultimate in experience. And it was this thirst that brought him enlightenment.

Excerpts from:

Dimesnions Beyond the Known
Be Still and Know
Only One Sky: On the Tantric Way of Tilopa's Song of Mahamudra
The Grass Grows By Itself
And the Flowers Showered: Talks On Zen Stories
Tao: The Golden gate vol. 2
The Discipline of Transcendence vol. 3
The Last Testament vol. 3
Om Mani Padme Hum
Vigyan Bhairav Tantra vol. 1

End notes:

1. *The Sound of Running Water: A Photo-Biography of Bhagwan Shree Rajneesh and His Work 1974-1978.*
    Ma Prem Asha, Rajneesh Foundation, 1980.

3

ENLIGHTENMENT

In 1951, after graduating from high school in Gadarwara at the age of nineteen, Osho went to Jabalpur, where he enrolled at Hitkarini College. He lived with his cousins Kranti and Arvind, who were about his age. Kranti and Arvind were the children of one of Osho's father's sisters, Ratnibai. Ratnibai died when they were young and their father remarried so they were brought up by their aunt Makhmalbai and her husband Kundanlal Samaiya, who had no children of their own.

Kranti was married at a very young age, but unfortunately her husband died just one year after the marriage. Osho felt very deeply for his widowed cousin and helped her as much as he could, encouraging her to pursue her education. She later became a school teacher. Arvind graduated from a business school and became a college professor. As long as Osho was in Jabalpur, all three stayed together. They earned enough, supported each other, and lived a comfortable life.

Osho continued to do in college what he had done in high school he remained as uncompromising, unconventional and forthright as ever. He willingly accepted whatever the consequences were for exercising his freedom. It did not take too long for him to get into trouble. Two years after he entered college he was on his way out.

Osho was particularly troublesome in his classes in philosophy and logic. No matter what the professor said, he would invariably question it and start a long but logical argument, so that the professor never got very far in covering the coursework. When admonished by the professor not to argue, Osho pointed out that this would defeat the whole purpose of being in a class on philosophy and logic. His questions and arguments, based on his keen sense of inquiry, pertained strictly to the prescribed coursework. But finally the professor could take it no more and delivered an ultimatum to the principal: 'Either Osho goes or I go.' The principal called Osho into his office and asked him to leave the college. He admitted that he was not really at fault, but he could not see one of his most senior and well-respected professors resign.

Osho understood the situation and agreed to leave, provided that the principal took the responsibility for gaining admission for him at another college—a difficult demand since the college year was almost at an end. The principal agreed to make contacts. Osho's reputation had already travelled all over the town and other colleges were reluctant to admit him. Finally, the principal of D. N. Jain College agreed to admit Osho, but on the condition that he will not question professors as he had before. Osho said that was impossible, and it would be better if he stayed home instead of attending classes. The principal allowed him to stay home and bent the attendance rules so that Osho was allowed to appear only for examinations.

Osho describes the situation as follows:

'In colleges I was expelled and the principals said to me, "We feel guilty for expelling you, because you have not done anything wrong. But you are a little strange."

'The first college I entered, I wanted to learn logic. And the old professor, with many honorary degrees, with many books published in his name, started talking about Aristotle, the father of Western logic. I said, "Wait a minute. Do you know that Aristotle writes in his book that women have less teeth than men?" He said, "My God, what kind of question is this? What has it to do with logic?" I said, "It has something very fundamental to do with the whole process of logic. Are you aware that Aristotle had two wives?" He said, "I don't know... from where are you getting these facts?" But in Greece it was traditionally known for centuries that women were bound to have everything less than men. Naturally, they couldn't have the same number of teeth as men.

'I said, "And you call this man Aristotle the father of logic? He could have at least counted—and he had two wives available, but he did not count. His statement is illogical. He has simply taken it from the tradition, and I cannot trust in a man who has two wives and writes that women have less teeth than men. This is a male chauvinistic attitude. A logician has to be beyond prejudices."

'Seeing the situation, the professor threatened the principal that either I should be expelled from the college or he was going to resign. And he stopped coming to the college. He said, "I will wait for three days." The principal could not lose an experienced professor. He called me into his office to say, "There has never been any trouble with that man, he is a very nice man. Just on the first day...what have you done?" I told him the whole story and I said, "Do you think it deserves expulsion from college? I was asking absolutely relevant questions, and if a professor of logic cannot answer, who is going to answer?"

'The principal was a good man. He said, "I will not expel you, because I don't see that you have done anything wrong. But I cannot afford to lose the professor either, so I will make arrangements for you in another college." But the rumour about me had spread in all the colleges. The city I was in had almost twenty colleges and finally it became a very prestigious university just by combining those twenty colleges. He sent me to another principal with a letter of recommendation, but he must have phoned him to say, "Don't believe in the letter of recommendation. I had to write it because

I have to get rid of that student. He is not wrong, but he is absolutely individualistic and that is going to create trouble."

'I went to see the other principal, and he was waiting. He said, "I can admit you only on one condition: that you will never attend the college." I said, "Then what is going to happen when it is time for my examination?" He said, "I will give you the necessary percentage for being present in the college, but this is a secret pact between me and you."

'I said, "It is perfectly good—anyway your professors are out of date. But can I enter the library?"

'He said, "The library is perfectly okay, but never attend any class because I don't want to hear from any professor the complaint that you are creating trouble." And I have never created any trouble! I was simply asking questions which...if they were really gentlemen they would have said, 'I will find out. For the time being, I don't know.' But this is the most difficult thing in the world to say, "I don't know."'

Osho used this free time to find a job at the daily newspaper as assistant editor. He stayed with the newspaper for only a few months.

However, this period was not particularly significant for either Osho's employment or his education. Rather, it was important because of the extraordinary intensity of his personal search for the eternal. This was the most critical time of his life. He was beset with doubts and feelings of terrible insecurity and emptiness. The situation was all the more painful because there was no one to guide him, to empathise with him—he was without a master, he was alone on the path.

As has been mentioned before, Osho would not accept anything without questioning. He was especially unwilling to accept anything about the existence of God without encountering that reality face-to-face, without personal experience of it. He questioned all, he rejected all—including enlightened beings such as Krishna, Mahavir, Buddha and Jesus, and scriptures such as the Vedas, Upanishands, *Bible* and *Koran*. Thus, now that he realised these sources could no longer help him, his search became fully personal and solitary and he almost went mad. In Osho's words:

'In every small matter, there was doubt and nothing but doubt… Questions remained without any answer. In one respect, I was as good as mad. I was myself afraid that anytime I might become mad. I was not able to sleep at night.

'Throughout the night and day…questions hovered around me…I was in a deep sea, so to speak, without any boat or bank anywhere. Whatever boats had been there, I had myself sunk or denied. There were many boats and many sailors, but I had…refused to step into anyone else's boat I felt that it was better to drown by oneself…than to step into someone else's boat. If this was where life was to lead me, to drowning myself, then I felt that this drowning should be accepted.

'My condition was one of utter darkness. It was as if I had fallen into a deep dark well. In those days I had many times dreamt that I was falling and falling and going deeper into a bottomless well. And many times I… awakened from a dream full of perspiration, sweating profusely, because the falling was endless without any ground or place anywhere to rest my feet…for me there was no clear path. It was all darkness. Every next step for me was in darkness—aimless and ambiguous. My condition was full of tension, insecurity and danger.'

There was no escape; there were no shortcuts for Osho. He knew full well that he was facing a very crucial time in his life with a little bit of unawareness or loss of patience, or lack of courage, he could go berserk. Again, the absence of a master is what made this situation so critical. He searched long and hard, but he could not find one. He confides:

'It is very rare to find a master, rare to find a being who has become a non-being, rare to find a presence who is almost an absence, rare to find a man who is simply a door to the divine, an open door to the divine which will not hinder you, through which you can pass. It is very difficult…Yes, sometimes it happens that a person has to work without a master. If the master is not available, then one has to work without a master, but then the journey is very hazardous.'

This tremendously intense and challenging situation lasted for one whole year. It put Osho into a most difficult state of mind. Osho gives a description of what he went through during this period:

'For one year it was almost impossible to know what was happening… Just to keep myself alive was a very difficult thing, because all appetite disappeared. Days would pass and I would not feel any hunger, days would pass and I would not feel any thirst. I had to force myself to eat, force myself to drink. The body was so non-existential that I had to hurt myself to feel that I was still in the body. I had to knock my head against the wall to feel whether my head was still there or not. Only when it hurt, would I be a little in the body.

'Every morning and every evening I would run for five to eight miles. People used to think that I was mad. Why was I running so much? Sixteen miles a day! It was just to feel myself…not to lose contact with myself…I could not talk to anybody because everything had become so inconsistent that even to formulate one sentence was difficult. In the middle of the sentence I would forget what I was saying; in the middle of the way I would forget where I was going. Then I would have to come back…

'I had to keep myself shut in my room. I made it a point not to talk, not to say anything, because to say anything was to say that I was mad. For one year it persisted I would simply lie on the floor and look at the ceiling and count from one to a hundred then back from a hundred to one. Just to remain capable of counting was at least something. Again and again I would forget. It took one year for me to gain a focus again, to have a perspective.

'There was nobody to support me; there was nobody to say where I was going and what was happening. In fact, everybody was against…my teachers, my friends, my well wishers.'

During these enormously difficult times, Kranti took great care of Osho and looked after his needs with love and dedication.

Osho often complained of severe headaches which caused her great worry. She and her brother Arvind wanted very much to do something, to find some cure for Osho's painful headaches, but he would tell them lovingly not to bother since there was nothing anybody could do about it.

Osho's father also mentioned Osho's headaches. Once the pain became so severe that Kranti and Arvind sent an urgent message to Gadarwara, and Dadda had to rush to Jabalpur. Dadda thought that the headaches were caused by the heavy reading Osho used to do. He remembered how, when in Gadarwara, Osho simply kept applying the pain-killing balm to his forehead and continued to read.

Osho's mother also recalled an earlier incident when Osho once had an excruciating pain in his head and blood started running from his nose. She got worried, but fortunately, after a while, the bleeding stopped. But the headaches of these early years of college did not seem to be related to his reading habits. Rather, they were due to the psychological state Osho was passing through.

Looking at his physical and psychological condition, the family began to suspect that the astrologer's prediction of Osho's death at twenty-one might come true. They took him from one doctor to another. Osho alone knew that these frantic efforts were meaningless. He insisted that there was no need to see a doctor, since no medicine would do him any good. Osho describes one remarkable visit to a physician:

'I was also taken to a vaidya, to a physician. In fact, I was taken to many doctors and to many physicians but only one Ayurvedic vaidya told my father, "He is not ill. Don't waste your time." Of course, they were dragging me from one place to another. And many people would give me medicines and I would tell my father, "Why are you worried? I am perfectly okay." But nobody would believe what I was saying. They would say, "You keep quiet. You just take the medicine. What is wrong in it?" So I used to take all sorts of medicines.

'There was only one vaidya who was a man of insight. His name was Pandit Bhagirath Prasad…That old man is gone, but he was a rare man of insight. He looked at me and he said, "He is not ill." And he started crying and said, "I have been searching for this state myself. He is fortunate. In this life I have missed this state. Don't take him to anybody. He is reaching home." And he cried tears of happiness.

'He became my protector—my protector against the doctors and other physicians. He said to my father, "You leave it to me. I will take care." He never gave me any medicine. When my father insisted, he just gave me sugar pills and told me, "These are sugar pills. Just to console them, you can take them. They will not harm, they will not help. In fact, there is no help possible."'

The physician's reading of Osho's condition was correct because his disease was unusual; he was not an ordinary patient. Osho knew his condition and its causes better than any medical practitioner.

'Now it was beyond me, it was happening. I had done something. Unknowingly, I had knocked at the door. Now the door had opened. I had been meditating for many years, just sitting silently doing nothing, and by and by I started getting into that space, that heart space, where your are and you are not doing anything; you are simply there, a presence, a watcher.'

The intensity of Osho's meditations continued to deepen. His experiences were leading him towards the big explosion. Of all the meditations he used to do, the one that involved sitting on the top of a tree turned out to be particularly powerful. This fascinating experience occurred at Saugar, in Madhya Pradesh, approximately one year before the big event took place. While studying in college at Jabalpur, Osho was invited to participate in a debating contest sponsored by Saugar University. Osho was there for three days, and he describes what happened:

'I used to sit on a tree and meditate in the night. Many times I felt that when I meditated sitting on the earth, my body became powerful and had the upper hand—perhaps because the body is made out of earth. The talk *about the yogis going to the mountain tops or the heights of the Himalayas is certainly not vain, but is definitely based on scientific principles.*

'The greater the distance between the body and the earth, the more the physical force or pressure of the body lessens…and the power of the inner force increases. That is why I used to climb up a tall tree and get myself engrossed in meditation for hours every night.

'One night I got so lost in meditation that I did not know when my body fell down from the tree. I looked about askance when I saw my body lying on the ground. I was surprised at this happening. How it happened that I was sitting on the tree and my body was lying on the ground. I could not understand at all. It was a very queer experience. A bright line, a glittering silver cord from the navel of my body was joined on to me up above where I was perched on the tree. It was beyond my capacity to understand or foresee what would happen next and I worried how I would return to my body. How long that trance lasted I do not know, but that unique experience was not known to me before.

'That day for the first time, I saw my own body from outside, and since that day the mere physical existence of my body finished forever. And from that day death also ceased to exist, because that day I experienced that the body and spirit are two different things, quite separate from each other. That was the most important moment: my realisation of the spirit that is within every human body.

'It is really very difficult to say how long that experience lasted. As morning dawned, two women carrying milk cans from some nearby village passed by that way and saw my body…lying there. I saw them looking at my body from the top of the tree beside it. They touched my forehead with their palms and in a moment, as if by sheer force of attraction, I returned inside my body and my eyes opened.

'I felt that a woman can create a charge of electricity in the body of a man and similarly a man can too in the body of a woman. Then I pondered over the coincidence of the woman's touch to my forehead and my instant return to my body. How and why did all that happen? Many more experiences of this sort occurred to me and I understood why in India those spiritualists who carried on experiments on samadhi (*an uninterrupted state of pure consciousness*) and the fact of death got women to collaborate with them.

'If in a deep and profound samadhi *the spiritual self,* tejas sharira, *has gone out of the man's physical body, it cannot return to the body without the cooperation and assistance of a woman. In the same way if it has gone out of a woman's body, it cannot return without the assistance of a man. No sooner do the bodies of a man and woman come in contact than a current is established and an electrical circle is completed, and that very instant the consciousness of the spirit which has gone out returns.*

'*Thereafter I experienced this phenomenon six times within the period of six months. During those eventful six months, I felt that my life span became less by ten years: that is to say, if I was to live seventy years, now with these experiences I would only live a life of sixty years. Such extraordinary experiences I had in those six months! The hair on my chest turned white and I failed to grasp the meaning of all those happenings. Then I thought, and I realised that whatever connection or link there was between this physical body and that spiritual being was interrupted and the adjustment that existed naturally between them was broken.*'[1]

As Osho entered deeper and deeper into the mysteries of meditation, his questions disappeared. His *doing* ceased; the search came to a point from which there was nowhere to go. As had happened years ago at the time of his grandfather's death, Osho was brought to his centre—but now it was forever. Osho recounts that deep down there was emptiness, there was no doer. He had lost ambition; he did not have any desire to become anybody, or to reach anywhere. He did not care for God or for nirvana. 'The Buddha-disease had completely disappeared,' says Osho.

The opportune moment had come. The doors were about to open, the dawn was not too far. In Osho's words:

'*One day a questionless condition came about. It is not that I received the answer—no! Rather, all the questions just fell away and a great void was created. This was an explosive situation. Living in that condition was as good as dying. And then the person died who had been asking questions.*

After that experience of void, I asked no questions. All matters on which questions could be asked became non-existent. Previously, there was only asking and asking. Thereafter, nothing like questioning remained.'

Osho himself did not reveal the event of enlightenment to anyone for about twenty years. The story came out rather dramatically one night while Osho was living in the Woodland Apartments in Mumbai. Kranti was often asked by friends if she knew when Osho was enlightened. She could not tell them because she did not know, but every time someone new asked her about it, she again felt the impulse to try to find out from Osho.

Kranti recounts her conversation with Osho:

'Last night, (27 November 1972), the curiosity that I had carried for so long became uncontrollable. It was about 11:30 pm. After taking his milk Osho had gone to bed. I also lay down in my bed and suddenly I felt like asking Osho when he had attained enlightenment. No sooner had the thought occurred to me than I asked, "When did you attain enlightenment?" Osho laughed and said, "Do you yourself feel inspired to know about it or is it because people keep on asking you?"

'I said, "Both things are true, please tell me." Osho started laughing again and said, "I'll tell you some other time." I said, "I want to know right now." He said, "Start thinking and you will come to know."

'I remained quiet for a while. Then I said, "I think you attained enlightenment at the age of twenty-one or twenty-two when you were studying in Inter (Intermediate: second year of college)." No sooner had I mentioned this than Osho said a little seriously, "At the age of twenty-one, not twenty-two." Then I became curious about the date and the year and asked about it.

'Osho said, "On 21 March 1953." After some time, I asked again, "Where did it happen? Did anything unusual take place on that day?"

'Osho said, "Try to recall, you will come to remember everything." I kept lying silently, and remembered a night twenty year ago. I said, "That night

when all of a sudden at twelve o'clock you told me you were leaving, and then returned at three o'clock."

'Osho said, "You got it exactly right, precisely on that night." I could not believe that what I was seeing was really true. And here was Osho telling me that it was indeed true. Could I see in the past? It was all his play. It was all his doing. While such thoughts were clamouring in my mind, yet another curiosity arose: At what time in the night, where and at which place did Osho become enlightened? I immediately asked, "Where did you go that night?"

'Osho said, "To the Bhanvartal Garden." No sooner had he said "to the garden" than I remembered a tree. I said, "You went to the garden and sat under the ashoka tree."

'He said, "No, I was under the maulshree." Then I asked, "Since you were in the garden between twelve and three, at what time in the night did the event take place?"

'He said, "Recall and you will remember it." I was quiet for a while and all the scenes of that evening began to appear before my eyes: how he left home, how he woke me gently and said he was going out, didn't know when he would return. He left just after telling me that much, while I stayed up the whole night waiting for his return.

'Then the whole event began to reveal itself to me. I could even recall his mudra (body posture). Somehow I felt that the event must have taken place at two o'clock. As I got the idea of two o'clock, I told Osho about it.

'He said, "It happened exactly at two o'clock. Now you are getting it all right." Once again I was full of amazement, but I was so filled with joy that it became impossible to sleep. Again and again I felt like waking up everyone and telling them what I had learned.'[2]

Osho himself gives the reason for not revealing the story of his enlightenment for almost twenty years as follows:

'Many people have asked me that if I became enlightened in 1953, why did I keep silent? For almost twenty years I never said anything about it to anybody unless somebody suspected himself, unless somebody asked me on his own…"We feel that something has happened to you. We don't know what it is, but one thing is certain: that something has happened, you are no more the same as we are and you are hiding it."

'In those twenty years not more than ten people had asked me and even then I avoided them as much as I could, unless I felt that their desire was genuine. And I told them only when they had promised to keep it a secret. And they all fulfilled it. Now they are all sannyasins…I said, "You wait, you wait for the right moment; only then I will declare it."

'I have learned much from the past Buddhas. If Jesus had kept quieter about his being the son of God it would have been far more beneficial to humanity.'

Osho had made it a point not to reveal it until he stopped travelling about the country, for to have it known would mean great risk to his life.

'For twenty years continuously I was moving, and there was not a single bodyguard. And I was in constant danger: stones where being thrown at me, shoes were being thrown at me. I would reach a town after travelling twenty-four hours in the train, and the crowd wouldn't allow me to get down into the station; they would force me to go back. There would ensue a fight between those who wanted me to get down from the train and those who did not want me to get down, in their town at least.

'If I had declared that I was enlightened, I would have been killed very easily; there was no problem in it; it would have been so simple. But for twenty years I kept absolutely silent about it. I declared it only when I saw that I had gathered enough people who would understand it…enough people who were mine, who belonged to me. I declared it only when I knew that I could create my own small world and I was no more concerned with the crowds and the masses and the stupid mob.'

After over twenty years, Osho described in his own words that incredibly powerful experience. He has articulated the experience in more detail than perhaps any other enlightened being has ever done before:

'I am reminded of the fateful day of 21 March 1953, for many lives I had been working—working upon myself, struggling, doing whatsoever can be done—and nothing was happening. Now I understand why nothing was happening. The very effort was the barrier, the very ladder was preventing, the very urge to seek was the obstacle. Not that one can reach without seeking. Seeking is needed, but then comes a point when seeking has to be dropped. The boat is needed to cross the river but then comes a moment when you have to get out of the boat and forget all about it and leave it behind. Effort is needed, without effort nothing is possible. And also with only effort, nothing is possible.

'Just seven days before 21 March, I stopped working on myself. A moment comes when you see the whole futility of effort. You have done all that you can do and nothing is happening. You have done all that is humanly possible. Then what else can you do? In sheer helplessness one drops all search.

'And the day the search stopped, the day I was not seeking for something, the day I was not expecting something to happen. It started happening. A new energy arose, out of nowhere. It was coming from nowhere and everywhere. It was in the trees and in the rocks and the sky and the sun and the air—it was everywhere. And I was seeking so hard, and I was thinking it is very far away. And it was so near and so close.

'...Seven days I lived in a very hopeless and helpless state, but at the same time something was arising. When I say hopeless I don't mean what you mean by the word hopeless. I simply mean there was no hope in me. Hope was absent. I am not saying that I was hopeless and sad. I was happy in fact, I was very tranquil, calm and collected and centered. Hopeless, but in a totally new meaning. There was no hope, so how could there be hopelessness. Both had disappeared.

'The hopelessness was absolute and total. Hope had disappeared and with it its counterpart, hopelessness, had also disappeared. It was a totally new experience—*of being without hope. It was not a negative state...It was absolutely positive. It was not just absence, a presence was felt. Something was overflowing in me, over flooding me.*

'And when I say I was helpless. I don't mean the word in the dictionary sense. I simply say I was selfless. That's what I mean when I say helpless. I have recognised the fact that I am not, so I cannot depend on myself, so I cannot stand on my own ground.

'...I was in...a bottomless abyss. But there was no fear, because there was nothing to protect. There was no fear, because there was nobody to be afraid.

'Those seven days were of tremendous transformation, total transformation. And the last day the presence of a totally new energy, a new light and new delight, became so intense that it was almost unbearable, as if I was exploding, as if I was going mad with blissfulness. The new generation in the West has the right word for it: I was blissed out, stoned.

'It was impossible to make any sense out of...what was happening. It was a very non-sense world—difficult to figure it out, difficult to manage in categories, difficult to use words, languages, explanations. All scriptures appeared dead and all the words that have been used for this experience looked very pale, anaemic. This was so alive. It was like a tidal wave of bliss.

'The whole day was strange, stunning, and it was a shattering experience. The past was disappearing, as if it had never belonged to me, as if I had read about it somewhere, as if I had dreamed about it, as if it was somebody else's story I have heard and somebody told it to me. I was becoming loose from my past, I was being uprooted from my history, I was losing my autobiography. I was becoming a non-being, what Buddha calls anatta. *Boundaries were disappearing, distinctions were disappearing. Mind was disappearing; it was millions of miles away. It was difficult to catch hold of it, it was rushing farther and farther away, and there was no urge to keep it close. I was simply indifferent about it all. It was okay. There was no urge to remain continuous with the past.*

'By the evening it became so difficult to bear it—it was hurting, it was painful. It was like when a woman goes into labour when a child is to be born, and the woman suffers tremendous pain—the birth pangs.

'I used to go to sleep on those days about twelve or one in the night, but that day it was impossible to remain awake. My eyes were closing; it was difficult to keep them open. Something was very imminent, something was going to happen. It was difficult to say what it was—maybe it is going to be my death—but there was no fear. I was ready for it. Those seven days had been so beautiful that I was ready to die, nothing more was needed. They had been so tremendously blissful. I was so contented, that if death was coming, it was welcome.

'But something was going to happen—something like death, something very drastic, something which will be either a death or a new birth, a crucifixion or a resurrection—but something of tremendous import was just around the corner. And it was impossible to keep my eyes open…I went to sleep near about eight. It was not like sleep. Now I can understand what Patanjali means when he says that sleep and samadhi are similar. Only with one difference—that in samadhi you are fully awake and asleep also. Asleep and awake together, the whole body relaxed, every cell of the body totally relaxed, all functioning relaxed, and yet a light of awareness burns within you…clear, smokeless.

'You remain alert and yet relaxed, loose but fully awake. The body is in the deepest sleep possible and your consciousness is at its peak. The peak of consciousness and the valley of the body meet.

'I went to sleep. It was a very strange sleep. The body was asleep, I was awake. It was so strange—as if one was torn apart into two directions, two dimensions; as if the polarity has become completely focused, as if I was both the polarities together: the positive and negative were meeting, sleep and awareness were meeting, death and life were meeting. That is the moment when you can say, "The creator and the creation meet."

'It was weird. For the first time it shocks you to the very roots, it shakes your foundations. You can never be the same after that experience; it brings a new vision to your life, a new quality.

'Near about midnight my eyes suddenly opened—I had not opened them. The sleep was broken by something else. I felt a great presence around me in the room. It was a very small room. I felt a throbbing life all around me, a great vibration—almost like a hurricane, a great storm of light, joy, ecstasy. I was drowning in it. It was so tremendously real that everything became unreal. The walls of the room became unreal, the house became unreal, my own body became unreal...That night another reality opened its door, another dimension became available. Suddenly it was there, the other reality, the separate reality, the really Real, or whatsoever you want to call it—call it God, call it truth, call it Dhamma, call it Tao, or whatsoever you will. It was nameless. But it was there—so opaque, so transparent, and yet so solid one could have touched it. It was almost suffocating me in that room. It was too much and I was not yet capable of absorbing it.

'A deep urge arose in me to rush out of the room, to go under the sky; it was suffocating me. It was too much! It will kill me! If I had remained a few moments more, it would have suffocated me, it looked like that. I rushed out of the room, came out in the street. A great urge was there just to be under the sky with the stars, with the trees, with the earth...to be with nature. And immediately as I came out, the feeling of being suffocated disappeared. It was too small a place for such a big phenomenon. Even the sky is a small place for that big phenomenon...It is bigger than the sky. Even the sky is not the limit for it. But then I felt more at ease.

'I was walking towards the nearest garden. It was a totally new walk, as if gravitation had disappeared. I was walking, or I was running, or I was simply flying; it was difficult to decide. There was no gravitation, I was feeling weightless—as if some energy was taking me. I was in the hands of some other energy.

'For the first time I was not alone, for the first time I was no more an individual, for the first time the drop had come and fallen into the ocean. Now the whole ocean was mine, I was the ocean. There was no limitation. A tremendous power arose as if I could do anything whatsoever. I was not there, only the power was there. I reached the garden where I used to go every day. The garden was closed for the night. It was too late, it was almost one o'clock in the night. The gardeners were fast asleep. I had to enter the garden like a thief. I had to climb the gate. But some thing was pulling me towards the garden. It was not within my capacity to prevent myself. I was just floating.

'That's what I mean when I say again and again, "Float with the river, don't push the river." I was relaxed. I was in a let-go. I was not there. It was there, call it God—God was there. The moment I entered the garden everything became luminous, it was all over the place; the benediction, the blessedness. I could see the trees for the first time—their green, their life, their very sap running. The whole garden was asleep, the trees were asleep. But I could see the whole garden alive, even the small grass leaves were so beautiful.

'I looked around. One tree was tremendously luminous—the maulshree tree. It attracted me, it pulled me towards itself. I had not chosen it, God himself had chosen it. I went to the tree, I sat under the tree. As I sat there things started settling. The whole universe became a benediction.

'It is difficult to say how long I was in that state. When I went back home it was four o'clock in the morning, so I must have been there by clock time at least three hours, but it was infinity. It had nothing to do with clock time. It was timeless.

'Those three hours became the whole eternity, endless eternity. There was no time, there was no passage of time; it was the virgin reality—uncorrupted, untouchable, unmeasurable. And that day something happened that has continued—not as a continuity—but it has still continued as an undercurrent. Not as a permanency—each moment it has been happening again and again. It has been a miracle each moment.'

In a way, the story of Osho ends right here. 'There is no story after that explosion,' says Osho, 'there are no events after it. All events are before the explosion. After the explosion there is only void.' His search came to an end and, in a way, the prediction of the astrologer finally came true. The man named Rajneesh Chandra Mohan died at twenty-one and yet the resurrection happened, the miracle happened. He was reborn, but not in the physical body; he attained something, but not of this world—he simply arrived home:

'...As if a dew drop slipping from a lotus leaf into the ocean. In one sense the dew drop disappears; in another sense it becomes the very ocean, it becomes oceanic. When the dew drop is slipping from the lotus leaf, there is a natural hesitation, that, "I am going to disappear into this vast ocean. There is still time, if I can hold." But once the dew drop has melted into the ocean, merged, there is tremendous joy because now the other side of the story opens up: now the dew drop is no more there, but an infinite ocean.'

The event was, in a way, a miracle, and yet there was nothing miraculous about it. The bud had flowered; the hidden had become manifest. The flowering is a miracle and not a miracle. It is a miracle in the sense that the seed has been transformed into something unbelievable; and not a miracle because it is the culmination of a natural evolutionary process. Osho has often quoted the mystic Kabir which aptly describes the state of Osho's enlightenment. He says:

'The universe is an expansion of energy, and life is the crystallisation of it. What we see as matter, what we see as stone, is also energy. What is seen as life, what is experienced as thought, what is felt like consciousness is also a transformation of energy. The whole cosmos, whether it is the waves of the sea or the pine trees of the forest or the grains of sand or the stars in the skies or that which is within us—all are manifestations of the same energy in infinite forms and ways.

'It is difficult to say where we begin and where we end. It is equally difficult to say where our body ends. The body which we take to be our limit is not limited in itself. If the sun, who is a hundred million miles away, cools down, we will instantly freeze to death. This means that the sun is ever present in our beings, he is a part of our bodies. As soon as he will lose his heat we will perish. The heat of the sun is the heat of our bodies

'There is an ocean of air currents all around us from which we draw our vital energy—the life breath. If it ceases to be available to us we would die immediately. Where does the body end? If you investigate fully then the whole universe is our body. Our body is limitless and infinite. And if you search rightly, you will find that the centre of life is everywhere and it is expanding everywhere. But to know it, to experience it, it is essential that we ourselves become energy that is tremendously alive.

'What I call meditation is another name for freeing in every way the flow of energy that has gotten blocked up within us. So when you enter into meditation the hidden energy may awaken with such force that it gets connected with the energy on the outside. But as soon as this connection is established we become like tiny leaves floating in the infinite ocean of winds. Then our separate existence is lost and we become one with the immeasurable.

'What is it that is known after being one with the immeasurable? Up to now man has tried in every way to say it, but it could not be said. Kabir says, "I searched for him and searched a good deal. And in the course of the search itself I lost myself. He was found for sure, but only when I was no more. Who can now say what it is that is found? And how to say it?" What Kabir said on having this experience for the first time he subsequently changed. When for the first time he experienced God, he said, "It seems that the drop has entered into the ocean." His own words are:

Searching on and on, O my friend,
Kabir lost himself.
A drop merged in the ocean;
how can it be found again?

'Kabir lost himself in the course of the search. The drop merged into the ocean; so how can it be recovered? But he changed it later, and the change is very significant. He said later that what he had said before was wrong; he was mistaken to say so. It was not the case of the drop entering the sea, but the sea itself had entered into the drop. If the drop had merged in the ocean there was a chance of recalling it, but recovery was far more difficult when the ocean had merged into the drop. And in the case of the drop entering the ocean, the drop would have said something about it. But it was now so difficult to say anything when the sea itself had merged in the drop. So he said later:

Searching on and on, my friend,
Kabir lost himself.
The sea merged in the drop,
so how can it be found again?'

Osho has repeatedly stressed that enlightenment is already present, it is already an integral part of our being—it is not a thing to be achieved somewhere in the future. As Osho points out, enlightenment is already available to us; one simply has to 'relax into it'. He explains:

'An enlightened person is not somebody who has reached to the pinnacle, who has reached to the topmost rung of the ladder. You are all ladder climbers…you need a ladder…Enlightenment is not the last rung of a ladder, enlightenment is getting down from the ladder, getting down forever and never asking for any ladder again, becoming natural.'

Osho warns us to beware of certain explanations about enlightenment since they can easily confuse seekers. Using Sri Aurobindo's description of 'supra-consciousness' as an example, Osho comments:

'Enlightenment is a natural state. It is not some supra-conscious state, supra-mental. Avoid Sri Aurobindo and his terminology; that is all mind games. It (enlightenment) is not something very special; it is very ordinary. It is so ordinary that there is nothing to brag about in it.'

The story that follows Osho's enlightenment is a new story, in the sense that it is not continuous with his past. From here on, he does not do anything because the ego—the sense of the *doer* and the *doing*—has ceased to exist. 'That night I became empty and became full,' says Osho.

'I became non-existential and became existence. That night I died and was reborn. But the one that was reborn has nothing to do with that which died, it is a discontinuous thing…The one who died, died totally; nothing of him has remained…not even a shadow. It died totally, utterly…That day of 21 March the person who had lived for many, many lives, for millennia, simply died. Another being, absolutely new, not connected at all with the old, started to exist.'

The experience of that 'death' was a religious one in its purest and most original sense. Osho continues:

'Religion just gives you a total death. Maybe that's why the whole day

previous to that happening I was feeling some urgency like death, as if I was going to die—and I really died. I have known many other deaths, but they were nothing compared to it; they were partial deaths. Sometimes the body died, sometimes a part of the mind died, sometimes a part of the ego died, but as far as the person was concerned, it remained. Renovated many times, decorated many times, changed a little bit here and there, but it remained; the continuity remained. That night the death was total. It was a date with death and God simultaneously.'

The event did not change either Osho's routine or his lifestyle, however. He continued to visit the college whenever he felt like doing so, but remained busy mostly reading and writing. The reading he did then and later was, however, for a different purpose. Before enlightenment, his reading was part of his own search, while after that happening, reading became part of his work to help those who were still searching. Reading made it possible for Osho to be familiar with current thinking, research, and terminology, and enabled him to communicate his thoughts and share his experiences in the most up-to-date manner, in the context of present-day living. Incredible as it may sound, he read during his lifetime more than 80,000 books on almost 400 different subjects. About his love for books, Osho says:

'I have been collecting books from my high school days. You will be surprised that by the time I was a matriculate (high school graduate) I had read thousands of books—and collected hundreds of books of my own—and great masterpieces. I was finished with Kahlil Gibran, Dostoevsky, Tolstoy, Chekhov, Gorky, Turgnev—the best as far as writing is concerned. When I was finishing my Intermediate, I was finished with Socrates, Plato, Aristotle, Bertrand Russell—all the philosophers I could find in any library, in any bookshop, or borrow from anybody.

'In Jabalpur there was one beautiful place where I was an everyday visitor. I would go for at least one or two hours. It was called the Thieves' Market. Stolen things were sold there, and I was after stolen books because so many people were stealing books and selling them and I was getting such beautiful books—I got Gurdjieff's first book from there, and Ouspensky's In Search of the Miraculous.'

Osho wrote for various newspapers and magazines in Hindi. His language and style were essentially poetic, and the thoughts were deep and profound. He was also in demand to give talks and to participate in debates in Jabalpur and other cities. His talks were original, fiery and authentic.

All this time, while Osho was at school in Jabalpur, his paternal grandmother was very eager for him to get married. She kept pushing the family, especially Osho's father, Dadda, to arrange his marriage. Dadda's friends also kept urging Osho's marriage, but Dadda was hesitant to even propose the idea to his son. He knew very well that suggesting to Osho to get married would mean taking a big chance, for if Osho said no, then that would be the end of the whole matter.

Nevertheless, when Osho came home after graduating form the university, indirectly through Osho's friends Dadda tried to find if he would be interested in marrying. Osho felt that Dadda himself should ask this question directly. Dadda was hesitant; finally, he asked Osho's mother to go and talk to him. As Osho tells the story:

'...One night she came to my bed, sat there, and asked me what I thought about marriage. So I said, "I have not married yet, so I have no experience. You know well, you have the experience, so you tell me. Take fifteen days: think over it, contemplate, and if you feel you have achieved something through it, then just order me. I will follow the order. Don't ask about my opinion. I have none, because I have no experience. You are experienced. If you were again given a chance, would you get married?"

'She said, "You are trying to confuse me."

'I said, "You take your time, at your own ease. I will wait for two weeks, then you order me. I will just follow, because I don't know."

'So for two weeks she was worried. She could not sleep because she knew if she said to marry, I would follow. Then she would be responsible, not I. So after two weeks she said, "I am not going to say anything, because if I look to my own experience, then I would not like you to move into that life. But I cannot say anything now."

'So this is how I remained unmarried. Sincerely, authentically, I was not ready to marry, I was not intending at all.'

Osho completed his BA in philosophy in 1955, and began working towards his MA at the well known Saugar University. At Saugar he lived in a student dormitory for two years. Osho got his master's degree in philosophy (first division) in 1957 and was recognised as an outstanding student of the university. Although he was awarded gold medal, the honour didn't matter to him much. Here is the story of the gold medal in Osho's words:

'I came first in the university and won the gold medal. But I had promised (that if he won the gold medal he would throw it in the university well right away), so I had to drop the gold medal down the well in front of everybody. The whole university was there, and I dropped the gold medal. I said to them, "With this I drop the idea that I am the first in the university, so that nobody feels inferior to me. I am just a nobody."'

He enjoyed those two years tremendously, because he could immerse himself completely in the vast collection of the university library, and at the same time enjoy a pleasant, natural setting surrounded by beautiful hills. Rather than attending classes, Osho spent most of his time reading in the library and roaming at night under the starry sky, enjoying the raindrops or walking in the hills. Even on holidays when the library was closed, he could be found reading on the library lawn or wandering with nature as his only company.

His life for these two years at Saugar remained as interesting as ever and reflected the same essential qualities of rebelliousness and experimentation that he had shown all along. It did not matter to him whether or not what he did conformed to the dictates of family, society, school, or religion.

Osho explains that one does not become integrated. One is already integrated deep inside, though on the periphery there is much turmoil; hence, one only needs to move inward. And the deeper one goes inside, the more one finds that he is already integrated. How to discover it? For this he suggests: 'Only do that which you enjoy doing. If you do not enjoy, don't do it.' He relates his own experiment:

'I used to do it in my university days, and people thought that I was crazy: suddenly I would stop, and...remain in that spot for half an hour, an hour unless I started enjoying walking again. My professors were so afraid that, when there were examinations, they would put me in a car and take me to the university hall. They would leave me at the door and wait there: had I reached my desk or not? If I was taking my bath and suddenly I realised that I was not enjoying it, I would stop. What is the point then? If I was eating and I recognised suddenly that I was not enjoying (it), then I would stop.'

Similarly, once during his school days in Gadarwara, he got up in the middle of his first mathematics class in high school and told his teacher he would not come back because he did not enjoy the class. 'And by and by,' points out Osho, 'it became a key. I suddenly recognised that whenever you are enjoying something, you are centred. Enjoyment is just the sound of being centred. Whenever you are not enjoying something, you are off centre.'

One can gain a perspective on Osho's life by understanding his experiment with the three *gunas*—the three basic qualities that make up the human personality. An individual of *tamas guna* shows inactivity, inertia, indolence; one of *rajas guna* exhibits intense activity or passion; and a person of *sattva guna* has the quality of serenity, calmness and wisdom. Lord Krishna has elaborated upon these *gunas* in the *Bhagavad Gita*. Osho's discourses on the *Bhagavad Gita* in Hindi contain a detailed explanation of these *gunas* or qualities.

Generally, all three *gunas* are present in all individuals in different proportions. The mixture of these *gunas* in each person contributes to the formation of each individual's personality. No matter how predominant one quality may be in a person, the other two are also there, even if dormant.

Commenting upon the past Buddhas—Jesus, Mohammed, Lao Tzu, Ramana Maharshi, and Krishna—Osho has this to say:

'Rajas *was the predominant medium of expression for Jesus and Mohammed. Tamas was the predominant quality of Lao Tzu and Ramana Maharshi. But Krishna made use of all the three qualities simultaneously as his medium of expression. Just as the equilateral triangle has three lines of equal length, in the personality of Krishna all three gunas are present and united in equal measure.'*

Because of this, Krishna is not consistent and, therefore, Krishna's life and actions have been very much misunderstood. In contrast, Buddha, Lao Tzu, Mohammed and Jesus are quite consistent, because they exhibit one predominant quality. Osho has exhibited all three *gunas* as Krishna did, but with one difference: he has used them sequentially rather than simultaneously. 'In my opinion this is the most scientific way of doing it, and that is why I have chosen this way,' says Osho.

Reflecting further upon the similarities between Krishna's personality and his own, Osho explains:

'In me also there will be inconsistency, but not so much as in Krishna. There is another possibility which I have utilised in my own experiments. All three gunas are present in every individual, and a personality can be complete and total only when all three are utilised. None of the gunas need be suppressed. Neither is Krishna in favour of suppression, nor am I in favour of suppression. Whatsoever there is in an individual must be utilised creatively.'

Throughout the early period of his life Osho was often regarded as lazy and of no help to the family. This, however, was due to the fact that he often experimented with the quality of *tamas* (inactivity, indolence).

'The first years of my life were spent like Lao Tzu, in experiencing the mysteries of the tamas guna. My attachment to Lao Tzu is, therefore, fundamental. I was inactive in everything; inactivity was the achievement sought by me. As far as possible, nothing was done—only as much as was unavoidable or compulsory. I did not do so much as move a hand or a foot without a reason.'

Osho gives an illustration:

'In my house, the situation was such that my mother sitting before me would say, "Nobody else can be found and I want to send someone to fetch vegetables from the market." I would hear this as I sat idly in front of her. I knew that even if the house was on fire, she would say to me, "No one else can be found and our house is on fire, who will extinguish it?" But silently, the only thing I did was to watch my inactivity as a witness, in full awareness.'

During this period, the quality of inactivity became significant for Osho in his overall experimentation with the three *gunas*.

'In my own experiments I chose to express one guna *at a time—only one in a single time period. First I chose* tamas…*because this principle is in the basic foundation of everyone. When a child is growing in the mother's womb for nine months, it is living in this* guna. *The child does not do anything on its own. It is in a condition of total inactivity.'*

Osho finds this *guna* not only the predominant one, but he also shows how the state of inactivity in the womb is significant in a spiritual sense.

'The child has known supreme silence in the womb. This memory is hidden deep down in the unconscious. That nine-month experience in the mother's womb was very blissful, because then there was nothing to be done…There was only existence for you—just being. This state is very similar to the state we call liberation.'

Osho thus teaches that the search for a silent and blissful state is not accidental—rather it is related to our deep unconscious; it is a search for the blissful state of the womb. But there is one crucial difference between life in the womb and any attempt to re-experience it. The state in the womb is part of the biological process of growth and the child is not conscious of the state, but in the remembrance or revival of that state at the peak of spiritual experience, the individual is fully conscious. Osho uses a metaphor to describe the function of *tamas guna*:

'Inactivity is the foundation, and blissful silence is the crest. This house which we call life is built on the foundation of inactivity. The middle structure is the active part and the dome of that temple is ultimate bliss. In my opinion, this is the edifice of life. That is why I…practised inactivity in the first part of my life.'

In Osho's experiments with each of the three *gunas*, one constant factor was his watchfulness, his awareness, his remaining a witness to each state, his being an unidentified observer. He describes the nature of this awareness by relating the following story:

'In the last year of my university education, there was one professor of philosophy. Like most professors of philosophy, he was obstinate and eccentric. He was obstinate in his determination not to see any woman. Unfortunately there were only two students in his class…myself and … a young girl. Therefore, this professor had to teach us while keeping his eyes closed.

'This was a very lucky thing for me, because while he would give a lecture I would sleep in class. Because there was a young girl in the class he could not open his eyes. However, the professor was very pleased with me, because he thought that I also believed in the principle of not looking at women, and that in the whole university there was at least one other person who did not see women. Therefore, many times when he met me alone he told me that I was the only person who could understand him.

'But one day this image of me was erased. The professor had one other habit. He did not believe in a one-hour period for his lectures. Therefore, he was always given the last period by the university. He would say, "It is in my hands when to begin a lecture, but it is not in my hands to end it." Therefore, his lecture might end in sixty minutes or eighty minutes or even ninety minutes; it made no difference to him…There was an understanding between the young girl and myself that she would wake me up when the period was near to end. One day, however, she had been called by someone for some urgent work during the middle of the period, and she went away. I kept on sleeping and the professor went on lecturing. When the period was over and he opened his eyes, he found me sleeping. He woke me up and asked why I was sleeping. I said to him, "Now that you have found me *sleeping I would like to tell you that I have been sleeping daily, that I have no quarrel with young women and that it is very pleasurable to sleep while you are lecturing."'*

During these years sleeping had become a sort of meditation for Osho. He came to know during his experiments with sleep what Krishna had conveyed to Arjuna: 'Even though the rest of the world remains asleep at night, the sage is always awake.' Osho experienced wakefulness, the witnessing state, in his sleep. This is different from the sleep in which one remains unconscious. Osho found out that if one persisted in sleeping more than the body requirement then, 'Someone inside you remains aware and becomes a witness of all that is happening around you…then within you a sort of wakeful sound begins to become audible.'

Osho describes his life at Saugar University during this inactive phase:

'I made it my first principle to refrain from doing anything. For the two years that I was in the university hostel, I never cleaned or swept my room. I kept my cot right at the entrance of my room so that from the door I could jump straight into my cot and from the cot I could jump straight out of the room. Why should the whole room be unnecessarily traversed, I felt. Neither did I want to enter into the room, nor was there any question of cleaning it. There was, however, a sort of joy in this.

'Things were left in the same way that they had been arranged prior to my living there, no change was made. No more was ever done than the minimum that was necessary. Because changing things around required that something be done, things were kept as they were. But due to this, some unique experiences began to dawn, as every guna has its own unique experience. No matter how much rubbish became collected in my room, it did not disturb me at all. I had learned to live with that condition just as I would live in a place which is meticulously cleaned.

'In the university where I was studying, new buildings were as yet not constructed. It was a newly established university, and military barracks were used as a hostel. Because the barracks were in a deep forest it was frequently common for snakes to appear. I used to watch those snakes while sleeping on my cot. The snakes came, rested in the room and went away. Neither did they disturb me at any time, not did I disturb them.'

In his experiments with sleep and inactivity, Osho also experienced the state of no-mind, or the experience of having no thoughts—the state of being a pure consciousness.

'In those days I used to go on lying upon the cot, vacantly watching the ceiling above. I came to know after a long time that Meher Baba had meditated in this manner only. I did this without any effort, because while lying down on a cot what else is there to do? If the sleep was over, I would just go on looking at the ceiling without even blinking the eyes. Why even blink the eyes? It is also a type of doing. It is also a part of activity. I just went on lying there. There was nothing to be done. If you remain lying down like that, just looking at the ceiling for an hour or two, you will find that your mind becomes clear like a cloudless sky—just thoughtless. If someone can make inactivity his achievement in life, he can experience thoughtlessness very naturally and easily.'

This state of non-doing and no-mind opened up the doors of divine glory to him.

'In those days I neither believed in God nor in the soul. The only reason for not believing was that by believing something would have to be done. For inactivity, atheism is very helpful, because if God is, then some work will have to be done for him. But without any belief on my part in God and soul, by my simply lying down silently, the effulgent splendour of both God and soul began to be visualised. I did not give up inactivity until inactivity left me. Until then, I had decided to continue on like that—just doing nothing.'

As seen earlier, Osho remained mainly in the state of *tamas*, inactivity, throughout his school and college years. But after obtaining his master's degree, he entered into the state of *rajas guna* and became very active. He remained in the fiery *rajas* throughout the following years until he began to manifest the cool *sattva guna* and finally settled down in Pune in 1974.

Excerpts from:

Om Mani Padme Hum
Dimensions Beyond the Known
Tao: The Pathless Path vol. 2
The Dhammapada: The Way of the Buddha vol. 11
The Discipline of Transcendence vol. 2 and 4
The Last Testament vol. 3
In Search of the Miraculous
Take It Easy vol. 1
The Rajneesh Bible vol. 3
Vedanta: Seven Steps to Samadhi

End notes:

1. *The Sound of Running Water: A Photo-Biography of
   Bhagwan Shree Rajneesh and His Work 1974-1978.*
   Ma Prem Asha, Rajneesh Foundation, 1980.
2. *Jyotishikha* no. 27

4

NEO-SANNYAS:
THE LOTUS IN A SWAMP

After he graduated from the Saugar University, Osho looked for a teaching job. But his defiance of social norms once again threatened his prospects. He narrates an interesting episode:

'When I passed out of the university, I applied for a government job. The education minister called me for an interview and asked me for some character certificates (references). I said, "I am here; you look at me. I can sit here, you can watch me. I can live with you for a few days if you like. But don't ask about certificates. Who can give me a character certificate?"

'He couldn't understand and said, "You can bring one from your vice-chancellor, or at least from the head of your department."

'I said, "If my vice-chancellor asks for a character certificate for himself, I cannot give it to him. So how can I ask for a character certificate *from him? So that is impossible. I can ask for a character certificate only from a man whom I can see is a man of character. But that will be absurd. That means that first I give him a character certificate—only then his character certificate becomes meaningful."*

'He totally failed to follow me. He said, "Then it will be difficult, because at least two character certificates are needed."

'So I wrote a character reference in the name of my vice-chancellor. Later I went to the vice-chancellor and said, "This is the certificate I have given to myself. You have to sign it."

'He said, "But this is absurd. How can you give a character certificate (to) yourself?"

'I told him, "If I cannot give my own self, then who can give one to me? I know myself more than anybody else knows me. You don't know me at all. If you can give a character certificate to me, then why can't I? This is the certificate. You have to sign it."

'He looked at the certificate and laughed, because I had written in the certificate that man is freedom, and character is always of the past, and the future remains open. I may have been a good man up to now, but next moment? Nobody knows! I may have been a saint up to now, but the next moment I can become a sinner. In fact, each moment I have to give a new lease to my character, again and again I have to hold it.'

By his explanation, Osho managed to impress those who were involved in the process of his hiring, and got a teaching position at Sanskrit Mahavidyalaya, Raipur (Raipur Sanskrit College) in 1957. In 1960, he moved onto becoming a professor of philosophy at the University of Jabalpur.

Throughout his teaching career, Osho was respected as a brilliant and wonderful teacher. He inspired interest and a spirit of curiosity in his students and encouraged them to search for answers on their own. He was so popular that at the university, students often missed other classes to attend his lectures. As Osho describes, 'I had only ten students in my class, but soon the vice-chancellor had to give me special permission for a bigger class because 200 students were attending who were not my students. The other teachers were angry because the students who should have been in their classes, were sitting in mine. They told me, "This is not right." I said, "You don't be bothered. You can also come," and in fact a few teachers started coming too.'

But Osho's rebelliousness could not remain under wraps for even a day. Right from the first day he started his job at Raipur Sanskrit College, he was asking uncomfortable questions and rendering the customs of the old college loose. The following incident narrated by Osho attests this:

'I was a professor in a Sanskrit university. The first day I reached the university I was not yet allotted quarter(s) so I had to stay in the hostel for a few days. Because it was a Sanskrit university, and nobody wants to learn Sanskrit nowadays…almost 90 per cent of the students were on government scholarships. They were there only because of the scholarships. They had no desire to learn Sanskrit, they were not interested in it, but they were poor students and they could not get scholarships anywhere else, so it was better than nothing. And because there were almost all scholarship holders, they were forced to pray every morning at four o'clock.

'When I reached the university it was wintertime, and at four o'clock they had to take baths with cold water to get ready for the prayer meeting and were shivering. No hot water was provided—Sanskrit scholars are not supposed to have such luxuries as hot water; they are supposed to live like the ancient rishis and their disciples. And they had to get up early, at four o'clock in the brahma muhurta (which is one of the most divine moments according to the Hindu mythology).

'That first day, they did not know that I was a professor. I loved to have a cold bath in the morning, so I went to the well to take a bath. And the students were so angry: they were using all kinds of four-letter words… not only for the vice-chancellor but also for God.

'I went up to the vice-chancellor and said, "This is not right. You are not teaching them prayers. After the cold bath they have to stand in a line and pray for hours in Sanskrit. Now, how can they be prayerful? They are angry with God. If they come across God they will kill him! And they are praying all that while. What kind of prayer can it be?"

'But the vice-chancellor was an old Sanskrit scholar. He said, "No, that's not right. They are doing it on their own; we are not forcing anybody."

'I said, "I know that they are doing it on their own, because if they don't do it their scholarships disappear. You are not forcing them in a direct, but an indirect way. And if you want to argue with me, then give me only one day and I will put up a notice saying that whoever wants to have a cold bath at four o'clock and pray can get up, and whoever does not want to, need not worry about the scholarship; it will be up to him."

'Now the vice-chancellor was caught. He had to agree. I went to the vice-chancellor at four o'clock and he himself was asleep! I dragged him out of bed and said, "Come on! What kind of vice-chancellor are you? Your students are praying, taking cold baths, and you are asleep!" He was very angry at me. I said, "The same is happening to them. Come on!"

'And there was not a single student, the well was empty and the prayer hall was empty. I told him, "Now take a cold bath with me, and we will both pray!"

'He said, "I cannot take a cold bath. I am an old man!"

'I said, "Okay then I will take the cold bath. You sit here and watch, and then we will go and pray."

'He said, "But I am feeling tired and I want to go to sleep!"

'"Then," I said, "I am the only person who will be praying—and I don't know Sanskrit at all! And God understands only Sanskrit! I was wrongly appointed to this university by the mistake of the Ministry of Education. They thought, looking at me, that I must know Sanskrit. I don't know Sanskrit at all. I am not interested in anything dead."

'So he went to his room and I went to my room, and everybody slept.

That morning the students came to me and they were very happy and thankful. I said to the vice-chancellor, "This is far more beautiful, this is far more prayerful—their coming to me and thanking me." I said to him, "Stop all this nonsense!"

'But rather than stopping the nonsense he made the government transfer me to another university, saying, "This man is dangerous! He will destroy my students' morality, character and religion."'

After a year, Osho was assigned as a faculty at the Jabalpur University. During this period, he focused on his body and spent time exercising and building it up. Keeping himself in excellent physical health was in line with greater plans, for over the next ten years growing *rajas* energy was required to keep him constantly on the move. He travelled all over the country with great passion and purpose. Osho was perhaps aware of what a toll the following years would take on his health.

The hectic travelling schedule that followed from 1960 onwards, shows the *rajas* phase of his life. This activity, according to Osho, is possible only when one has thoroughly lived out or transcended the inactivity phase. Then it develops automatically and flows naturally from within. Osho explains that this sort of activity is tangentially different from the anxiety-ridden or the tense kind that, for example, a politician experiences. Unlike the latter's, this activity is not motivated by desire but by compassion. Osho fully lived through this activity phase before he settled down in Mumbai in 1970. In the book, *Dimensions Beyond the Known*, Osho describes this phase of his life: 'When this second phase—that of *rajas*—began, I moved throughout the country. As much as I have travelled within the span of those ten to fifteen years, no one can, even in two or three lives (births). As much as I have spoken during those ten to fifteen years, would ordinarily require (someone else) ten to fifteen lives. From morning till night, I was on the move, travelling everywhere.' Stating the purpose and nature of this phase in the same book, Osho adds:

'With or without reason, I was creating controversies, because more the controversies, quicker this transition through the second phase of activity is. I therefore began to criticise Gandhiji. I began to criticise socialism.

Neither did I have any relationship with these subjects, nor was there any attachment to politics. I had no interest whatsoever in these. But when the entire population of the country was absorbed in these tensions, there seemed, even if just for fun, a necessity to create controversies. Therefore, during the transition of my second phase of activity, I engineered a number of controversies and enjoyed them.

'If those controversies had been created due to tension-filled actions motivated by desire, it would have brought me unhappiness. But as all this was just to develop the rajas guna, *just for its expression, there was fun and interest in it. These controversies were just like the acting of an actor.'*

Osho's travels were hectic, where he was on the go from three weeks out of a month. Osho had spoken very little, when he was passing through the phase of inactivity. But he says: 'During the period of activity, I myself went up to people just to speak, and my language was full of fire...That fire was not mine. It came out of the *rajas guna*. That was the only way to burn out the fire of the *rajas guna*. It must burn in full ferocity so that it can quickly turn to ashes. The milder the fire, the longer it takes to burn out.'

In 1964, Osho held his first camp to introduce meditation to followers. It was a ten-day meditation camp held in the hills of Rajasthan, at a place called Muchala Mahavir. He taught several kinds of meditation techniques that could be practised early in the morning, during the day, as well as in the evening and before going to bed. Some of the meditation techniques such as Vipassana, Nadabrahma, and Whirling (Sufi) meditation are well known to different traditions as well.

Osho has explained what meditation is in innumerable ways and in great depth. He calls meditation essentially 'a state of no-mind', which is a state of cessation of thoughts, a state of silence:

'Ordinarily, your consciousness is full of too much of rubbish, just like a mirror covered with dust. The mind is like constant traffic: thoughts are moving, desires are moving, memories are moving, ambitions are moving— it is constant traffic, day in and day out. Even when you are asleep, the mind is functioning; it is dreaming; it is still thinking; it is still in worries

and anxieties. It is preparing for the next day; an underground preparation is going on. This is a state of no meditation—just the opposite of meditation. When there is no traffic and thinking has ceased, no thought moves, no desire stirs, you are utterly silent—that silence is meditation. And in that silence truth is known, and never otherwise. Meditation is a state of no-mind.

'And you cannot find meditation through the mind because mind will perpetuate itself. You can find meditation only by putting the mind aside, by being cool, indifferent, unidentified with the mind—seeing the mind pass, but not getting identified with it, not thinking that "I am it." Meditation is the awareness that "I am not the mind." When the awareness goes deeper and deeper in you, slowly, slowly a few moments arrive—moments of silence, moments of pure space, moments of transparency, moments when nothing stirs in you and everything is still. In those still moments you will know who you are, and you will know the mystery that this existence is.'

Contrary to the popular idea of meditation, Osho looks at it as an experience of non-activity, non-seriousness, joy and playfulness: 'Mind is very serious, and meditation is absolutely non-serious. When I say this you may get bewildered, because people go on talking about meditation very seriously. But meditation is not a serious thing. It is just like play. Sincere, but non-serious. It is not something like work; it is more like play. Play is not an activity. Even when it is active, it is not an activity. Play is just pleasure. The activity is not going anywhere; it is not motivated. Rather, it is just pure, flowing energy.' After his first meditation camp in 1964, Osho conducted many more such camps all over the country. He usually chose places in a natural setting away from crowds and city noise. His meditation camps and discourses became instantly popular and he began to stir the nation out of its lethargy. He made significant impressions on people from all walks of life, and more and more people fell in love with him.

Osho's frequent travels, his style and originality, his sharp wit and rebellious nature often annoyed the university administration; however, because of his popularity and reputation, they could not do much. His friends often insisted that he give up his job to devote himself totally to his work. But Osho's response would be to wait when the time is right.

In August 1966, he felt that the time had come for him to free himself from the university job. But it was mutual. He was creating enough controversy to make the university uncomfortable. The time was ripe. Osho had just returned from a tour. The dispute cropped up on his dressing style. For a number of years, Osho had been wearing a lungi (a long piece of cloth wrapped below the waist) and *chadar* (cloth draped on the upper body). Although college officials had previously expressed their dislike of this style of dress, the principal chose Osho's return from his tour to press the issue. Since Osho had never objected to the kind of clothes the principal wore, he felt it was unjust for the principal to object to his style of dress. When pressed by the principal, Osho immediately submitted his letter of resignation which, incidentally, he always carried with him.

Free from his teacher's job at the Jabalpur University, Osho began to unravel his *rajas* energy by speaking out on sensitive issues as Mahatma Gandhi, sex, orthodox Hindu religion and socialism. He openly and boldly criticised Mahatma Gandhi, his ideas and those who followed him, during the Gandhi Centenary Year, 1968-69. Osho's criticism of Gandhi was two-fold: first, he found Gandhi to be a man of ethics, not of religion. Osho did not see a religious man in Gandhi, even though that is how Gandhi is popularly viewed in India. According to Osho, Gandhi's whole concept of religious synthesis was not free from his bias towards Hinduism. In Osho's words Gandhi knew nothing of meditation, but he tried hard to create a certain façade of synthesis. Basically, he was a Hindu and he remained a Hindu all his life, to the very end.

'He calls the Bhagavad Gita his mother, but he never calls the Koran his father—nor even an uncle. Although he says that the teaching is the same, the way he manages it is absolutely political—clever, cunning, but not authentic...Whatever he finds in the Koran, in the Bible, in the Dhammapada, which is in agreement with the Gita, he immediately picks up and he says, "Look! All religions teach the same thing!" But there are many things which go against the Gita in the Bible, which go against the Gita in the Koran, in the Dhammapada. He does not take any notice of them, he ignores them and so his synthesis is bogus. In fact, he reads the Gita everywhere, wherever he can find Gita's echoes, he immediately says, "Look! They are saying the same thing!" But what about the differences? What about the totally opposite stand points?

'Gandhi chooses only pieces from religion and then makes a hodgepodge which he calls the synthesis of all religions. But this synthesis has never happened. Neither the Muslims were convinced by him, nor the Hindus.'

Describing his own concept of religion and explaining his work in that context, Osho said in March 1971:

'I am not a synthesiser like Gandhiji. I do not call for any synthesising of religions. I am saying that all religions with their own distinct individualities are acceptable to me…The Koran and the Gita are not one, but a link can be made to join the two. So I would like to spread a network of sannyasins who are such that they would form the links. Theses sannyasins will do namaz in a mosque, say prayers in a church and will also do kirtan in a temple. They will walk on the path of Mahavir, meditate as Buddha and even experiment with the Sikh tradition, thus establishing connecting links —a living chain of human links. All will be struck by the one religious feeling that all religions, though separate, are one: not that all religions are one and inseparable, but that though they are separate, they are one in their inner harmonious march towards the goal. They are one in the sense that they lead you towards the one super consciousness.

'The overall perspective which I have before me is this: that I would like to help each one to move according to his capacity, his stage of evolution, his culture, according to what has already got assimilated in his blood. Then it will be much easier for him to achieve his truth. Therefore, I have neither any religion of my own, nor any path of my own, because now one exclusive path or religion will not work for the future.'

Osho found Gandhi's view of society and his solutions to its problems primitive and non-scientific. He found them regressive because they were rooted in tradition. Osho points out that Gandhi was more in favour of the old means, such as the spinning wheel which he propagated, than the modern, advanced technological means.

'For twenty years I have criticised Mahatma Gandhi and his philosophy. No Gandhian has answered back. Many Gandhians have in fact come up to me and said, "Whatever you say is right, but we cannot say it in public, because if we say that whatever you say about Mahatma Gandhi is right, we will lose. The public believes in Mahatma Gandhi." So utter nonsense has to be supported because Gandhi was anti-technology. Now, this country will remain poor if it remains anti-technology; this country will never be in a state of well-being. And there is no need for technology always to be anti-ecology, there is no need. Such technology can be developed which will be in tune with the ecology. Technology can be developed to not destroy nature, but help people at the same time. But Gandhi is against technology.

'He was against the railways, he was against the post office. He was against electricity, he was against machines of all kinds. They know this is stupid but they go on paying homage to Mahatma Gandhi because they have to get votes from people. And people worship the Mahatma, because the Mahatma fits with their ideas of how a mahatma should be.

'Mahatma Gandhi fits in with the Indian mob. The Indian mob worships him. The politician has to follow the mob. Remember always: in politics the leader follows the followers. He has to. He only pretends that he is leading; deep down he has to follow the followers. Once the followers leave him, he is nowhere. He cannot stand on his own, he has no ground of his own.

'Gandhi worshipped poverty. Now if you worship poverty, you will remain poor. Poverty has to be hated. I hate poverty! I cannot say worship it. That would be a crime. And I don't see any religious quality in being poor. But Gandhi talked much about poverty and its beauty; it helps the poor man's ego; it massages his ego. He feels good. It is a consolation that he is religious and simple and that he is poor. He portrayed, that though he may not have riches but he has some spiritual richness. Poverty in itself is not a spiritual richness; no, not at all. Poverty is ugly and poverty has to be destroyed. And to destroy poverty, technology has to be brought in.

'Mahatma Gandhi was against birth control. Now if you are against *birth control (India) will become poorer and poorer. Then there is no possibility.'*

Osho's views on Gandhi created a furore all over India, and especially in Gandhi's home state, Gujarat. The anger and protests were so intense that many who claimed to be Osho's friends left him. Also a promise of 600 acres of land to Osho by the Gujarat government was revoked; the land would have provided Osho with an ideal location to conduct meditation sessions.

Osho added more fuel to the fire on 28 August 1968. He was invited by a group of friends to give a series of lectures on love. The lecture was held at Bharatiya Vidya Bhavan, one of the prominent cultural and educational centres in Mumbai (then Bombay). The lecture was in Hindi and what Osho said in this lecture left everyone stunned. The main theme of his lecture was that sex is divine.

'The primal energy of sex has the reflection of God in it. It is obvious: it is the energy that creates new life. And that is the greatest, most mysterious force of all. End this enmity with sex. If you crave a shower of love in your life, renounce this conflict with sex. Accept sex with joy. Acknowledge its sacredness. Receive it gratefully and embrace it more and more deeply. You will be surprised that sex can reveal such sacredness; it will reveal its sacredness to the degree of your acceptance. As sinful and irreverent as your approach will be, the sex that will confront you will be equally ugly and sinful.

'If you want to know the elemental truth about love, the first requisite is to accept the sacredness of sex, to accept the divinity of sex in the same way you accept God's existence—with an open heart. And the more fully you accept sex with an open heart and mind, the freer you will be of it. But the more you suppress it, the more you will become bound to it.'

The organisers were shocked to hear Osho speaking so openly about sex. They became so upset about it that they cancelled the rest of the lecture series. Osho returned to Jabalpur. But despite the fact that in this lecture, Osho jolted orthodox Indian beliefs, taboos, and attitudes about sex, he nevertheless created enough interest in some people who had listened to him. Therefore he was invited once again to continue with the lectures. Exactly a month later, Osho returned to Mumbai and lectured on the same subject in an open public meeting before 50,000 people at Gowalia Tank Maidan.

In these lectures, Osho dealt with many aspects of sex and love, although his emphasis remained on transcending or purifying the sex energy so that one could experience the divine. He strongly rejects the idea of celibacy, because for him celibacy is usually sexual suppression and not a healthy, natural transformation of sex. He teaches that sex is a natural phenomenon and that people should experience it lovingly and meditatively so that it can become the first step on the way to superconsciousness. Osho does not teach 'free sex' or sexual indulgence, as is widely misunderstood. On the contrary, he has declared in unequivocal terms that sex, understood correctly, does not allow self-indulgence.

When these speeches were published, they brought Osho nothing but rejection, anger and abuse from the public and the Indian press. But no one could give a sensible, intelligent, and unbiased response to the issues and aspects of sex discussed by Osho. These discourses were translated into English in the book *From Sex to Superconsciousness*, published in 1979.

In March 1969, Osho was invited to speak at the Second World Hindu Religion Conference held at Patna. The conference was presided over by the highest religious priest of the Hindus, the Shankaracharya of Puri. He was angry and agitated about Osho's presence on the same podium, and objected to it. The organisers pleaded with him and the Shankaracharya, somewhat mollified, allowed Osho to have forty five minutes. But in his typical courageous and fiery style, Osho began lashing out at organised religions, the priests, and the hypocrisy of religion. In front of all the audience, including the Shankracharya, Osho said, 'Any religion which considers life meaningless, full of misery and propagates hatred towards life is not a true religion. Religion is an art that shows how to enjoy life. Liberation is not in running away from life, but rather in enjoying fully the life and the world. But these shops being run in the name of religion do not want a person to become truly religious. Because then these shops will have to be shut down, and there will no longer be any need for a priest or a world teacher.'[1] Osho had hardly spoken for ten minutes when Shankaracharya and his colleagues demanded that the organisers stop Osho's speech. Osho asked the audience whether he should stop or continue. The audience shouted back that he should continue. At the conclusion of his lecture, the audience gave him a very warm and loud applause, which angered the Shakaracharya even more.

Osho also expressed his disagreement with the socialist ideals of the leaders of the Congress party, including Nehru, became committed to after India's independence from British rule. He considered it disastrous for any country to talk about socialism without first building a capitalist economy, as he did not regard capitalism and socialism as opposite systems. In July 1969, Osho spoke in Jabalpur on 'India and Socialism.' In his words:

'*Socialism is the ultimate result of capitalism. It is a very natural process There is no need to go through any revolution. In fact, capitalism itself is a revolution that brings about socialism. Capitalism has shown, for the first time in the world, how to create wealth.*

'*I believe that in India socialism is inevitable, but fifty, sixty, or seventy years hence. India should apply all its efforts in first creating wealth. The poverty in this country is so chronic, it has lasted for so long, that unless this country develops a capitalist system for the next fifty or one hundred years, this country will remain poor forever. Capitalism would make it possible to distribute wealth. At present, in the name of socialism, what we have for distribution is only poverty.*'[2]

Osho's criticism of socialism and his support for capitalism brought an instant reaction: he was branded anti-nationalist and called a CIA agent. Thus, with his talks, debates, and discussions, Osho touched upon issues at the core of India's problems and maladies. Even at the risk of his own life, Osho made bold and frank statements for one reason: he strongly felt that India could no longer afford to push its dirt under the carpet. Someone had to take the lead in exposing the evils and stupidities that engulfed the country. Osho could provide that leadership and with his insight also a glimpse of the vision he was going to unfold in the next ten years.

On his visits to Mumbai, between 13-16 April 1970, Osho held meditation sessions at Palm Beach High School. During these sessions, Osho surprised all those who had come prepared for his regular 'relax' meditation. He introduced for the first time his own technique of meditation, Dynamic Meditation. Having conducted 'relax' meditation for many years, Osho found that technique did not really suit modern people. He explains:

'I was working for ten years continuously on Lao Tzuan methods, so I was teaching direct relaxation. It was simple for me, so I thought it would be simple for everyone. Then, by and by, I became aware that it is impossible...I would say "relax" to people. They would appear to understand the meaning of the word but they could not relax. Then I had to devise new methods for meditation which first created tension and more tension. The technique created such tension that you would go mad. And then I would say "relax".'

So the day he introduced Dynamic Meditation, everyone was taken aback but fascinated at the same time. The Indian press expressed its shock at watching the participants scream, shout and take off their clothes. The whole scene appeared incomprehensible. But it was very intense. On the fourth day, which was the last day of the session, Osho said, 'I have given you a very valuable technique. Do it regularly!'

The technique of Dynamic Meditation consists of elements from the Yoga, Sufi and Tibetan traditions as well as findings of contemporary psychology. Osho has pulled them together into one unique prescription to suit the needs of individuals in our contemporary society. Osho explains the meaning of Dynamic Meditation as follows:

'Dynamic Meditation is a contradiction. Dynamic means effort much effort, absolute effort. And meditation means silence, no effort, no activity. You can call it a dialectical meditation. Be so active that the whole energy becomes a movement; no energy is left static in you...Become dynamic... You are more like energy...Put total energy to work ...

'When everything is moving and you have become a cyclone, then become alert. Remember, be mindful and in this cyclone suddenly you will find a centre which is absolutely silent. This is the centre of the cyclone. This is you—you in your divinity, you as a god.

'Effort and effortlessness, movement and no movement, activity and no activity, matter and the soul, these are the banks. And between these two, flows the invisible. These two are visible. Between these two flows the invisible—that is what you are.'[3]

Besides Dynamic Meditation, other techniques taught by Osho are equally simple and yet powerful, intense and yet playful. Music and movement are the two main components of these meditations, and the principle of the transformation of energy, by arousing activity and silently witnessing it, is at the core.

Throughout his travels, Osho spoke to people of all professions, castes, religions and class. He held discussions with politicians and industrialists, writers and artists, people from the entertainment industry and students from universities, members of Lion and Rotary clubs, priests and pundits. He spoke to vast audiences consisting of 50,000 people and to small groups huddled in smoke-filled rooms.

Besides the fact that Osho's quality of *rajas* (activity) was being dissipated and spent in travelling, controversial lectures, discussions and debates, he also came to realise that he was not making any substantial progress. Hence, these travels became less and less meaningful. In Osho's words:

'I talked to millions of people in this country; then I had to stop. I was talking to thousands—to 50,000 people in a single meeting. I travelled in the country for fifteen years, from one corner to the other. I simply became tired of the whole thing, because each day I would have to start with the ABCs. It was always, ABC, ABC. And it became absolutely clear that I would never be able to reach XYZ. I had to stop travelling.

'Once I was talking on Krishna in a meeting, and people were sitting with their backs towards me, talking to each other. That was the last day, the

last straw. In the middle, I left. The president of the meeting asked, "Where are you going?" I said, "I am going forever. I am finished with these stupid people. I am talking about Krishna, they have invited me to talk to them, and nobody seems to listen."'

Throughout his travelling phase, Osho repeatedly went back to Jabalpur to find a space for himself to be alone for a while. But soon that was also becoming more and more difficult. Almost after four years of resigning from the university in 1966, Osho left Jabalpur. He cut short his travels, reduced the number of meditation camps, and began packing up his personal library. His friends were eager and ready to find a place for him in Mumbai where he could find his own space and also be able to meet people.

He was given a farewell reception on the evening of 29 June 1970 at the Shaheed Smarak Bhavan in Jabalpur. The reception was attended by the vice-chancellor of Jabalpur University, along with prominent journalists, writers, professors, editors of newspapers, and other leading citizens. After all the speeches were made, Osho was asked to speak. He said:

'People say that I have become a mahatma (great soul). But it would be appropriate if you called me a wanderer instead. Today I am here, tomorrow in Bombay, and the day after I may go to New York. Wherever the divine takes me, I will follow. I have hurt the feelings of many people and will not forget Jabalpur for this reason also. I have been chopping off their erudite talks with my reasoning which has caused many wounds. In Bombay I will see that these wounds do not heal up for I don't want you to sit quietly. I am here to cause wounds, so that you keep thinking. This country never thinks. And remember, the country in which thinking and reflection stops, the race of that country dies. So I will see to it that as soon as your wounds begin to heal, I will come back again and hit...I am not going anywhere (on my own will). It is up to the divine will. I would like to say only this much: keep thinking. Once the flow of thought stops, the water will turn into a dirty pool, and if it remains flowing, it will be a river.'[4]

Osho arrived in Mumbai on 1 July 1970. There he began what was a totally new activity for him. He started conducting regular evening discourses, on spiritual and esoteric matters, with fifty people. He delved into secrets hidden in various spiritual traditions; he enjoyed answering questions based on previous lectures and went deeply into his answers. It was a very intense, live, powerful dialogue, most of which has been compiled and translated from Hindi in the book, *The Mystic Experience*.

Those who were close to him during this period say that his radiance and force was such that just by being near him one would feel a lot of energy and begin to shake or cry. People felt this very intensely during one of his meditation camps held in August 1970. He disclosed at this camp that he wanted to initiate into *sannyas* those who felt inwardly connected to him. Thus, at a meditation camp held from 25 September to 5 October 1970, at Manali, a beautiful resort in a valley of the Himalayas, Osho initiated six people into *sannyas*. He gave new names to these individuals and formally began the Neo-*Sannyas* International Movement. The revolutionary concept of neo-*sannyas*, or Osho's idea of *sannyas*, can be summarised briefly in the following excerpts from his discourses:

'My sannyas is life-affirmative. Nothing like this has ever flowered on the earth. It is a totally new phenomenon. All the old ideas of sannyas were based on escapism, on renunciation. My sannyas has nothing to do with escape. It is against escape, because to me God and life are synonymous. It has never been said that God and life are synonymous. God has always been put against life: you had to drop life to attain God. And I say to you, you have to live as totally as possible, as intensely as possible, as passionately as possible if you want to know God at all.

'Each and everyone is there to become a god. That is everybody's destiny. You can delay it, but you cannot destroy it. By giving you sannyas I am trying to hasten it. Giving you sannyas means I am persuading you not to postpone it any more. Giving you sannyas is nothing but helping you not to delay it any more.

'It is out of great respect, because I see the Buddha inside you. The Buddha has already waited too long, and you have not looked at it. When I ask you to become a sannyasin, I am saying, "Now the time has come. You take the plunge." Try this new way of life. You have lived in the old way, nothing has happened out of it or whatever has happened has proved only superficial and futile. Try this way too.

'The old concept of sannyas all over the world was to give you a rigid discipline, to give you a character, to give you a certain form, a pattern, a lifestyle. My sannyas is not like that at all—it is a radical change. I don't give you any character, because to me the man of character is a dead man, I would like to take all character away from you so you are left in a creative chaos...so each moment one has to respond to life, not out of a certain pattern.

'To respond in the moment without any pattern, just out of spontaneity—whatever the feel of the moment decides to act just like that—is what I call "creative chaos"—a characterless consciousness, a present without past, a freedom unhindered by any discipline.

'To live that way is to live the life of a sannyasin. It is utterly beautiful, utterly blessed, but great courage is needed because you don't have a guide, you don't have a particular form, you cannot depend on the past. One has to move from the unknown to the unknown, there is no security in it...it is pure adventure.

'The older concept of sannayas was very life-negative—it was utterly against life—but my idea or concept is absolutely life-affirmative. Nothing has to be dropped—everything has to be transformed. So this old sannyas was an unholy sannyas: it accepted only part of life and denied the remaining part. It accepted the mind but denied the body; it accepted love but it denied sex; it accepted God but it denied the world. And they are all together.

'So the old sannyas was an unholy sannyas because it never led anybody to the wholeness of life. It was very perfectionistic. I am not perfectionistic at all. So my sannyas is absolutely life-affirmative. Hence, it is holistic rather than perfectionistic. I am utterly in love with life. It is non-perfectionistic, it is non-guilt-creating; it does not teach you to condemn anything in you or in anybody else. It makes you more and more aware of all the limitations of life and yet helps you to enjoy with all those limitations.

'*Let this sannyas be a great love affair with life itself…and there is no other God. If you can find life, you have found God…*'

The initiation into *sannyas* included:

- Changing one's name.
- Wearing a *mala* (a necklace of 108 beads) which had a locket with Osho's picture framed in it.
- Wearing clothes of ochre colour (later changed to maroon).

Osho has explained in detail the significance of these changes. About the new name he says, 'I give you a new name only to make you feel that names are not important. Your old name can simply disappear because it was only a label, it can be changed. You are not the name.' A name, even though given to us by others, enters deep into consciousness and we become identified with it, says Osho. But by giving *sannyas*, Osho destroys this and other identifications as well. He explains, 'When you become a *sannyasin*, I want to destroy that identity, because this is the beginning of the destruction of all identities. First I destroy the identity with the name, then I will destroy the identity with the body, then the identity with the mind, then the identity with the heart. When all these identities have been destroyed, you will be able to know who you are: the unidentified, the nameless, the formless or the indefinable.'

Osho also chose to title his disciples as Ma or Swami as the case maybe. He explains the reason behind it: 'The path of masculine is that of awareness and awareness brings you to a point where you become master of your own being. That is the meaning of Swami. The feminine path is that of love and love brings you to an ultimate point where you can mother your whole existence. And that is the meaning of Ma.'

Pointing out that each colour has its own psychology and impact, Osho explains the reason for selecting the ochre colour: 'One reason is that it makes you feel just like the sunrise in the morning. It is the colour of the sun rising; the rays of the sun in the morning are ochre-coloured. The colour creates a living atmosphere, something alive and vibrating. This colour was chosen so that you vibrate with divinity. You must be alive with divinity; no sadness should have any shelter within you; no sorrow should be allowed to have any shelter. You must be in a dancing mood twenty-four hours. Ochre is a dancing colour.'

Explaining the meaning and significance of the *mala*, Osho first distinguishes it from the cross. 'The *mala* represents life,' he says. 'The cross represents death. The *mala* represents a certain art of making life a garland.' Going even deeper into its meaning, he gives this elaborate explanation of the *mala* and the locket with his picture: 'Unless your life knows what eternity is, your life will be just a heap of beads or a heap of flowers, but it will not be a garland; it will not be a *mala*. It will not have any inner harmony. The beads will remain unrelated. It will be a chaos; it will not be a cosmos. There will be no order, no discipline. But the discipline should be invisible like the thread…The *mala* represents time as beads, visible, and the thread as eternity, the invisible.'

Osho explains further that the 108 beads of the *mala* represent 108 methods of meditation. According to him, 108 methods of meditation are the fundamental ones out of which hundreds of other methods can grow. As for his picture in the locket: 'The picture is not mine. Had it been mine, I would have hesitated to put it there. The picture only appears to be mine; it is not. No picture of me is possible, really. The moment one knows oneself, one knows something that cannot be depicted, described, framed. I exist as an emptiness that cannot be pictured, that cannot be photographed. That is why I could put the picture there.'

In an interview Osho made the following prophetic statement in connection with his initiating people into *sannyas*:

'The last part of this century, will be very definitive. The latter part of this century will decide the fate of the centuries to come. This is going to be a definitive period, definitive in the sense that the belief that human beings are only machines, natural mechanical devices, may become prevalent.

If this belief becomes prevalent, it will be difficult to come again to the living current...Each day there are fewer and fewer people who know the living current, who know the inner reality, who know consciousness, who know the divine...This century, the last part of this century, will be decisive. So, those who are in any way ready to begin, I will initiate them. If 10,000 are initiated and even one reaches the goal, the trouble is worth taking...'

As Osho began to attract more and more people and initiate them into *sannyas*, people started reacting adversely to him. First, those who called themselves 'progressive' and 'intellectuals' became very unhappy with Osho, for they could not accept Osho as a guru and began to part from his company. In a way, Osho welcomed this situation, since he wanted only those people around him who loved him, who were open to him. He never cared for those who came just to satisfy their intellectual curiosity or to find yet another support for their beliefs or ideology. Opposition to Osho stemmed from the fact that, with the number of *sannyasins* increasing around him, he was seen as a potential threat to those in the society whose vested interests Osho had been exposing all along in his countrywide travels and talks. Regardless of negative reactions to him and his *sannyas*, Osho kept drawing more and more admirers not only from within the country, but now from the West also. Although between 1968 and 1970 only very few seekers from the West had contact with him, but after he settled down in Mumbai, more began to approach him. Some English translations of his talks began to appear in the form of booklets.

With the increase in the number of people wanting to see him, it soon became necessary for him to look for a larger place. He moved to Woodland Apartments in December 1970. Also, he appointed Ma Yoga Laxmi and Swami Yoga Chinmaya as his secretaries. Laxmi was to see to the organisational matters and Chinmaya, who has a very wide and rich experience in yoga and meditation, would conduct classes.

First, as Osho's secretary and later as the managing trustee of the Osho foundation in Pune, Laxmi was largely instrumental in the expansion and growth of Osho's work. She came from a prominent and well known Jain family in Mumbai. Her father was a very successful businessman and was a member of the Indian National Congress. He was close to many leaders in the Congress, including Gandhi, Nehru and Patel, and was deeply interested in India's independence movement. But since his children were still young, he helped the movement mainly from behind the scenes.

Laxmi also took keen interest in Indian politics, especially from 1962 to 1965. She heard Osho for the first time at an All India Congress Women's Conference, when she was its secretary. When she saw him, she said, something unusual happened: a thrill passed through her body, something clicked and the next moment, she was crying and couldn't hold back. She had never experienced such deep feelings of love and reverence towards anyone before. Later, she and her family became better acquainted with Osho.

In 1969, at a meditation camp held by Osho in a beautiful resort called Nargol, Laxmi had an incredible experience. Osho gave lectures in the evening and the following morning conducted meditations. She describes that in the course of a lecture, Osho said, 'You don't know why I have come, but I do!' These words struck the inner chords of Laxmi's heart, and she felt more deeply for Osho. At night while she lay in her bed, all of a sudden the silent question 'Who am I?' started vibrating throughout her body and became increasingly intense. Then she broke out into uncontrollable laughter. Her maternal uncle came out from the next room and seeing Laxmi in that unusual state, became very worried. She was laughing hysterically. Then Osho came and put his hand on Laxmi's head, and she slowly calmed down. For the entire next day, she was in a state of bliss, but at night again the laughter began and remained until morning.

Even though she remained without food and water for three days, her energy did not dissipate. The whole episode brought a sharp awareness in her and changed her life completely. Since that time, she worked unceasingly under Osho's guidance in giving concrete shape to his vision. Osho once said, 'Always remember that Laxmi never does anything on her own. She is a perfect vehicle, that is why she is chosen for this work…Whatever is said, she does.'[5]

After this camp, Laxmi often accompanied Osho on his travels. But yet another significant thing happened to her in Mumbai while Osho was away in Jabalpur. One day, while meditating, the colour ochre appeared in her vision. When she told her mother about it, her mother said that traditionally that was the colour of *sannyas*. Laxmi said she liked the colour so much that henceforth she would wear only clothes of that colour. Her mother said it was all right to wear ochre-coloured clothes, except that once she chose to wear them, she would have to wear them forever. Laxmi made new clothes in ochre and even attended a women's conference wearing them. It created quite a stir among the delegates attending the conference.

When Osho returned from Jabalpur on 1 July 1970, his friends gathered at the railway station to receive him. When the train slowly came to the platform, Osho stood at the compartment door greeting people with his customary folded hands. He spotted Laxmi in the crowd wearing her new clothes. When the train stopped, Osho called out to her and asked casually what the change in clothes was about. Laxmi said she could not explain how or why the change occurred. Osho said smilingly, but in a very clear and firm tone, that she was to become his first disciple, the first *sannyasin*, he named her Ma Yoga Laxmi. Thus, Laxmi became the first *sannyasin* of Osho's, although the formal beginning of initiation of others into *sannyas* occurred several months later at the Manali camp.

Osho also initiated a few Westerners after moving to Woodland Apartments. They started spreading the word about Osho in the West. There are many fascinating stories of how people from the West were drawn to him but one common factor in their stories is that they recognised Osho as a living Buddha or Christ. After taking *sannyas* they returned to their respective home countries where they obviously faced opposition, but remained committed to the cause. They formed the first close group of Western disciples, and with that, a communal life began to develop.

Osho remained in Mumbai, and every day the stream of Westerners increased. Slowly and gradually, Osho reduced his public contact, stopped lecturing in open public meetings, and spoke only before small groups at his residence, he stopped giving press interviews and meeting with leading citizens or highly placed people of the society. His travels also became rare.

Instead, he now preferred to put his energy into those who were sincere and courageous in their search. He very clearly expressed his wish in letters written in early 1971. Here are a few of them.

16/1/71

My Beloved,

Love!

In the previous birth I promised many friends that when the truth was found, I would let them know. I have done so. Hence my travels in India are now over.

Certainly, there are also friends other than the Indians with whom I am building contacts. Although these friends have no idea of the promise— even you do not have— it is still essential that I do what I know has to be done. Henceforth, generally I shall stay in one place. This way I shall be able to pay more attention to the seekers. And thus I shall be of much help to those who are truly in need.

16/1/71

My Beloved,

Love!

My travels are now almost over. The promises which I made to others in some previous birth, I have kept. From now on I shall stay in one place. Those who want to come, will come. They always come. And perhaps this way I may be of more help to those who really need me. I have completed the broader scope of my work. Now I will be doing deeper work. I went and called from one town to another; now I wait for them. This is now the inner command. And I have never done anything different from the inner command, nor can I do it now.

Neo-Sannyas: The Lotus in a Swamp | 113

My Beloved,

Love!

Until now, the well reached out to the thirsty, but from now on, this may not be possible. Now the thirsty will have to come to the well. And perhaps this is also according to the law. Is it not? I have almost stopped travelling. The message has been delivered. Now the one who wants to find me will find me, and the one who does not want to find me, I have knocked at his door as well.

16/2/71

My Beloved,

Love!

I am ceasing external travels. But to those who truly call, I will open the doors of inner journey. No, no one will be kept out, I shall enter your heart, and I shall speak to you. And that which you could not understand through outer language, you will be able to follow through inner speech. I have said enough about the subtle through the gross. Now the subtle has to be conveyed through the subtle alone.

In early 1971, a remarkable event took place—Osho's mother received initiation from him and became his disciple. Osho gave her a new name, Ma Amrit Saraswati. Those who were present at the occasion were moved to see the son touching the feet of his mother, and the mother bowing down and touching the feet of her son—now her master.

When once asked how she felt being Bhagwan's mother, she replied, '...He is my son, and he is Bhagwan. And so when I bow down to him I feel he is Bhagwan, and at the same time there is a feeling that he is my son; that warmth is there. And that feeling of prayer is also there ...(that feeling) that he is God.'[6] As his travels and public exposure decreased, Osho was able to see more and more people who came from the West. One of the first to come (from Frankfurt, Germany) was Christine Woolf, later known as Ma Yoga Vivek and one of Osho's attendants. She is none other than his girlfriend, Shashi who had died when Osho was seventeen. Osho revealed the mystery in the following words: 'I had a girlfriend when I was young. Then she died. But on her deathbed, she promised me that she would come back. And she has come back. The name of the girlfriend was Shashi. She died in 1947. She was the daughter of a certain doctor, Dr Sharma, of my village. He is also dead now. And now she has come as Vivek—to take care of me.' 'Vivek' is a Sanskrit word which means 'awareness', or 'consciousness', and it is with constant awareness that she looked after Osho, a very challenging and yet rewarding task. Osho explained how he gave her this name and what it means in an interview given on the day Vivek took *sannyas*, 16 April 1971.

'Yesterday someone came to me in the morning. I told her to take sannyas. She was bewildered. She asked for time to think and decide, at least two days. I insisted, "Take it today, this moment." But she was not decisive, so I gave her two days. The next morning she came and took it...I asked her, "Why? You have been given two days: why have you come so soon?"'

'She said, "At three o'clock in the night, suddenly I woke up, and something deep within told me, 'Go, take sannyas."'

'Here it is not a decision that she has made, but a decision that has been made by her deep-rooted mind. But the moment she came in the room, I knew her, that mind which she came to know only twenty hours later. So when I say, "Take sannyas", there are so many reasons with every person to whom I say it. Either he has been a sannyasin in his last life, or somewhere in the long journey, he has been a sannyasin.*

'I had given her another name yesterday, but today I had to change it because I gave her that name in her indecision. Now I am giving her a different name that will be a help to her. But when she came this morning she herself was decided; that name was not needed at all. And I have given her the name Ma Yoga Vivek, because now the decision has come through her vivek, her awareness, her consciousness.*

'Vivek is so close to me that she is constantly on the cross. She has to be; it is difficult. To be so close to me is arduous. The more you are close to me, more the responsibility. The more you are close to me, the more you have to transform yourself. The more you feel the unworthiness, the more you start feeling how to become more worthy—and the goal seems almost impossible. And I go on creating many situations. I have to create them because only through friction does integration happen. Only through harder and harder situations does one grow. Growth is not soft, growth is painful. You ask me, "What do you do with Vivek? It is a cross to be with me, and the task is hard.'

As Osho cut down the number of travels, speeches and other outside engagements, his life and work began to take on a totally new form. It was in May 1971, recalls Swami Yoga Chinmaya, when Osho told him that since the work had gone much deeper, a new dimension had to be given to it. Osho was known until then as 'Acharya', which means teacher. He asked Chinmaya to find a new name for him. Chinmaya suggested a few names, out of which he selected Bhagwan, which is literally translated as God. It is a symbolic name, however, and signifies qualities related to heart, love, and devotion. It was meant to symbolise heart-centred work, work that henceforth would happen more in terms of love, in tune with the spirit of Bhakti, Sufism and Tantra.

The new dimension that Osho wanted to point out was this dimension of heart or love. His emphasis was no longer on the intellect, or on appealing to large numbers of people. The *Acharya* (teacher) had communicated enough through the head; he now wanted communion to take place heart to heart with those who were in love with him. From then on Acharya Rajneesh came to be known as Bhagwan Shree Rajneesh.

'I loved the term. I said, "That will do. At least for a few years it will do; then we can drop it...I have chosen it for a specific purpose and it has been serving well, because people who used to come to me to gather knowledge, they stopped. The day I called myself Bhagwan, they stopped. It was too much for them, it was too much for their egos, somebody calling himself Bhagwan..."

'They stopped. They were coming to me to gather knowledge. Now I've changed my function absolutely. I started working on a different level, in a different dimension. Now I give you being, not knowledge. I was an acharya and they were students; they were learning. Now I am no more a teacher and you are not here as students.

'I am here to impart being. I am here to wake you up. I am not going to give you knowledge. I am going to give you knowing—and that is a totally different dimension.

'Calling myself Bhagwan was simply symbolic; now I have taken a different dimension to work. And it has been tremendously useful. All wrong people automatically disappeared and a totally different quality of people started arriving.

'It worked well. Chinmaya's choice was good. Only those who are ready to dissolve with me remained. All others escaped. They created space around me. Otherwise, they were crowding too much, and it was very difficult for the real seekers to come closer to me. The crowds disappeared. The word bhagwan functioned like an atomic explosion. It did well. I am happy that I chose it.'

Since the day he adopted the name, he has been asked many times why he calls himself God. What does it mean? And Osho has answered these questions with elaborate explanation.

'Because I am—and because you are. And because only God is. The choice is not between whether to be a God or not to be a God; the choice is whether to recognise it or not. You can choose not to call, but you cannot choose not to be.

'When you call this life God, you bring poetry to it. You bring a vision, you open doors. You say, "More is possible." You say, "We are not the end." Higher realms of possibilities arise in your vision. You start dreaming. The moment you say this existence is divine, dreams become possible. Then you can live a life of adventure. God is the greatest adventure…the greatest pilgrimage.

'There are only two ways to give a label to life. One is the way of the realist—he calls it matter. The other is the way of the poet, the dreamer—he calls it God.

'I am an unashamed poet. I'm not a realist. I call myself God. I call you God. I call rocks God, I call trees God, and the clouds God...with God you can grow, with God you can ride on great tidal waves; you can go to the other shore. God is just a glimpse of your destiny. You give personality to existence.

'Then between you and the tree it is not emptiness. Then between you and your beloved it is not emptiness—God is bridging everything. He surrounds you, he is your surrounding. He is within and he is without.

'When I call myself God, I mean to provoke you, to challenge you. I am simply calling myself God so that you can also gather courage to recognise it. If you can recognise it in me, you have taken the first step to recognising it in yourself.

'It would be very difficult for you to recognise it in yourself because you have always been taught to condemn yourself. You have always been taught that you are a sinner. Here I am to take all that nonsense away. My insistence is that it is only one thing that is missing in you—the courage to recognise who you are.

'...By calling myself God, I am not bringing God down, I am bringing you up. I am taking you for a higher journey. I'm simply opening a door towards the Himalayan peaks. Once you start recognising that you are also divine, you become unburdened. Then there may be errors, but there are no sins anymore, you are not a sinner. You may be mistaken, you may be wandering, but you are not a sinner. Whatever you do, you cannot lose your godhood—that is your nature.

'The Indian term for God, bhagwan, is even better than God. That word is tremendously meaningful. It simply means "the blessed one", nothing else. Bhagwan means "the blessed one"—one who is fortunate enough to recognise his own being.

'It has no Christian associations. When you say "God", it seems as if I have created the world. I deny all responsibility! I have not created this world.

I am not that much a fool. The Christian idea of God is one who has created the world. Bhagwan is totally different, it has nothing to do with creating the world. It simply says one who has recognised himself as divine. In that recognition is benediction. In that recognition is blessing. He has become the blessed one.

'I call myself Bhagwan because I respect myself. I am tremendously fulfilled as I am. I am the blessed one. I have no discontent. That is the meaning of Bhagwan—when you have no discontent, when each moment of your life is a fulfillment…when you don't desire anything in the future; your present is so full, overflowing…when there is no hankering.

'That's why we call Buddha, Bhagwan. He has denied God in his cosmology. He says there is no God, no creator. Christians become very puzzled when Buddha says there is no God, no creator. Then why do Buddhists call him Bhagwan?

'Our meaning of bhagwan is totally different. We call him Buddha, Bhagwan, because he has now no more desires. He is contented. He is happy and at home. He has come home—that is his blessedness. Now there is no conflict between him and existence. He has fallen in accord in harmony. Now he and the whole are not two separate things. They vibrate in the same way. He has become part of the orchestra of the whole. And by becoming a part of this great orchestra of stars and trees and flowers and winds and clouds and seas and sands, he has become blessed—we call him Bhagwan.

'When I call myself Bhagwan, I am simply saying to you, "Look at me–the roses have bloomed. And what has happened to me can happen to you. So don't feel desperate and don't feel depressed. Look at me and your hope will come back, and you will not feel hopeless."

'Calling myself Bhagwan is just a device. I can drop it any day. The moment I see it has started working, the chain has started. The moment I see that now it is no more needed…a few people have become aflame; then they will be enough proof. There will be no need to call myself Bhagwan. They will be enough proof. If a few of my sannyasins start blooming, I will stop calling myself Bhagwan. The device will have worked.'

Throughout his travels, Osho had quietly found those who were going to become part of his family in the subsequent years. Through his meditation techniques, he was able to gather a number of courageous followers who shared his vision and were eager to explore the new world they only glimpsed. The message was delivered, the path was shown, the distant call to awakening was sounded. Now was the time to sit and watch the stream grow into a river.

As for his drawing more and more people from the West, it was clear that he had begun expanding his attention and compassion on a much wider scale, as if he were opening up a huge gate through which the whole world could pass through. Or, he himself had become the gate through which one could find many avenues open for continuing one's own search. Osho was fully aware of the nature, depth and quality of the seekers coming to him. He was also prepared for the forthcoming experiments, in minute detail, to bring about a transformation in the lives of these seekers.

His years in Mumbai from 1 July 1970 to 20 March 1974, were the years of personal and intense encounters with selected individual seekers. He met each individual directly, intimately, face-to-face. During these days, one could get to see him almost any time of the day. He appeared to have started his work with these early disciples— as if he were spreading his roots, as if his roots were searching for a ground to launch a worldwide movement of spiritual awakening.

Of the first few hundred Western seekers who came in contact with Osho, almost 90 per cent remained his lifelong companions. Most of them came to India only as short-term visitors. They came for a short period, met Osho, and then went back to their countries to sort out their personal problems and get ready to become a part of Osho's work. They served as mediums through which he travelled around the world—they were divine conduits who had conveyed Osho's spiritual message all over the world. The hundreds who came in contact with these early initiates came to be with Osho, sooner or later, got involved with him, and became part of his expanding 'family'.

These early disciples displayed the same qualities that Osho had shown all along—they were very courageous, rebellious, creative, and had great potential for giving birth to a new religious consciousness. The seekers from the West who first came in scores while Osho was in Mumbai, and later in thousands after he shifted to Pune, came from different cultural and family backgrounds, religious denominations, and spiritual beliefs, but they had one thing in common: their psyches were ripe and ready to receive Osho's energy and guidance. Osho had by now begun to unfold his creative energy in devising all sorts of methods, approaches, and experiments that would be instrumental in transforming their lives.

In one of Osho's earlier experiments, his Western disciples were sent to live in a work-farm commune away from Mumbai. Swami Anand Veetrag, who came from South Africa to be with Osho in 1973, was made the leader of this group which started with thirty–five *sannyasins*, male and female. Another commune named, Samarpan, was set up in the outskirts of Baroda, 290 kilometres northeast of Mumbai in the state of Gujarat. Some of the *sannyasins* were sent to this commune. The farm and lodging/boarding were made available by Swami Swarupanand Bharti and Ma Swarupanand Bharti. The site was located in the middle of Maharashtra in western India. It was a very primitive, rural setting. The nearest village was a kilometre away, from the farm, the nearest town, Sarli, about ten kilometres, and the nearest city, Chandrapur, about seventy kilometres away. Another farm, Kailash, situated on the River Vanganga, was made available for this experimental work by its owner, Ma Anand Mayi.

The commune and its environment were a real test for these people who were accustomed to independent, affluent lives. They lived out in the field in small huts and had to get along with each other although they came from different countries, different backgrounds, and were not known to each other before. The commune was meant to create a situation where the disciples had to learn how to surrender their ego. This surrender or dropping of the ego is different from the general understanding of surrender. It does not mean submitting to a tyrant or an enemy out of weakness, or giving away one's freedom, body, mind, or belongings at the whim of a leader. In the spiritual sense, what is being tested in the disciple is the extent of his commitment and ability to submerge or surrender the ego or the ego-attachment to possessions, people, and conditioning in full awareness on the journey towards experiencing total freedom and joy.

Surrender in this sense is not giving up one's responsibility; rather, it is abandoning one's old beliefs and values and going on a new adventure by dedicating oneself to the vision given by an enlightened master who has transcended the ego and become one with the universe. It is only through this kind of dedication and devotion that in a spiritual commune there is no longer any work; it is only allowing something to happen through you. The work acquires an aesthetic quality, and a climate is created for everyone to fall in harmony with each other.

At first, the whole thing was chaotic—there was no proper equipment or materials available, no one in the commune knew the native language, and above all, there were no clear guidelines or directions given by Osho. He wanted Swami Veetrag to figure out for himself what needed to be done. The work was hard. It included working in the fields, making bricks, gardening, shopping for supplies in the town. The day began at four o'clock in the morning with Dynamic Meditation, followed by housecleaning and then breakfast. The morning chores lasted until ten o'clock. The temperature by then sometimes reached 49° C, so during midday the *sannyasins* cooled themselves in the river. At four o'clock they resumed work and stopped at seven o'clock in the evening. After supper, there would be either Sufi dance or Whirling Meditation. They went to bed at nine o'clock.

As Swami Veetrag puts it, 'It was Gurdjieff-style—there was nothing else to do except work, no need to think, work was the main thing. The entire focus was on work with the spirit of surrender. Gurdjieff's "work" was the main factor that guided or influenced the commune.' Commenting on the situation, Veetrag continues, 'It was tough, people did react to the conditions strongly; but they also learnt how to live in a commune in love and acceptance. Those who could not take it, they left.'

The whole experiment was a kind of prototype of what was to unfold later at Pune. The commune lasted for ten months, until August 1974. When Osho moved to Pune, the commune members began to leave Kailash and gather around the master in Pune.

When Western *sannyasins* were sent to communes like Kailash and Samarpan, Indian *sannyasins* were sent in small groups to different towns and villages. Each of the small groups was called *kirtan mandali*. The *sannyasins* sang devotional hymns and songs, conducted meditation, and played tapes of Osho's discourses in Hindi. For these *sannyasins* the experiment was the same—how to surrender the ego, and how to live in love and acceptance under adverse conditions, in an unfamiliar or uncongenial environment. These groups also lasted until Osho moved to Pune.

The intensive travelling of the past years coupled with poor and irregular eating conditions of that period began to take their toll on Osho's health. His diabetes and asthma worsened. It also became evident that a much larger, permanent place was needed. Laxmi was sent out to look for a site suitable for a large ashram. She chose Pune, 130 kilometres southeast of Mumbai, situated on high hills and very well known for its pleasant climate, historic significance, orthodox community, and for its association with enlightened beings, the most recent being Meher Baba. Osho's friends established a public trust, the Rajneesh Foundation, which bought a place spread over about six acres in beautiful and luxurious surroundings on the outskirts of the city of Pune.

Exactly twenty-one years after his enlightenment, Osho arrived in Pune on 21 March 1974, with seven disciples to begin a new phase of his work. The celebration of the anniversary of Osho's enlightenment day and of his arrival took place at 17 Koregaon Park, Pune. The place was named Shree Rajneesh Ashram.

Excerpts from:

Come Follow To You vol. 3
Socrates Poisoned Again After 25 Centuries

Zen, Zest, Zip, Zap and Zing
The New Alchemy: To Turn You On
Philosophia Perennis vol. 2
Tao: The Golden Gate
Dimensions Beyond the Known
The Secret of Secrets
From Sex to Superconsciousness
The Book of Wisdom
Hallelujah!: A Darshan Diary
I Am That
I Am The Gate
The Book of Books vol. 6
Discipline of Transcendence
The Ultimate Alchemy: Discourses on the Atma Pooja Upanishad vol. 1

End notes:

1. *Jyotishikha* no. 13
2. *Dekh Kabira Roya*
3. Rajneesh Foundation Press Office Files, 1975-1981
4. *Yukrand* no. 5 & 6
5. *The Sound of Running Water: A Photo-Biography of Bhagwan Shree Rajneesh and His Work 1974-1978.* Ma Prem Asha, Rajneesh Foundation, 1980.
6. *Sannyas* no. 6

5

SHREE RAJNEESH ASHRAM: A PLACE OF CONFLUENCE

Before moving to Pune in March 1974, Osho gave indications of his entering a new 'phase'. He explained how the fire of the *rajas guna* and its explosive force had come to an end and the quality of *sattva* had begun: 'Now *that* fire is quenched. Now, just as the sun withdraws its rays in the evening, as a fisherman withdraws his fishing net, I am slowly withdrawing too. It is not proper to say that I will withdraw. The withdrawal will automatically happen, because the third phase–that of the *sattva guna*–has begun. Therefore, you may be watching my gradual withdrawal from activities.'

It also seemed that with the change of climate his health further deteriorated. He suffered from acute asthma and this made him very sensitive to allergies. But, in spite of his delicate health, he continued to hold *darshans*, or meetings held in his presence, on the lawn in the mornings. He talked only to those disciples who were either arriving or leaving. The meetings were informal and Osho would sometimes remind his disciples:

'...When near me on the lawn, be sincere and true. Don't bring questions which are intellectual. They are useless. Don't bring any metaphysical questions. They are not true; they don't belong to you. Bring your nonsense out, whatever it is. And don't try to manipulate it, don't try to rationalise it or polish it; let it be as raw as possible, because before a master, you must be naked: you should not wear clothes and you should not hide yourself.'[1]

In April 1974, Osho gave eight discourses on the *Bhagavad Gita* (Chapter 16) in Hindi, in spite of his illness. After the series was over, Osho went into almost complete silence. He did not seem interested in giving further lectures. He also appeared uncomfortable in Pune and astonished everyone by asking that an alternative site be found near Mumbai. His plan was that while the ashram in Pune was to remain a meditation centre with residential facilities, Osho himself would reside in the alternative site.

Meanwhile, meditations began at a place called the Empress Botanical Gardens, located close to the ashram. The place was suitable for the two main group meditations: Dynamic Meditation at six o'clock in the morning and Whirling (Sufi) Meditation in the evening.

To everyone's delight, Osho slowly began to recover. He often strolled in the garden and seemed to enjoy the surroundings. It was announced on 30 April that Osho would stay in Pune after all, and that negotiations were under way so that the property adjoining the ashram could also be acquired. There was a new energy, joy, and a sense of direction in the air. His first series of English discourses in Pune began in May 1974, and when published was entitled, *My Way: The Way of the White Clouds*.

Osho's withdrawal however, continued, and after June 1974, he stopped directing meditations in person. Instead, an empty chair was brought in and placed on the podium. It marked the beginning of a new phase of his work. The master was present, but now his disciples had to feel him on a more subtle level. He explained:

'I cannot always be in this physical body with you; one day or another the physical vehicle has to be dropped. My work is complete as far as I am concerned. If I am carrying this physical vehicle, it is just for you; some day, it has to be dropped. Before it happens you must be ready to work in my absence, or in my non-physical presence which means the same. And once you can feel me in my absence you are free of me, and then even if I am not here in this body the contact will not be lost.'

A typical day for *sannyasins* in the ashram began with one hour of Dynamic Meditation at six o'clock in the morning. After this the *sannyasins* got ready and assembled to listen to Osho's discourse for the day. Osho arrived in Chuang Tzu auditorium, a part of his residence known as Lao Tzu House, at eight o'clock. The discourse lasted for about two hours, alternating from month to month between English and Hindi. After the discourse, *sannyasins* had breakfast, after which they busied themselves with assigned jobs (maintaining the ashram premises, working on Osho's books and lectures, handling his public relations, etc.), working at least six hours every day. From the eleventh of every month, a ten-day meditation camp was held which included five daily group meditations. Visiting *sannyasins* and non-*sannyasins* who came from all over the world participated in the meditation camp. From 1975 onwards, therapy groups were also conducted during and after the meditation camp.

The flow of people coming to the ashram increased steadily, especially from the West. Several Westerners who had come in contact with Osho in the early seventies were well known group therapy leaders; they had now settled down in Pune. These therapists had given up all rewards of wealth and prestige available to them in Europe and America, because they found something in Osho that was lacking in them—the quality of meditativeness. They came to learn from him how to be meditative. They found him to be the only spiritual master who fully knew holistic psychology, and one who could use it as a means of bringing individuals to higher levels of meditativeness.

Some of these well known therapists were Swami Ananda Teertha, formerly Paul Lowe, founder of Europe's first and biggest growth centre, 'Quaesitor', Swami Anand Somendra, formerly Michael Barnett, author of the much acclaimed book, *People Not Psychiatry* and Swami Prem Siddha, formerly Leonard Zunin, a California psychologist and a member of the American Board of Psychiatry and Neurology. The encounter and primal therapy groups began in April 1975. Osho has explained the need for therapy, saying that it is needed because people have forgotten now to be religious. Keeping this need in mind, Osho made it essential for his *sannyasins* to go through these therapy sessions. 'In my commune I have made it a must,' he says, 'that everybody should pass through therapy. They will help you to unburden the garbage that you have repressed within yourself. They will clean you, and only in a clear, clean heart is prayer possible. And when prayer arises, the miracle happens.'

Some of the techniques at the ashram were designed specifically to encourage exploration of repressed feelings and emotions such as anger, fear, jealousy and greed. This constitutes the first stage of the process, removing emotional blocks which in turn allows the energy to flow without impediment. After this stage, one can move into more advanced groups that will help one's energy to flow through all aspects of one's being: physical, emotional, mental and transcendent. Essentially, the therapy process, for Osho's *sannyasins*, is an initial step towards transformation. It is not an end; it is the beginning of the search for ultimate freedom.

Despite introducing therapy, Osho's emphasis has always been to become a seeker and to move from therapy to meditation. He explains:

'The mind is your only problem. All other problems are just offshoots of the mind. Meditation cuts the mind from the very roots. And all these therapies—Gestalt and Voice Dialogue and Fritz Perls—we can use them for those who have not yet entered into meditation so that they can develop a little understanding of the mind and can find the door from where to get out. We are using all forms of therapy which are helpful, but not for the meditators. They are only helpful in the beginning when you have not

yet become accustomed to meditation. Once you are meditative you don't need any therapy, no therapy is helpful then. But in the beginning, it can be helpful, and particularly for the Western sannyasins.'

Almost all major branches of holistic psychology were included in the ashram groups: encounter, primal therapy, Reichian therapy, Gestalt, bioenergetics, rolfing, massage including many techniques which are unique to the ashram. These had been designed to work on human energy. The crowd of thousands who came each year included doctors, lawyers, artists, journalists, businessmen, psychologists, priests and others who were searching for personal transformation through the ashram's group process.

The basic difference between groups that are conducted in the West and those that were held at the Rajneesh Ashram was the presence of Osho who gave his insights into human nature. Swami Anand Rajen, formerly Alan Lowen, who gave up postgraduate research work in psychology at Oxford University, reflects upon this unique characteristic of groups at the ashram, 'Good therapists are always on the lookout for someone who understands the human psyche better than they do it themselves. In this sense, an enlightened master like Osho is the ultimate therapist. By becoming a *sannyasin* and practising therapy under his guidance I am allowing him to take me beyond the limits of my previous understanding.'[2]

A therapist knows how the mind works, but a master goes beyond the mind and touches the deepest core of one's being; hence, a master is not just an 'ultimate therapist'; he is far more. The therapists in the West have begun to project themselves as masters, but qualitatively a master and a therapist are two entirely different things. Distinguishing between a master and a therapist, Osho explains:

'You are not your surface. You are your depth. Neither the physician nor the therapist can touch that depth. That depth can only be touched by a master, because he is that depth. A master is a no-mind. And that is the greatest difference possible. The master is a no-mind. He has no know how. He makes his nothingness available to the disciple, but the nothingness is a healing force. The psychotherapist tries to heal, but never succeeds. The master never tries to heal, but always succeeds. His love is his therapy…Just to be with a master is to be in a healing presence. The master is not a therapist, but his presence is therapy. His presence heals, and heals wounds of so many lives. But his process of healing is not psychological: it is existential.'

The ashram groups were also unique because they transcended the usual limits set by society and personality. They functioned in freedom and with greater intensity. The freedom and intensity of these groups, however, has been misunderstood, both in India and in the West, as indulgence and promiscuity, and a great controversy arose regarding these groups. The controversy centred more on those groups that helped bring out sexual repressions and tried to transform sex energy (according to the tantric tradition) into love, and even higher, into prayer. Osho has spoken of these group experiments:

'These are not new experiments. These have been tried by seekers of Tantra for centuries. For ages, Sarahapa and Tilopa and Kanhapa tried it. For the first time, I am trying to give these experiments a scientific base. These experiments were conducted in secrecy for so long. These experiments are described in the scriptures, but the common man was never informed about them because the common man was not considered worthy of that respect. I am giving him respect. I ask why the common man should be so ignored. Even he should be given an opportunity to avail himself of these experiments. Why should he not know that there are ways to take his energy upwards? Why should he be deceived? Why should the energy which is dissipated through the sex organs not be given a chance to rise upwards to reach the highest chakra, the sahasrar or the lotus flower?

'I am revealing that which has been hidden up to now; that is my only offence. For this, I am facing thousands of difficulties. But I am not going to stop these experiments at any cost. I will intensify these and they will reach more and more people. To all those who are willing to listen, who want to understand how life's energy can be transformed form the baser to the higher, these experiments will be made available.'[3]

It is Osho's observation that when one loves naturally, that is, when one accepts his senses and emotions, including the baser ones, he moves towards transformation. But, he adds, before this natural state can be attained, one must first see that which is unnatural in him, with courage and honesty. And this is where the groups help. Osho explains this in reply to a question: Is the purpose of the therapy groups to bring the participant to his natural self?

'The purpose of the therapy groups is not to bring the participants to their natural self. Not at all! The purpose of the therapy groups is to bring you to the point where you can see your unnaturalness. Nobody can bring you to your natural self; there can be no method, no technique, no device, which can bring you to your natural self, because all that you do will make you more and more unnatural.

'Then what is the purpose of a therapy group? It simply makes you aware of the unnatural patterns that you have evolved in your being. It simply helps you to see the unnaturalness of your life, that's all. When you start seeing it, it starts disappearing…Seeing the unnatural, you cannot support it any more. The natural can exist without your cooperation, but the unnatural cannot exist. Once you have seen that it is unnatural, your grip on it becomes loose. Your fist opens of its own accord.

'The group is not a device to open your fist. It is just to help you see what you are doing is unnatural. In that very seeing, the transformation happens.'

On several occasions, Osho had been asked why he did not encourage Indians to participate in therapy groups. In reply, Osho points out that the needs of Western people are different from those of Easterners. Also, the psychology of the East differs significantly from the West. He explains:

'In West, the psychology that has grown down the ages is extroverted; it is outgoing. The psychology that has been developed in the East is introverted; it is in-going. For a real Eastern person growth groups are not needed. He needs meditations like Vipassana or Zazen in which he can forget the whole outside world and just drown in his own being. He does not need any relationship. Relating is not needed. He needs only to unrelate himself from the world…The growth group is needed because you have a tremendous need to relate, to love, to communicate. In the West the basic problem is

how to communicate, how to relate…This is a different psychology. Both are ways to reach the ultimate: one is meditation, another is love. The East has developed the mind for meditation; the West has developed the mind for love. Love means relationship, meditation means non-relationship.'

Osho saw real possibility of going beyond the differences between the East and West. Hence his experiments with groups or with meditations are directed at dissolving those differences and creating a new human being, one who will be free of all patterns and conditionings of behaviour, Eastern or Western. The only way this can be accomplished is by creating what Osho calls a meditative space; this is the ultimate purpose or goal of the therapy groups and the meditations.

After Osho settled down in Pune, his parents visited the ashram occasionally, and although Osho's mother took initiation from him in 1971, Dadda had not felt spiritually ready until several experiences of deep meditation. The feeling became intense during one of his visits on 19 October 1975, when he became Osho's disciple and was given a new name—Swami Devateerth Bharti.

It was indeed a rare phenomenon: a father becoming a disciple of his own son. About his father's initiation, Osho says, 'Jesus' father never came to Jesus to be initiated. John the Baptist initiated many, but his own father never came to be initiated. Krishna's father was not a disciple of his. My father is rare, not because he is my father; he is simply rare.'

While Osho was bringing peace to the inner world of the seekers and leading a quiet revolution, the country had slipped into turmoil. India was about to witness its biggest political upheaval since its independence from the British rule in 1947. The political parties who opposed the policies of Prime Minister Indira Gandhi and her government united under the leadership of veteran leader Jaya Prakash Narayan and mobilised a countrywide opposition to Mrs Gandhi's government.

The situation became so critical that Mrs Gandhi declared a state of emergency at the end of 1975, under which many civil rights were suspended, the press censored, leaders of the opposition imprisoned, and stern measures taken against those who dared to create trouble for her government.

But this subversion of the democratic process resulted in even more agitation and hostility towards her. She faced harsh criticism in the foreign press. The pressure mounted and finally forced her to hold general elections. The public mandate went overwhelmingly against Mrs Gandhi. Her party lost the elections and the coalition of opposition parties under the name of the Janata Party achieved a landslide victory. The new Janata Party came into power in the middle of 1977.

One of the senior leaders of this party, who also became the prime minister, was Morarji Desai. Desai epitomised a conservative and narrow view of religion. All through his years in power, Desai harassed Osho and his followers. Revealing the cause of Desai's hostility towards him, Osho said in 1978, 'Morarji Desai has been against me all along. The conflict continued at least for fifteen years...Now he is in power, so the fascist in him surfaces...Once, when I started criticising Mahatma Gandhi, he wanted to prevent my entrance into his province of Gujarat...But he could not do a thing about it and he has held this wound about me in his heart for fifteen years.'

Desai carried out a kind of campaign against Osho and the ashram. Because of his strong adherence to Gandhism, his puritanical and orthodox attitude, and his vehement opposition to Osho's views, he used his influence to create as much trouble as possible for the ashram and the *sannyasins*. Osho was forthright in his response to Desai's accusations, stating clearly, 'My feeling is that he does not understand a bit what is happening here...All he knows is just playing the game of politics.'

The situation was further exaggerated by the Indian press which ran stories about Osho and the ashram that were sensational and inaccurate. Further, leaders of a number of religious sects also began to criticise Osho and his teachings. Osho responded to all these distortions by explaining the reasons for this negative public reaction, and also his vision and the nature of his work.

'With me they're all angry because I am not a hypocrite. I live the way I like to live. I say things that go in tune with my life. For example, I am not against life and its joys, that's what I say, and that's how I live. They would have loved me very much if I was living like a beggar on the surface, if I was starving naked on the road…I am not an ascetic. I am living herenow in paradise. And I teach you also to live herenow in paradise: this very earth is the paradise, this very body is the Buddha.

'I am teaching my people to live a single, unitary life…Be natural. I want Buddha, Gautam the Buddha, and Zorba the Greek to come closer and closer—to become one. My sannyasin has to be "Zorba the Buddha."

'I am a materialist-spiritualist. That is their trouble. They cannot even imagine this. They have always thought that materialism is something diametrically against, opposite, to spirituality. And I am trying to bring them closer. In fact, that is how it is. Your body is not opposed to your soul, otherwise, why should they be together? And God is not opposed to the world, otherwise, why should he create it?

'That's my whole work here, and I can understand why Morarji (Desai) strongly dislikes it. He is a traditionalist, an orthodox Hindu, with no vision, with no insight into life. He is just a fascist Hindu, and my approach towards life is that of individual freedom—utter freedom for the individual.

'The individual should not be interfered with unless he becomes dangerous to other people…Each individual has to be himself and has to be given space enough to be himself. That, the fascist mind cannot allow.'

While Desai and his government remained in power, bureaucratic obstacles prevented the ashram's efforts to buy land where a new commune could be established to fulfill Osho's vision. The Indian government also instructed its foreign embassies to deny visas to anyone who wanted to visit the Rajneesh Ashram in Pune. It became evident that the very people who had criticised and opposed Mrs Gandhi for suppressing democratic rights, and who came into power by pledging publicly to support democracy, secularism, and free press, were themselves engaging in the practices contrary to these principles where Osho and the Rajneesh Ashram were concerned.

Regardless of how the world outside treated Osho and the ashram, activities in the ashram moved ahead smoothly, growth continued, and more and more people came to see him. His daily schedule included his meetings with a small group of ashram *sannyasins*, *sannyasins* visiting from other parts of India and from abroad, and occasionally non-*sannyasin* visitors. These *darshans* provided intimate communion with the master, who initiated seekers into *sannyas* and explained the meanings of the new names; he chatted with *sannyasins* who either had arrived or were returning to their homes (reaching closer to their truths), talked with individuals very lovingly and compassionately and helped them if they had any problems or questions.

After February 1979, these *darshans* were given a new form and dimension. They were called 'energy *darshans*' and the format was changed. Instead of responding directly to the problems or questions of *sannyasins* in *darshan*, Osho would read letters from them and then send his replies through Ma Yoga Laxmi to them. The giving of *sannyas* remained as before, except that now Osho went into more elaborate detail when explaining the meaning of the new name. The arrival and departure *darshan* were changed to 'blessing *darshans*', in which there was no conversation with Osho; Osho would press his thumb or forefingers in the centre of the forehead (also known as the 'third eye') of the *sannyasin* (who sat with closed eyes before him) as energy was transferred from the master to the disciple. After the 'blessing *darshan*', *sannyasins*, especially the regular ashram workers, received an even more intense experience of energy and ecstasy. During this part the atmosphere would be filled with joy and festivity. While Osho pressed the 'third eye' of a particular *sannyasin*, other *sannyasins* danced ecstatically around him in a semicircle and the group swayed to the music. The whole experience was like opening out or being totally receptive to the flow of energy.

In June 1979, Osho's health, which had been fairly good since he arrived from Mumbai, gave way, and he had to stop giving discourses and *darshans*. *Sannyasins* participated in a silent music meditation with him in Buddha Hall from 11 to 20 June 1979. Osho did not speak, as his body was not well. He rested for a few days; there were no lectures and no evening *darshans*, and by the third day all was well. Still, he did not come to speak. The hall was filled with expectant disciples enjoying music that was being played as part of the meditation in Osho's absence. At the front of the lecture hall was his poignantly empty chair. On the fourth day Osho came, a fragile, gentle breath of love floating into the lecture hall, onto the dais, into the chair, accentuating the empty space with his emptiness.

It was a very beautiful experience for the disciples, although they could not help but worry about the master's health. They felt him even more intensely, lovingly and prayerfully. Osho recovered from the illness and resumed his morning discourse on 21 June. He spoke to the disciples that morning quite intimately and more specifically about himself. He talked elaborately on silence, on the value of sitting in silent communion with him, and gave a hint of the fact that he might stop talking in the near future. (He did stop talking about two years later.) The following excerpts are from the discourse of 21 June 1979:

'My beloved bodhisattvas...The time is ripe, the time has come for it. My whole work here consists in creating a Buddhafield, an energy-field where these eternal truths can be uttered again. It is a rare opportunity. Only once in a while, after centuries, such an opportunity exists...don't miss it. Be very alert, mindful: listen to these words not only by your head but by your heart, by your every fibre of being. Let your totality be stirred by them.

'And after these ten days of silence, it is exactly the right moment to bring Buddha back, to make him again alive amongst you, to let the winds of Buddha pass through you. Yes, he can be called back again, because nobody ever disappears. Buddha is no more an embodied person; certainly he does not exist as an individual anywhere but his essence, his soul, is part of the cosmic soul now.

'I am immensely glad, because after these ten days of silence I can say to you that many of you are now ready to commune with me in silence.

That is the ultimate in communication. Words are inadequate; words say, but only partially. Silence communes totally.

'And to use words is a dangerous game too, because my meaning will remain with me, only the word will reach to you and you will give it your own meaning, your own colour. It will not contain the same truth that it was meant to contain. It will contain something else, something far poorer. It will contain your meaning, not my meaning. You can distort language—in fact it is almost impossible to avoid distortion—but you cannot distort silence. Either you understand or you don't understand.

'And for those ten days, there were only two categories of people here; those who understood and those who did not. But there was not a single person who misunderstood. You cannot misunderstand silence, that's the beauty of silence. The demarcation is absolute, either you understand or you simply don't understand, there is nothing to misunderstand.

'These ten days have been of strange beauty, and of a mysterious majesty too. I no more really belong to this shore. My ship has been waiting for me for a long time—I should have gone. It is a miracle that I am in the body still. The whole credit goes to you—to your love, to your prayers, to your longing. You would like me to linger a little while longer on this shore, hence the impossible has become possible.

'These ten days, I was not feeling together with my body. I was feeling very uprooted, dislocated. So it was strange to be in the body when you don't feel that you are in the body. And it was also strange to go on living in a place which no more belongs to you—my home is on the other shore. And the call comes persistently! But because you need me, it is out of the compassion of the universe—you can call it God's compassion—that he is allowing me to be in the body a little more.

'Words are becoming more and more difficult for me. They are becoming more and more of an effort. I have to say something, so I go on saying something to you. But I would like you to get ready as soon as possible so that we can simply sit in silence…listening to the birds and their songs, or listening just to your own heartbeat. Just being here, doing nothing.

'Get ready as soon as possible, because I may stop speaking any day. And let the news be spread to all nooks and corners of the world: those who want to understand me only through words, they should come soon, because I may cease speaking any day. Unpredictably, any day, it may happen—it may happen even in the middle of a sentence. Then I am not going to complete the sentence! Then it will hang forever and forever... incomplete.

'But this time you have pulled me back.'

While *sannyasins* enjoyed energy *darshans*, living in celebration, and working creatively, they were unaware that an experience of great intensity and meaning was to occur shortly—the death of Osho's father, Dadda. Dadda and most of the family, including Osho's mother, brothers and their wives and children, had left Gadarwara and had been living at the ashram since 1978. It was almost impossible not to notice Dadda, the white haired man who was old in body but whose face showed vitality and joy. His bright and laughing eyes showed inner peace and contentment. He was a delightful host during the *kirtan* celebrations that were held every week at his residence.

Dadda had not been in good health for some time. He had six heart attacks since 1975, and was admitted to the hospital for heart failure about a month and a half before he left his body. The following is a personal account of how I experienced the incident.

It was one of those damp evenings of the monsoon season in September. After supper, I was working in my office. I had been working for half an hour when I heard a female voice: 'Swami, Dadda is dead. We are going to have a celebration in Buddha Hall.' The message came like a jolt. I immediately put my papers aside, got up, and joined other *sannyasins* in the Buddha Hall. The news cut me off from everything else; it just pushed me into the moment, and I remained seated silently in Buddha Hall.

Just a week before, I had met with Dadda in his hospital room. I had an appointment with him. In fact, it was agreed that we would talk about Osho and he would tell me stories, incidents from Osho's childhood. He looked as cheerful as ever and also seemed to have greatly recovered from an attack of paralysis. He had now been hospitalised for about five weeks. Doctors had assured his release within the next few days. But as I sat, touching his feet, he looked at me and said: 'I don't feel like saying anything more than what has already been said previously by me (about Osho). I don't like to see people anymore. I don't even feel like eating anymore. I feel sorry for this, since you have come from such a long distance especially for this.'

I told him not to feel sorry, and said that we could arrange a meeting later when he was fully recovered and back at the ashram. I chatted briefly with Ammaji (Osho's mother) and Shailendra and Amit (Osho's brothers). With the help of his sons, Dadda walked slowly out of the room, feeling very hot and exhausted. We brought him back to the room and laid him down on the bed. He closed his eyes and went to sleep. I returned to the ashram.

Dadda left his body on 8 September 1979, at 8:45 pm. But this was the death of his physical body. He had attained the state of *samadhi*, the state of detachment of mind from body, early that day at three o'clock in the morning. And with that first glimpse of the eternal he became aware that he was going to die. He sent a message to Osho to come as he wished to say goodbye to him. However, immediately thereafter he sent another message that Osho need not bother and need not come. Osho went to see his father anyway.

This death was extraordinary, but then again so was the meeting of father and son, the master and disciple. Two beings—one already one with the whole, and the other stepping into it. It was their last meeting. The father had loved his son immensely. Osho had served him lovingly since childhood. At one of my meetings with Dadda, he remembered fondly how once during an illness, Osho, when he was fifteen, used to give him a massage and, despite the doctor's prohibition, bring sweets to him secretly and feed him. But now this illness was the last one, and father and son were no longer the same. It was an incredible meeting of two beings in an intimate yet unattached relationship.

So a great celebration began in Buddha Hall at about nine that evening.

Disciples were crying, dancing and singing 'Hallelujah'. That is the way Osho wanted it to be. Because, as he says, 'He left the world in utter silence, in joy, in peace. He left the world like a lotus flower. It was worth celebrating. And these are the occasions for you to learn how to live and how to die. Each death should be a celebration—but it can be a celebration only if it leads you to higher planes of existence.'

Around 10:30 pm, Dadda's body was brought into the hall and laid on a marble stage from where Osho gave his discourses. Osho's mother and other family members, full of tears, were near the body. There was a distinct glow on Dadda's face and he looked to me more as though he was deep in meditation, rather than dead.

After a while, Osho came. As usual he smiled and signalled greetings to everyone with hands pressed together in a *namaste*. Then he placed a garland of leaves around Dadda's neck and knelt down. It was a remarkable scene; the energy in the hall was intense. Osho touched his father's head at two spots. In his lecture later that day, he explained what he was doing.

'*I had touched his body at two spots, one on the agya chakra because there were only two possibilities, either he could have left his body through the agya chakra, in which case he would have had to take one more birth, though only once more. And if he had left through the seventh chakra, sahasrar, then he would not have to take birth again. First I checked his agya chakra. I put my hand on his agya chakra with a little concern because the chakra through which life departs opens up like a bud which blossoms into a flower. And those who have experience of chakras can immediately feel, just by touching, from where life found its way out. I was very happy to see that his life had not passed through the agya chakra. Then I touched his sahasrar, which is also known as the 'thousand petal lotus', and found it open. He flew away through the seventh door.*'

In a few minutes Osho left the hall smiling, and a little after that the body was taken to the nearest cremation ground, followed by the hundreds of ochre-robed *sannyasins* chanting, 'Rejoice, rejoice!' Around two o'clock in the morning the body was placed on the pyre and the fire was lit. As the chanting and dancing reached its peak, the orange-coloured flames engulfed the body and the whole cremation ground lit up in its glory.

Celebrating life and death in the same spirit, the ashram continued to grow. More and more creative activities were added to the ashram routines. For the disciples, creativity and artistic expression became an integral part of their daily meditation. To Osho's disciples, *sannyas* meant living in the world without being attached to it and sharing the bliss of meditation with others through creating beautiful arts and crafts. Hence, many different kinds of arts and crafts flourished at Shree Rajneesh Ashram. The ashram pottery acquired considerable reputation. The weaving studio became equally well known and produced a wide range of ponchos, jackets, shawls, blankets and children's toys. Dresses and robes designed and manufactured at the ashram became very popular.

The Rajneesh Theatre Group won critical acclaim from the Indian press with its colourful production of Shakespeare's delightful comedy, *A Midsummer Night's Dream* in July1979, in Mumbai. The group also toured other cities in India. Encouraged by its continued success, the group presented *A Midsummer Night's Dream* and *Twelfth Night* in New Delhi in March 1980.

The ashram's health centre was equipped with a modern laboratory, surgical facilities and staffed by qualified doctors. The staff of the health centre carried out extensive research in controlling indigenous diseases such as hepatitis, which especially affected people coming from the West.

The tape department used highly sophisticated instrumentation to record Osho's daily discourses. It was run by *sannyasin* electronic engineers. *Sannyasins* also experimented with new ways of utilising power, including the construction of houses fitted with solar heated panels.

The ashram also produced detergents and soaps that were not detrimental to plant life when recycled into the environment. It manufactured a wide range of soaps, shampoos and creams, from non-animal fats and natural oils. In the canteen, a wide range of excellent vegetarian food was always available, including egg-less cakes and pastries, homemade curd, cheese and peanut butter. The *sannyasins* also showed a remarkable achievement in the area of hydroponics.

By 1979, more than one 100 therapy groups were being conducted within the Department of Psychology of the emerging Rajneesh International Meditation University (RIMU). These groups were later consolidated into twenty major groups, residential and non-residential. In addition, a variety of special classes were held: Tai Chi, Karate, Indian dance, English and Hindi language, and chamber music.

The innovative programmes of RIMU could not find government support for recognition. In April 1981, the name of the university was changed to Rajneesh International No-University (RIN-U) and it was announced by the Rajneesh Foundation that RIN-U would function in freedom and not seek recognition from any state, country, government, nation or educational authority. 'It is not prepared to compromise its revolutionary approach to education in order to gain official recognition...While not seeking any recognition itself, the No-University will recognise certain schools, colleges, institutes, and universities around the world.'[4]

It soon became impossible for this rapidly expanding experiment in communal living to be limited to the six acres of land at Shree Rajneesh Ashram in Pune. Efforts were intensified to acquire 400 acres of largely barren land, thirty-two kilometres from Pune, in a valley known as Jadhavwadi, in a town called Saswad.

Plans were made to build the 'Rajneesh Neo-*Sannyas* International Commune', where 10,000 *sannyasins* could live and work together in love and meditation as a self-contained, self-sufficient community. The process of acquiring the place began by leasing an old castle adjoining the property in order to house handicraft industries and residential therapy groups. Also, the ashram *sannyasins* began cultivating some of the land. Efforts were made to get permission from the Maharashtra State Government to use part of the land for non-agricultural purposes.

The new commune at Jadhavwadi was inaugurated on 11 December 1979, Osho's forty-eighth birthday. Over 6,000 *sannyasins* and visitors drove out to the site in a convoy of buses, cars and motorbikes. At the highest spot of the property, the specially designed flag of 'Rajneeshdham' was raised. This spot was to be saved for building a beautiful meditation temple. Forty-nine different departments of the new commune were announced. The plan included meditation halls, therapy chambers, a university, a five-star hotel, a cinema and film institute, colleges of dramatic art, crafts, music, dance, painting and sculpture and many other facilities.

However, the hurdles created by bureaucracy did not allow the commune to expand and grow. Consequently, the Rajneesh Foundation made further efforts to acquire land in the area of Kutch (in the western state of Gujarat) as well as in the north, but the efforts proved unsuccessful.

Osho's vision sees a commune as a framework within which its members can experience spiritual awakening. The commune and its environment, which Osho calls a 'Buddhafield', would allow things to be done in a relaxed, creative, and loving way. There would no longer be any work, in its literal sense. This way, the work would no longer be serious business; instead, it would become continuous *leela* (play). The whole idea was to foster spiritual growth by allowing individuals to be open to change. In this way communal life would acquire an aesthetic quality. In this commune no one would function in a stereotyped, established role or position; each person, instead, would be seen as having undiscovered potential and would be provided opportunities to discover his divinity. The commune would be more of a laboratory than an organisation, where experiments would be carried on to see which method, path, technique, or insight could best bring Buddhahood to the earth. Osho discussed this vision in great detail in the book, *From Sex to Superconsciousness*.

Osho continued to sharply criticise orthodox religions and the hypocritical leaders of the society with their vested interests. As we have seen, his sole concern has always been to see things as they are and reveal the truth regardless of how anyone else feels about it. Because of this, he invited trouble and opposition from every direction. The most violent and dramatic reaction to his discourses and work, however, occurred on 22 May 1980, when a religious fanatic attempted to assassinate Osho during his morning discourse.

On that day, the activities in the ashram began as usual. Osho was then speaking in Hindi. Thousands had gathered in the Buddha Hall on the pleasant summer morning and were listening to his discourse. Suddenly, at about 8:30 am, a young man stood up in the audience and started running towards Osho, shouting in Hindi, which when translated into English meant, 'Bhagwan Rajneesh, you are speaking against our religion, we won't tolerate it.' His path was immediately blocked by the ashram guards, but before they could seize him he managed to throw a large knife that passed in front of Osho and landed on the concrete floor of the hall.

Minutes before this incident, the ashram security had received a tip-off from the Pune police that an attack was imminent. While the attack was under way, a police squad arrived at the ashram gate. The assailant, who was later identified as Vilas Vitthal Tupe, a member of an extreme Hindu organisation based in Pune, was gently apprehended by the guards, removed from the hall in silence, and handed over to the police. A wave of shock passed through the *sannyasins* sitting in the hall, but there was no panic.

Osho remained seated throughout the attack, calm and absolutely unperturbed. In fact, he in turn calmed the audience, requesting everyone to remain seated and continued his discourse.

The ashram *sannyasins* were shaken by this event. Ma Yoga Laxmi, managing trustee of the Rajneesh Foundation, stated in a press release: 'Today, in the Buddha Hall, the history of assassination, abuse and hostility which has been India's reaction to all its great mystics and seers repeated itself. These are the people who stoned Buddha, tortured Mahavir and who now wish to silence Osho…These fanatics thought they could dispose off Osho in the same way that they disposed off Gandhi, but the divine grace of existence decreed otherwise. Osho will continue to speak the truth, no matter how many attempts are made to prevent him from doing so.'

Not surprisingly, considering the government's attitude towards Osho, the accused, the would-be assassin, was charged, tried and acquitted. Regardless of threats to Osho's life and the negative reactions from the press, priests, pundits and politicians, the ashram activities functioned normally. The energy-field continued to grow. Security, though, in and around the ashram was tightened. Osho's health also remained very good. The remaining part of the year 1980 passed relatively calmly.

Excerpts from:

Dimensions Beyond the Known
A Bird on the Wing
The Secret of Secrets vol. 2
The Invitation
The Perfect Master
Take It Easy
Tao: The Pathless Path
Come Follow To You vol. 2
The Secret
The Dhammapada: Way of the Buddha vol. 1 & 2

End notes:

1. *The Sound of Running Water: A Photo-Biography of Bhagwan Shree Rajneesh and His Work 1974-1978.*
   Ma Prem Asha, Rajneesh Foundation, 1980.
2. Rajneesh Foundation Press Office Files
3. *ibid*
4. *ibid*

6

THE SILENT SAGE

The year of 1981 will perhaps be recalled as the most eventful year for the ashram. It began with one more disciple of Osho's attaining enlightenment. Thirty-three-year old Swami Anand Vimalkirti, formerly Prince Welf of Hanover, reached enlightenment on the evening of 9 January 1981. He died and attained *Mahaparinirvana* (freedom from birth and death) on 10 January 1981. The story of this event, in brief, is as follows.

On 5 January, while Vimalkirti was doing his daily 'warm-up' exercises, he collapsed due to a cerebral hemorrhage. He was put on respiratory machines in a Pune hospital for five days. His mother, Princess Sophia, and his brother, Prince Georg, came from Germany to be with him. Osho paid his tribute to Vimalkirti in the morning discourse in the following words:

'*Vimalkirti is blessed. He was one of the few chosen* sannyasins *who never wavered for a single moment, whose trust has been total the whole time he was here. He never asked a question, he never wrote a letter, he never brought any problem. His trust was such that by and by he absolutely merged with me. He has one of the rarest hearts. That quality of the heart has disappeared from the world. He is really a prince, really royal, really aristocratic. Aristocracy has nothing to do with birth, it has something to do with the quality of the heart. And I experienced him as one of the rarest, most beautiful souls on the earth.'*

Osho wanted Vimalkirti to be kept on the respiratory machines for at least seven days, because, as Osho explains, 'He was just on the edge—a little push and he would become part of the beyond…Hence I wanted him to hang around a little more. Last night he managed. He crossed the boundary from doing to non-doing…'

Osho also explained that because of his meditative quality, Vimalkirti succeeded in disidentifying from his body and thus attaining consciousness beyond the body.

All members of Vimalkirti's family including his wife, Ma Prem Turiya (formerly Princess Wibke of Hanover, also a *sannyasin*), daughter, Ma Prem Tania (formerly Princess Tania of Hanover), his father, Prince Georg Wilhelm of Hanover, mother, and brother, joined thousands of *sannyasins* in carrying his body to the cremation ground. While Vimalkirti's body was burning on the pyre, everyone danced and sang in celebration. Messages of condolence were received from Queen Elizabeth II of England, H. R. H. Prince Charles of England (Vimalkirti was a nephew of the Queen and so a cousin to Prince Charles), Queen Fredericka of Greece, Mrs Indira Gandhi, and many other prominent people.

8 September was declared *Mahaparinirvana* Day, to be celebrated annually in memory of Osho's father and Vimalkirti and all those *sannyasins* who have left their bodies (people who have died) and who will be leaving their bodies in the future.

The spirit of celebration not only continued as ever in the ashram, but it began to spread to other parts of the world as well. The biggest celebration ever, organised by disciples of Osho outside Pune, took place at London's prestigious Cafe Royal on 14-15 March 1981. It was called 'The March Event' and was in response to growing British interest in Osho and the activities of Shree Rajneesh Ashram, Pune. Over a thousand people, including journalists and many other prominent people, participated in this two-day programme of meditation and group therapy. Seven expert *sannyasin* group leaders conducted the programme.

Following the overwhelming success of the 'The March Event', plans were made to hold similar types of celebrations in San Francisco, Sydney, Berlin and Munich. This is precisely what Osho had envisioned, that his message and work should be spread in the world through his *sannyasins*. He had said before that, the time had come to extend his 'Buddhafield'—the energy-field created by the Enlightened master— all over the world. Since he himself had attained enlightenment, he left no stone unturned to make the phenomenon of enlightenment available to as many people as possible. His work and story stands a proof to the same. He has declared: 'I will be sending you to the four corners of the earth. You will be my ambassadors at large, you will function for me, I will see through your eyes, and I will speak through your tongues, and I will touch people through your hands, and I will love through your love.'[1]

Osho's message of love came through once again on the twenty-eighth anniversary of his enlightenment—21 March 1981. 'My message to those thirsty for godliness is this: this is a tavern and not a temple,' said Osho. He explained in the morning discourse that his religion has no name because love has no name: love is neither Christian, nor Hindu, nor Muslim, nor Jain, nor Buddhist. And if love has no name, how can religion—which is the ultimate in love—have a name? Don't ask for a name; the drunk have no religion, they have only drunkenness, only bliss.

In reference to the ashram and its organisation, he added: 'Even a tavern needs a little organisation. Someone has to see that the thirsty are not left thirsty, and that the non-thirsty are not allowed to trespass.'

No one had the slightest idea that the master was just about ready to reveal a new dimension of his work, and that from now on he was going to be available to only those who were ready to drink without the help of his words—in silence. For many years, Osho had been telling his disciples that truth could never be expressed through words. He said repeatedly that the disciple could enter into communion with the master only through profound silence: 'Words are too profane, too inadequate, too limited. Only an empty space, utterly silence, can represent the being of the Buddha. Because you cannot understand silence, it has to be translated into language—otherwise there is no need.'

The evening *darshan* on 23 March 1981 turned out to be of immense significance—it was Osho's last *darshan* to disciples and visitors. The discourse next morning also turned out to be his last. It so happened that on 24 March several cases of chicken pox were spotted in the ashram, and extra precautions were taken and the persons affected by the disease were immediately quarantined. Evening *darshans* were cancelled, and instead of morning discourse, silent music meditation began in Buddha Hall two days later.

At the last *darshan* of 23 March, Osho talked about the origin of words and language. He mentioned in particular the classic statement made in the *Bible* that, 'In the beginning was the Word, and the Word was with God and the Word was God.' Osho responded to this statement by saying, 'I say categorically no! In the beginning was silence and also in the end is silence. Silence is the stuff the universe is made of. And I can say it authentically because if one goes within oneself, one comes to the beginning of everything, because you contain both the beginning and the end.'

Despite the spread of chicken pox, cancellation of the *darshans*, and absence of early morning discourses of the master, the ashram activities continued as usual. Everyone expected Osho to come out on 11 April, when the next meditation camp was to begin and Osho was to start the lecture series in English. However, on 10 April, Ma Anand Sheela, one of the trustees of Rajneesh Foundation, called a meeting of all department heads of the ashram and announced that Osho was entering into a new and ultimate stage of his work—he was entering into silence. She was among the first ones to hear of Osho's decision and was shocked to hear the news. She said, 'But Osho said there was no need to be shocked, he said we should all be happy and celebrate. And he asked me to convey it to others with the same feeling of joy which he felt.'

In the ashram, the news spread like wildfire. It came as a great surprise to many. But within a few hours everyone in the ashram was singing and dancing. The disciples soon realised that the time had come for them to go to a deeper level and have a real communion with the master.

In a historical declaration, the Rajneesh Foundation announced that Osho had begun the ultimate stage of his work. From 1 May 1981 onwards, Osho would speak only through silence, which he had described as 'the language of existence'. Instead of verbal communication there would be a *satsang*, a silent heart-to-heart communion, it was announced. It was further stated that a certain number of disciples were ready to receive Osho in silence; hence, he would make himself available only to them. The disciples were now able to enter into a silent spiritual communion with the master, on a deeper and more profound level. *Satsang* would take place every morning in Buddha Hall.

The announcement also stated the beginning of a new phase in the evening *darshan*s at the ashram. Osho himself would no longer be physically present. Ma Yoga Laxmi, Swami Ananda Teertha, and Swami Satya Vedant (when Laxmi was away) were declared to be the mediums for this work. When the announcement was made, Laxmi was out of town for Foundation work, hence evening *darshan*s, *sannyas*, blessings and energy *darshan*s for Indian friends were given by Vedant and for the Western friends by Teertha.

After having astounded the public with his revolutionary and original views on almost every possible subject under the sun, Osho's decision to enter into silence produced reactions all across the world that ranged from surprise to complete disbelief and cynicism. Nevertheless, the fact remained that Osho had been waiting for this moment. He had been preparing disciples for this ultimate phase of his work; he had been preparing them for independence. His decision showed clearly that the disciples had become receptive enough for this new dimension, so there was a feeling of joy and of silent mystery among them. Although there was also a deep feeling that they would miss his voice and his insights which used to make their day flow, there was no alarm. In fact, there was a feeling of gratitude amongst them, because Osho had found them worthy enough to share the last phase of silence.

The new phase provided everyone with the opportunity to experience Osho's energy independently from his physical presence in the evening *darshan*, and also without the aid of his communication through words in the discourses. He withdrew even further from his disciples, as far as this outer part of his being was concerned, but entered into a deeper intimacy with them. He had pointed this out to them long before:

'*The day you are able to see this chair empty, this body empty, this being empty, you will have seen me; you will have contacted me. That is the real moment when the disciple meets the master. It is a dissolution, a disappearance...the dewdrop slipping into the ocean, or, the ocean slipping into the dewdrop. It is the same! The master disappearing into the disciple and the disciple disappearing into the master. And then there prevails profound silence. It is not a dialogue.*'

On 1 May1981, Osho gave his first *satsang* as a 'silent sage' to an audience of 10,000 disciples and visitors in the Buddha Hall. This was his first appearance since he stopped giving the daily discourse on 24 March 1981. The *satsang* lasted for one hour—it was a wordless, heart-to-heart communion between the master and his devotees. The *satsang* began with the chanting of a mantra which was used once before by the commune of (disciples) *bhikkhus* who gathered around Gautam Buddha 2,500 years ago:

Buddham sharanam gachchami
Sangham sharanam gachchami
Dhammam sharanam gachchami

I go to the feet of the Awakened One. I go to the feet of the commune of the Awakened One. I go to the feet of the ultimate truth of the Awakened One.

After chanting of the mantra soft, meditative music was played, interspersed with periods of silence. In between, passages from the *Isha Upanishad* and Kahlil Gibran's *The Prophet* were read. At the end, the mantra was repeated and Osho left the hall. The *satsang* continued to take place every morning. Osho would sit in silence with his *sannyasins* for one hour. Vivek would accompany him on the podium and sit at his feet. Osho had explained the meaning and purpose of *satsang* as a close proximity of the truth; it means near the truth, it means near a master who has become one with the truth—just being near him, open, receptive and waiting.

Withdrawing further from activities, Osho's silence, in a way, brought his being in the state of the third *guna*—*sattva*. He had already passed through the first two *gunas*—*tamas*, and *rajas*. Osho's silence, however, had an added dimension—the dimension of music. Explaining the relation between music and silence, Osho says, 'Music in a sense is absolutely silent. Sounds are there, but those sounds only make the silence deeper, they help the silence…Noise is just sound which does not lead you to silence. Music is sound that becomes a door to silence…The being of a master is the being of music, poetry, song. But they all lead to silence, and truth can only be conveyed in silence.'

While the disciples experienced the loving and blissful company of their master in this deep, new dimension, the world outside grew more and more hostile and violent towards Osho, the disciples and the ashram. There was an alarming increase in the number of threatening letters and telephone calls received at the ashram. They included life-threats on Osho as well as against some individual disciples. For example, an offer of a quarter of a million pounds was made to a man in Sri Lanka to assassinate Osho. A letter received on 3 May by a *sannyasin* at the ashram revealed this information.

The news release issued by the Rajneesh Foundation press office on 10 May brought this alarming situation to the attention of the press. The news release mentioned, among other things, that a threat had come from a group called 'Roman Catholics of Bombay and Pune', who warned that they would hurt Osho and bomb the ashram. A message was received that implied that a secret organisation was to launch a campaign of violence against the ashram.

The fear of the threats started to turn into reality. A fire occurred at Rajneeshdham, Jadhavwadi Fort, Saswad, in the early morning hours of 27 May. Twenty-four hours later, on 28 May, arson destroyed a Rajneesh Foundation book storage warehouse located near Pune. Several explosions were heard in rapid succession and fire spread quickly through the stacked books. The blaze started around three o'clock in the morning. At about the same time an explosive device detonated at the Foundation's medical centre. Fortunately, no one was hurt.

In spite of the attacks, the morning *satsang* with Osho continued to take place as usual in Buddha Hall. Before the *satsang* began, a gathering of thousands of disciples and visitors raised their arms in a demonstration of protest and condemnation against the outrage. The foundation issued a clear statement: our only concern is for Osho. But whatever the risk may be, what he is offering to humanity will continue to be offered. His message to the world is so important that it cannot be stopped by fanatics.

The disciples had taken the events of arson and hostility calmly and with increasing trust and devotion towards their master. They remained near him in silence, in prayer, in deep love and surrender. The work and activities of the ashram continued without interruption. But Osho's health again began to fail and it was clear that he would have to go to the West for medical treatment. Consequently, Osho's last *satsang* took place on the morning of 1 June1981. He bid goodbye to his beloved disciples the same afternoon and left Pune as quietly as he had arrived seven years earlier.

Osho was asked occasionally whether or not he would ever leave India, and every time his answer was that he would not. He explained the reasons for his not leaving India in a discourse on 30 August 1978.

'It is difficult for me to leave India. India has something tremendously valuable. It has the longest, deepest search for truth. Many Buddhas have walked on this land, under these trees; the very earth has become sacred. To be here is totally different from being anywhere else. And what I am trying to bring to you is more easily possible here than anywhere else.

'India has fallen from its peaks. It is no more its past glory. It is one of the ugliest spots now on the earth, but still, because a Gautam Buddha walked, and a Mahavira and a Krishna, and millions of others...

'No other country can claim this. Jesus is very alone in Jerusalem. Mohammed is very, very alone in the Arabian countries. Lao Tzu has had a very small company—Chuang Tzu and a few others. They tried hard to create something. But India has the longest spiritual vibe. At least for 5,000 years the search has been deepening. And still the waters are flowing.

'This India that you see in the newspapers, this India I have left already. The India that you know, I have left already. Have you ever seen me going out of the gate? I live in my room. Whether this room is here or anywhere else, I will live in the room. It will be the same. I am not concerned with this India that you come to know through radio, television, newspapers—the India of the politicians, of the hypocrites, of the masochistic mahatmas. I have already left it.

'But I cannot leave. There is a hidden India, too, an esoteric India too, where Buddhas are still alive, where you can contact Mahavira more easily than anywhere else, where the whole tradition of the awakened ones is like an undercurrent. I can't leave that. For me, there is no problem—I can leave; I will be the same anywhere—but for you it will not be the same.'

But Osho did leave India. Why? Part of the answer was revealed just one month before he stopped speaking in public. One question he was often asked was what would happen after he leaves his body. To this question, he gave an elaborate and clear reply.

'I am living my moment. I don't care a bit about what happens later on. It may look very irresponsible to you but my criterion of responsibility is diametrically opposite to people's idea of so-called responsibility. I am responsible to the moment, to existence—and responsible not in the sense of being dutiful to it, responsible in the sense that I respond totally, spontaneously. Whatsoever the situation is, I am utterly in tune with it. While I am alive I am alive, when I am dead I will be dead. I don't see any question at all.

'The moment I die, the whole world dies for me; then whatsoever happens, happens. I have not taken on the whole responsibility for existence. Who can take it? But there have been people who have tried it and they have all utterly failed.

'I am not controlling anybody—I am not a politician. I am not interested in controlling anybody today or tomorrow. And when I am not there, what can I do? Fools are fools. Whether they worship me or somebody else will not make much difference. If they want to worship they will worship.

'Every institution is bound to be dead, only a man is alive. No institution is ever alive. How can an institution be alive? By its very nature it is going to be dead.

'As far as I am concerned, I am not at all interested in the next moment. Even if this sentence remains incomplete, I will not make any effort to complete it. I will not even put a full point to it. I have no desire to dominate, but I cannot go on saying to people, "Don't worship me," because that is the way to create worship.

'People always misunderstand. While the master is alive they will not come to him because while the master is alive, they cannot be allowed to misunderstand. They will come to him only when he is no longer there, because a dead master can be controlled, manipulated.

'First, I am a man who is consistently inconsistent. It will not be possible to make a dogma out of my words; anybody trying to make a creed or dogma out of my words will go nuts! You can make a dogma out of Mahavira—he is a very consistent man, very logical. You can make a philosophy out of Buddha—he is very mathematical. You can make a philosophy out of Krishnamurti—for fifty years he has been simply repeating the same thing again and again; you cannot find a single inconsistency in him.

'It is impossible with me: I live in the moment and whatsoever I am saying right now is true only for this moment. I have no reference with my past and I don't think of the future at all. So my statements are atomic; they are not part of a system. And you can make a dead institution only when a philosophy is very systematic, when there are no more flaws, when no fault can be found, when all doubts are solved, all questions dissolved and you are given a ready-made answer to everything in life.

'I am so inconsistent that it is impossible to create a dead institution around me because a dead institution will need the infrastructure of a dead philosophy. I am not teaching you any doctrine, I am not giving you any principles. On the contrary, I am trying to take away all the philosophies that you have carried all along. I am destroying your ideologies, creeds, cults, dogmas and I am not replacing them with anything else. My process is of pure de-conditioning. I am not trying to recondition you. I leave you open.

'I am simply sharing my vision, my joy. I am enjoying it, and whosoever wants to enjoy it with me is welcome. Naturally, when I am gone there will be a few fools who will try to figure it out, to make a system, although I am making it almost impossible.

'These people who are wondering what will happen are the same people who will create a dead institution. My people cannot create a dead institution—it is impossible. Those who have been in communion with me will have learnt one thing absolutely, categorically: that life cannot be confined to institutions; the moment you try to confine it to institutions you destroy it. So, while I am alive they will celebrate. When I am gone they will still celebrate. They will celebrate my life, they will celebrate my death; and they will remain alive.

'I am preparing my people to live joyously, ecstatically, so when I am not here, it won't make any difference to them. They will still live in the same way and may be my death will bring them more intensity.

'I am not leaving anything to anybody. I have declared myself Bhagwan. Why should I leave it to anybody? I know I am the Blessed One, and only I can know. How can anybody else know it? And I am trying to seduce my people into understanding this immensity: that they are also the Blessed Ones. It is impossible to deify me—I have already done it! What else is left for you? I don't depend on anybody.'

It was widely reported in the American media that a new location of 64,000 acres has been bought by the Rajneesh Foundation International near Antelope, Oregon. This was to become the place for the realisation of Osho's vision as seen in the excerpts from his discourse:

'The new commune is not going to be of any religion. It will be religious. But the religion will not be unearthly, it will be very down to earth; hence it will be creative, it will explore all possibilities of being creative. All kinds of creativity will be supported, nourished.

'The real religious man has to contribute to the world. He has to make it a little more beautiful than he found it when he came into the world. He has to make it a little more joyous. He has to make it a little more perfumed. He has to make it a little more harmonious. That is going to be his contribution.

'The new commune will be on a big scale: 10,000 sannyasins living together as one body, one being. Nobody will possess anything; everybody will use everything, everybody will enjoy. Everybody is going to live as comfortably, as richly, as we can manage. But nobody will possess anything. Not only will things not be possessed, but persons also will not be possessed in the new commune. If you love a woman, live with her—out of sheer love, out of sheer joy—but you don't become her husband, you can't. You don't become a wife. To become a wife or a husband is ugly because it brings ownership; then the other is reduced to property.

'The new commune is going to be non-possessive, full of love—living in love but with no possessiveness at all; sharing all kinds of joys, making a pool of all the joys…When 10,000 people contribute, it can become explosive. The rejoicing will be great.

'Jesus says again and again: "Rejoice! Rejoice! Rejoice!" But he has not been heard yet. Christians look so serious, and they have painted Jesus also in such a way that it doesn't seem that he ever rejoiced himself. Christians say Jesus never laughed! This is ridiculous. The man who was saying "Rejoice!", the man who used to love good food, good wine, the man who used to feast and participate in festivals, the man around whom there was always feasting—he never laughed? Christians have given a false Christ to the world.

'In my commune, Buddha is going to laugh and dance, Christ is going to laugh and dance. Poor fellows, nobody has allowed them that up till now! Have compassion on them—let them dance and sing and play. My new commune is going to transform work into playfulness, it is going to transform life into love and laughter.

'Remember the motto again—to hallow the earth, to make everything sacred, to transform the ordinary, mundane things into extraordinary, spiritual things, the whole life has to be your temple; work has to be your worship, love has to be your prayer.

'This very body the Buddha, this very earth, the Lotus Paradise.'

Excerpts from:

Zen, Zest, Zip, Zap, and Zing
The Sound of One Hand Clapping
The Secret of Secrets
Bahutere Hain Ghat
The Dhammapada: The Way of the Buddha, vol. 1 & 2
The Goose is Out

End notes:

1. 'Journey Into Silence,' Rajneesh Foundation Press Office

7

Rajneeshpuram in America

Osho's health was becoming more of an issue in the early eighties. It was actually at the end of 1980 that he suffered a recurrence of an old back problem. The pain was acute and required proper care and treatment, and it became obvious that he needed surgery. It was decided that he required neurosurgery for the disc that was protruding onto the nervous tissue of his spine. Therefore, if Osho needed surgery, especially of an emergency nature, it was decided that he should be close to the best and safest facilities in New York which at the time had some of the best neurosurgical units in the world.

Thus on 1 June 1981, Osho left for New York with a small group of *sannyasins*. They stayed at a house purchased by a handful of disciples during the time required for Osho's medical care. The relatively clean environment obviously suited him and his condition stopped deteriorating. His disciples waited and watched. The hospital was notified, and an intensive care facility was set up at the house in

Montclair, New Jersey in advance. His disciples were concerned and prepared for a possible emergency.

While *sannyasins* were busy refurbishing the house, Osho gradually started showing signs of recovery. Initially, he tried a variety of American foods, but soon returned to his favourite rice and dal, vegetables, fruit and yogurt. As his condition improved, he started slow walks around the house and grounds. Once in a while he also took a ride in an open top Rolls Royce startling others on the freeway with the sight of his now famous beard and hat.

For security reasons, it was decided to try and keep his presence in Montclair quiet. But Osho was not easy to hide and soon the word got out. *Sannyasins* began to trickle in to see their beloved master, to offer to help with the work, and to sit with him. A musical troupe always accompanied Osho. Whenever he sat with his people, the musical *satsang* used to start.

Osho's secretary, Ma Anand Sheela, noticed the definite improvement in his overall health in the US and persuaded him to stay there longer. His main idea was to be with his people; where that would be was of secondary importance. If he were to stay in the US, his first choice was a disused airbase in Woodstock, near New York. There were enough buildings and other facilities available at this place and his people would be able to move in immediately. His secretary, however, had other ideas. Osho never imposed his ideas or preferences on anyone. If asked, he merely stated his views. If others had a different opinion, they had the freedom. And then, it was their responsibility: he was their guest.

Soon land was found in the middle of Oregon, a 64,000 acre spread, earlier a cattle ranch known as the 'Big Muddy', but now defunct. The land was overgrazed and ranchers in the neighbouring areas found it foolish to buy good-for-nothing property. A video film of the site was shown to Osho and he agreed to go along. When asked what he would like to call the new place, Osho suggested 'Rancho Rajneesh'. But people around him did not like the name, so he instead called it, 'Rajneeshpuram'. Later, a part of the land became the city of 'Rajneeshpuram' while the wider area of the property itself became 'Rancho Rajneesh'. So after about four months of arriving in the US, Osho was fit enough to travel, and was flown by a private jet to the ranch in Oregon.

Meanwhile, at Rajneeshpuram, there was a frantic last-minute rush to complete Osho's house. It was basically a deluxe version of a trailer, a double trailer with a living room and a small bedroom. There was also an adjoining trailer for the *sannyasins*, who had travelled with him to look after his needs, including his caretaker, cook, doctor and seamstress. Osho arrived at the ranch in September 1981. Final touches to the new lawn were given and exhilarated *sannyasins* sat quietly to welcome Osho with hearts full of love and dance. Osho stepped out of the car and sat in silence under an awning while his musicians played the *satsang* music.

For many it was their first glimpse of Osho since his departure from India. Being with the master in the middle of nowhere was a new adventure for them. Osho's improved health and his shower of love and compassion brought tears of joy and gratitude to their eyes. In fact, they deeply felt his very presence; his loving energy would transform this barren land into an oasis, which it eventually did.

Osho's love for nature, animals, plants, trees, rivers, mountains was profound. Here at the ranch, it was a very lifeless world, almost a desert. The only trees were windswept junipers, the last remnants of what had once been lush green pastures. 'And where are the trees?' Osho was heard asking. It was a question that gave a distinct feeling that this was not the place he would prefer to be in. But that was the subtlety and compassion of Osho. On the one hand he made his wishes very clear, and on the other, he gave his full and total energy to whatever existence brought. So when it became apparent that there were no trees there, he immediately saw a potential, another possibility, an opportunity to apply one's creativity and turn this wasteland into a paradise.

Osho began to live a secluded life. His contact with the outside world was through his secretary. He communicated only through her.

He would come out of his residence, Lao Tzu House, once a day for a drive in a Rolls Royce purchased by his friends and admirers so that he had the greatest comfort while driving. Osho loved to drive. And he drove the Rolls Royce with the same grace and joy, with the same non-attachment as he had while riding a bicycle or driving an Ambassador back in India.

These daily 'drive-bys' were full of dance and celebration. They were the high point of everyday life in Rajneeshpuram. Just after lunch, disciples, admirers and friends of Osho, lined up besides the road singing, dancing and playing musical instruments. Around two o'clock, Osho's car would emerge from the Lao Tzu House. Spreading his love and joy all around, he often stopped to encourage the musicians with his hand movements, faster and faster, pushing everyone to a climactic totality, then smiled serenely and drove on. Their faces shining with love and gratitude, *sannyasins* brought their hands together in a *namaste* to their master. Some lovingly placed a rose on the hood of his car which moved slowly.

During a major celebration, the line was miles long stretching off into the distance. A helicopter showered rose petals onto his car from above. Just to reach the end of the line and back often took three hours. Sometimes he stopped and gave presents to the children, or to some *sannyasin* he had seen after a long time. Occasionally he just chatted briefly with someone. Always unpredictable, always at ease, always graceful and smiling, and always love in those deep, twinkling yet intense eyes.

Visitors who had never seen him before, were so moved by his presence and the mutual love between the master and his disciples that they often ended up crying or laughing with delight as he passed them. Obviously, there was something in the complete acceptance of himself that was infectious, that seemed to give others permission to just be themselves in a way most people had never experienced in the competitive and judgmental world they came from.

To give a concrete shape to Osho's universal vision, new corporations were created: the Rajneesh Foundation International, the Rajneesh

Neo-*Sannyas* International, and the Rajneesh Investment Corporation. While the *sannyasins* were engaged in this experimental leap into the unknown, their efforts were being hampered by the residents of Antelope, a local village of some fifty people. Even before Osho had arrived at the ranch, they wrote letters to the government and the media to prevent the experiment from taking place. The local mayor had begun her campaign weeks earlier in an attempt to stir up prejudice and fear amongst a rather conservative group of ranchers, politicians, media and the government authorities.

The disciples soon found themselves in the middle of an ancient Oregonian battle between the 'conservationists', who were anti-growth and did not welcome the outsiders, and those who wanted to see Oregon grow economically. To put it in perspective, the western half of Oregon consists of a coastal, plain of rich soil which is rapidly being consumed by the spread of urbanisation. It is also the seat of power where all the big cities are located. The state introduced strict conservation codes to prevent this urban spread. The rest of Oregon consists of a desert plain with poor soil and little industry. In fact, it is Oregon's policy that anyone posing a threat of urbanisation to the rich soil is pushed to move to the under-populated east zone so that the state's best soils do not get buried under concrete.

Being a state, however, Oregon applies these conservation rules to both halves of its jurisdiction with some adjustments. This resulted in considerable resentment between the conservationists, headed by a 'watchdog' group called the 1000 Friends of Oregon, and the rural ranchers of the east. But the arrival of Osho's disciples changed the face of that conflict. Motivated by vested interests, both the groups joined hands against the disciples. The so-called 1000 Friends of Oregon, on the pretext of 'saving the state from urbanisation', put a whole lot of legal impediments in the way of Rajneeshpuram's development, an action that under any other circumstance would have had the eastern ranchers reaching out for their ever-ready rifles.

The 1000 Friends of Oregon told the disciples that they could not develop Rajneeshpuram because all the facilities they want, such as, telephone lines, housing, commercial outlets were available only in Antelope. However, the residents of Antelope also had no desire to see any *sannyasins* there, neither did the *sannyasins* have any interest in Antelope. Caught in this dilemma, *sannyasins* thought it better to incorporate the land at Rajneeshpuram into a city. It was a perfectly legitimate option open, according to the state of Oregon law, to any group of 180 or more Americans who wish to live together as a community.

The 1000 Friends of Oregon instigated by the ranchers on the one hand supported by conservative elements of the state, spoke up in the courts to strangle Rajneeshpuram's development. At the same time, publicity seeking politicians also jumped onto the bandwagon and began to add fuel to the fire. Under normal circumstances, any state would have been delighted to have an overgrazed, neglected piece of land developed, but this was not so. It was of no economic value to anyone and had remained for sale for decades.

Only an unusual and enthusiastic group such as Osho's people would have been able to develop such a useless and out-of-the-way property, which needed a totally original concept, to make any economic sense. Rajneeshpuram was just such a concept. Incredibly, in that race against time which lasted some three years and hundreds of hours of legal arguments, the city of Rajneeshpuram got somewhat built. (But a final stay order was brought in to stop all further development, until the Supreme Court decided the legalities of the entangled issue.)

In order to create the city, the residents worked day and night for about fourteen hours a day for those three years, constructing the entire city themselves. Perhaps the city's most famous building is the world's largest greenhouse of 2.2 acres. It was converted into a meeting hall for the annual festivals that were the most joyous events of those few years. *Sannyasins* from all over the world arrived at Rajneeshpuram to spend some precious days or weeks on the spiritual oasis. They too worked hard in their respective countries and sometimes sent money to support this gigantic endeavour for the future of humanity.

By 1985, the city of Rajneeshpuram was almost 5,000 strong. It had its own airport with its own airline. It had the third largest fleet of buses in Oregon. Comfortable, centrally heated and air-conditioned townhouses were built for its residents. An enormous dam was also constructed to cover any future water shortages in that desert region. Miracles of water management were performed by building a series of small dams along the creeks so that the receding water table could be restored effectively. The city had its own water pipelines, electricity grid, sewage disposal system and was about to complete a novel water recycling program that would have allowed all the sewage to get purified naturally and become reusable for irrigation.

The paint shops recycled all their oil-based paints, the gas station allowed no spillage or leakage into the soil. A truck farm down by the river provided enough organically grown fresh vegetables for the whole community. All garbage was recycled and only very few diesel cars used. Almost everybody travelled in the community buses. Miles of roads were constructed by the *sannyasins*. Green housing was intensely promoted to provide year-round sprouts and other out-of-season vegetables to its residents. An elaborate reforestation programme which included creating nurseries, together with a complex land rehabilitation scheme, started transforming the desert into an oasis. Even long before the concern for ecology became fashionable, it was taking shape in a remote Oregon area. The ecological vision given by Osho and its practical application by this highly motivated community is infact a remarkable example of dedication and commitment for the sustainable development.

In addition, the *sannyasins* built everything necessary to create a city. The infrastructure included farm buildings, office buildings, a university complex, a medical facility, warehouses, a cinema theatre, an air terminal, restaurants, a shopping mall, a dairy farm, stables, a crematorium and even a lakeside leisure centre. For those who can appreciate such astounding creativity, this is a model community where ecological values and land care are of a level, perhaps unparalleled anywhere in the US.

Even more extraordinary than the physical buildings, was the social fabric that evolved here. There was no police force, only a peace force.

No prison, no crime, no homelessness, no unemployment. Medical care was available to everyone. Everyone's basic needs were taken care of. There was no need for 'social workers' that exist in a normal society. Generally speaking, everyone knew what was happening to the other person, just like in a family. Perhaps, it must be the only place in the US where people of every different colour, creed and background were living peacefully together and a single woman or child could walk anywhere at night without fear. So remarkable and complete was the city of Rajneeshpuram.

But this was possible because a totally different premise was at work here, different from the rest of the social matrix generally seen around the world. That is why Osho's people could solve the problems that no one else could even dare to tackle. No wonder it attracted so much of resentment. That premise was based on meditation, the ever-present undercurrent in Osho's vision and work.

While Osho had worked on individuals in the sixties and on groups in the seventies, here in Oregon he was working on the collective unconscious, on the collective habits and patterns of our culture. These are the very impediments that have paralysed humanity and prevented this earth into turning into a living paradise. Osho's work is precisely to help us make this possible.

This miracle visible in Rajneeshpuram, financially however, had been an enormous undertaking. Millions of dollars had been lovingly poured by Osho's disciples into humanity's greatest experiment of the twentieth century. The resources, meanwhile, were also applied for developing an economic base in Portland, Oregon. Disciples acquired a hotel there and renovated it into a flourishing commercial enterprise. However, the *sannyasins* had to pay hugely for this. It was an endless struggle for survival. The efforts in Portland met with similar hurdles and hostility which climaxed in the bombing of the hotel by a religious fundamentalist.

Metaphorically speaking, the bombing of the Portland hotel was the last turning of the other cheek. The Rajneeshpuram administration now turned strict and used their legal rights, as an incorporated city, to create an armed force, normally called a police force but chosen to be called a peace force here. Several *sannyasins* earned special recognition for their accomplishments at the Oregon Police Academy. The idea of 'religious' seekers being armed, caused a disconnect in the conventional American mind which incidentally is no different than the traditionalists who were disturbed seeing a neo-*sannyasin* of Osho living a worldly life.

But the effect was dramatic. The armed peace force worked remarkably as a deterrent and not a single violent incident occurred after the hotel bombing.

8

SHEELA AND THE HOVERING CLOUDS OVER RAJNEESHPURAM

In an interview that Ma Anand Sheela, Osho's secretary, gave in 1995 to *Viha Connection*, a monthly magazine published by the Osho Viha Meditation Centre in Mill Valley, California, she said, 'I had nothing to do with meditation before; I have nothing to do with meditation now.' In this forthright statement she sums up the very genesis of the calamity that was going to fall on Rajneeshpuram. As the leader of the project Rajneeshpuram, she was clearly the most powerful, fearless and talented individual. Tragically, however, she had to shoulder the heavy responsibility of being Osho's secretary, but this gave her an outrageous sense of egotism and vanity—the ugliness of which only a meditator can be aware of.

Instead of being aware, watching the incredible creativity unfold, remaining committed to something without getting consumed by it, she fell into the worst of all possible traps—that of passionately identifying her work with her own perception, as opposed to Osho's work and his vision. Unprotected by the intense consciousness raising powers of meditation, her sensitivity diminished, and her intelligence became biased. Faced with a bizarre, kafkaesque bureaucracy, she could possibly be forgiven for being aggressive and manipulative to get around silly laws, but when it came to showing total disregard for peoples' lives and feelings, she went a bit too far.

From community meetings, it was clear how far removed she was from the reality of the ashram—the reality which was far removed from ego and was about surrendering to the master. For example, while conveying a message from Osho to his disciples, she would often say, 'your master has said…' Or, she would say, 'He is your master…' In short, she almost never saw herself as Osho's disciple. She looked upon herself almost always on an equal footing with him. She started to think that Rajneeshpuram was 'hers' to 'give' to Osho. She somehow rationalised that she knew better than he; that he maybe the wise man but, she was the practical one who was acquainted with the ways of the world. It was an absurd assumption.

She failed to understand that Osho did not have a 'goal', such as building an ecological utopia in the desert. He lived in the moment—neither in the past nor in the future.

Osho's focus was to use any situation as a device to help his people learn about themselves. Meditation, however, was the key to opening the locked doors of our unconscious, in any given situation. Meditation for him was the only means to turn every opportunity, every challenge into a growth process. He has often talked about the mystic George Gurdjieff who earlier in the twentieth century had worked towards helping people experience the different energy levels by applying one's totality and patience. Osho compared this process to someone who comes home, completely tired and discovers that the house is on fire. Suddenly the tiredness goes away and a whole new level of energy begins to work.

Working fourteen hours a day, for years on end, certainly took his disciples through these levels of energy. Such is the totality required for the spiritual search. But it has certainly nothing to do with building a city per se. For Osho, whatever the outcome, the important thing was one's level of involvement. He had no goals as such, no deadlines to meet. He simply lived each day as it came with a totality others could hardly envisage, and helped others to experience the same.

Sheela laboured under the misconception that if Osho wanted a city, and anything done to that end was justified. In a wild attempt to fight for the city in the summer of 1984 she embarked on a plan to ship in homeless people from all over the US so that they could vote in the Wasco County election that had become so critical for the city's survival. Suddenly that tranquil land of disciples became crowded with thousands of people for whom the food, clothes, shelter, all given free, was not only too good to be true but worth crossing the country. Of these street people, a good many were ex-convicts, some even hardened criminals. The *sannyasins* did their best to detox them, offering them loving and tender care, even introducing some to meditation. But the whole plan was so far away from Osho's work and vision, that it was concerning.

On 30 October 1984, after a silence of 1,315 days, Osho started to talk and opened his heart before his disciples once again. When Osho began speaking, the need for it slowly started to become clear. These meetings, addressed to the 'chosen few', were dynamite. A totally new phase of his work began from there. When he went into silence, in 1981, he had said he wanted to get rid of all those who were with him simply for intellectual reasons. Now he wanted only those who could be with him in silence.

'First, my silence was not because I have said everything. My silence was because I wanted to drop those people who were hanging around my words. I wanted people who can be with me even if I am silent. I sorted out all those people without any trouble. They simply dropped out.

'Three years was enough time. And when I saw all those people—and they were not many, but they were hanging around my words. I don't want people to just believe in my words; I want people to live my silence. In these

three years it was a great time to be silent with my people, and to see their courage and their love in remaining with a man who perhaps may never speak again.

'When the work was done, when those people had left, there was no need to remain silent. I am back again, and I have much more to say—and I will always have much more to say.'

In those few months of night discourses to a select group, he methodically tore apart the history of humanity into pieces. God, heaven, hell, Jesus, figures on whom he had talked highly in the past, along with all the religions and societies now came under severe criticism. He would give praise where it was due, but also criticise where it was necessary. He had waited nearly a decade to do so.

In his discourses, Osho is particularly severe on Christanity as a religion—shredding it piece by piece, myth by myth, contradiction by contradiction. This did little to put out the flames of hatred burning in the powerful Christian fundamentalists in Oregon, and elsewhere, who already viewed this city as an outrage to all they stand for. Ultimately, it came down to this: here was an alien, a non-white, a non-Christian mystic from a third world country, who wore an unusual dress and a strange kind of hat, who drove a fleet of fancy foreign cars around a city named after him in Sanskrit, had inspired a commune where there is no private property, no crime, no rape, no welfare, where people work for love and not money, where everyone was a vegetarian, where everyone wore red, where people danced on the streets every day out of sheer joy, where some of the brightest people came not only from the US but from all over the world—and all this happening right in the middle of fundamentalist Christian cowboy country.

Besides the religious fundamentalist, another section of the society whom Osho made extremely uncomfortable by his crystal clear insight were the politicians, particularly American politicians. What he had done to Indian politicians in the past, he was now doing it to Americans. He speaks highly of American Constitution, but this only adds to the force with which he exposes the politicians for trampling on it. Faith, hope, liberty, charity—all the icons of the American dream are left in shreds. He exposes each hypocrisy in clear, concise detail until his listeners can only shake their heads in realisation of the trick that has been played on them by their religion and the society. He held press conferences and answered questions from the world media, and continued his powerful attacks on the religious, political, and social institutions and their failing values.

He exposed the hypocrisy of the great American dream, with its much-touted notion of freedom of the individual, constitutionally enshrined freedom of expression, freedom of assembly, and freedom of religion. This came as a major shock to Osho's American disciples and friends. They obviously found this out through Osho's uncanny insights and exposures, how the people in America were being duped by the government.

His very presence was the ultimate challenge for the system, not simply because he was offering a real alternative to the old, but in effect showing precisely, as is evident in Rajneeshpuram, how the dream of 'life, liberty, and pursuit of happiness' *can* truly be realised. While the rest of the urban US was facing violence and alienation, here young Americans were caring for each other and living the very dream. It was something that was a threat to the flag-bearers of the society and so could not be permitted to succeed.

This attracted the storm clouds. The federal government was determined that this experiment should be terminated as soon as possible. Some seventeen government agencies had been instructed to get information on Osho and his *sannyasins*, anything that could convict them and get them out of US. Public opinion had already been manipulated with the usual clichés of 'religious cults', and therefore they knew that they will find support in whatever they choose to do.

The Reagan administration was in power then. It was most determined to do whatever it could to destroy the city and throw Osho out of the US. The Attorney General, Edwin Meese, later made it clear that he never wanted to hear Osho's name again. Ironically, it was the same administration that would later find scores of its members convicted under various crimes. Edwin Meese himself would later leave office under a cloud of criminality. At the time when that government was planning the destruction of Rajneeshpuram, they themselves were embroiled in a major abuse of their own Constitution. No American could ever imagine how perversely corrupt their own government was.

The hostility and attack against Rajneeshpuram was simply a symptom of that deep-seated, endemic abuse of power. As the pressure from the government mounted and the hostility from the press along with the vested interests in Oregon became intense, Sheela and her confidants began to feel desperate and took more and more extreme measures to hold on to power. Finally, she and her disoriented group came to realise that they had taken their power, their authority and the whole process too far and were about to be apprehended by the government. Suddenly without prior warning, in September 1985, Sheela left with a small group of her aids. Within hours, stories of their activities started to emerge from a couple of people close to the group. These revelations proved to be traumatic to the residents of Rajneeshpuram. Everyone, at a personal level, were aware of the powerful forces trying to destroy the city, but that Osho's secretary and her group should have so misunderstood him, set in motion an incredible internal self-appraisal.

All along, Osho's work has always been about the means, never about ends. Yet, in some twisted way, this tiny coterie had imagined that his work was of a 'city in the desert' and hence thought that any means to make it were justified.

In their zeal and lack of meditative awareness, they failed to see that the building of a city was simply an opportunity for Osho's *sannyasins* to energetically function as a collective body in a spiritual endeavour and that it was essentially an experiment for them to understand the collective unconscious. These basics, obviously, eluded them. The creation of a city was simply the by-product, not the main event. It is not for nothing that Osho always described the work around him as that of a mystery school, where the surface phenomenon are never the real work. The real work is always invisible and is basically all about transformation.

These extraordinary events put the *sannyasins* through an incredible process. The *sannyasins* knew nothing about serious crimes. However, they tolerated callous, arrogant and disdainful treatment meted out to them and had allowed these same people (Sheela and her group) in power to ride roughshod over them. It is a lesson that few will ever forget or not be grateful for having learnt.

Osho handled the situation peacefully and also taught them that the world around them is full of authoritarian abuse of power, and the run-of-the-mill way to contest this has always been of reaction, which naturally leads to more action and reaction. The state of the world is ample testimony to the failure of this process. Here in as small a place as Rajneeshpuram, they could see at close quarters how the success of all ruthless, totalitarian system is always based on fear. And that the way to fight it out lay in an individual's ability to recognise his freedom and the responsibility to deal with this fear through understanding and not through reaction. Osho's work was to hold a mirror to those around him. In this case, the mirror was the fear in the collective unconscious.

Throughout all the increasing confrontation, Osho remained supremely himself, never perturbed for a moment even. He led his usual isolated existence—eating simple meals, listening to music, swimming in an indoor pool, driving in the afternoon, seeing his secretary and giving discourses. By now, his health was also keeping very good thanks to the clean desert climate. His back problem has stabilised; his asthma and diabetes were under better control also.

With the support of physical energy, Osho started interacting with the press who had come from all over the world to talk to the man at the centre of the cyclone, more actively and regularly. Whenever he held a press conference, the huge meditation hall, Rajneesh Mandir, was a blaze of lights, cameras and technicians, not to mention the dancing *sannyasins*. To pin-drop silence, Osho used to expose all that he had heard. He invited the police to come and investigate the whole mess and convict those found guilty. Once the police were invited to the city by Osho, who encouraged all his *sannyasins* to cooperate fully with them, they had all they needed.

Nevertheless, the authorities arrived but acted very strangely. It was quite obvious that they were not interested in investigating the alleged crimes, but in working on ways to dismantle the city, the community of Osho's *sannyasins* and friends. Clearly, they wanted Osho out of there, even if on the flimsiest excuse. There main agenda, as laid down by the US Attorney, was to get them out. And the removal of Osho for them was the principle objective.

Rajneeshpuram was essentially an energetic phenomenon where almost everything was transparent and yet nothing was tangible. Dramatic changes would take place at the physical, structural, emotional and energy levels. Never a dull moment, nothing was certain. It was a training in being here and now. What a gift!

Under all adversities, challenges and pressures the spirit at Rajneeshpuram remained alive. No one could destroy that spirit. What seems hard for people to grasp about the Rajneeshpuram phenomenon, however, is that it was essentially an experiment, not the ultimate answer. It was an experiment into the unknown. Nothing went wrong in the process, everything happened as it would in a dynamic, alive and human environment.

On Osho's part, Rajneeshpuram is a *leela*—a playful manifestation of energy. *Leela* has no ultimate purpose, or end. It is sufficient unto the moment while it is happening. Such a dynamic, purposeless play can be very difficult to appreciate if one were to take it seriously or view it through one's ego. In both cases, one may end up either condemning the phenomenon or outright destroying it.

Rajneeshpuram was indeed a powerful expression of creativity. I learnt from my experience of Rajneeshpuram that creativity remains a source of joy only as long as we do not identify ourselves with what is being created. When we dis-identify ourselves, the very means becomes the end, every step and effort keeps us growing, and as Osho points out, 'in tune with the existence'.

But before it could get over, another extraordinary event took place. In early 1984, Osho gave a message to the world about the newly discovered disease, AIDS, warning that it would become a worldwide epidemic. It was a devastating announcement which took even his disciples aback.

'This is the greatest responsibility that man has ever faced. But remember, the greater the responsibility, the greater the challenge, the greater is the possibility for you to come to your highest intelligence, potential, capabilities, creativity…I am hammering continuously on these two things, AIDS and nuclear weapons, for the simple reason that perhaps this is the moment when you would not like to continue sleeping. This is the moment you would like to know something deeper than life and death itself. That's the world of peace. And it belongs to you, you just have to claim it.'

Osho gave a few spiritual yet practical, guidelines to safer sex, advocating safe sex practices. The press made fun of the fact that at the Rajneeshpuram five-star hotel, every room was stocked with a condom. Had Osho's advice been taken, of course, the number of lives that could have been saved is incalculable.

It will be years before the wisdom of his insight is understood. He deserves the credit for being the first to warn humanity of the perilous consequences of an irresponsible and licentious attitude towards sex. Osho's advice turned out to be spectacularly effective. To this day, his disciples have yet to see any of his people who followed his guidelines, become infected. This stands as a proof to Osho's vision when there is a new case in the world every few seconds. The AIDS experiment alone, just in terms of its subsequent proven life-saving potential, should have been enough for Rajneeshpuram to be welcomed by any intelligent person on the planet.

Excerpts from:
The Last Testament vol. 1
Death to Deathlessness

9

TRAVESTY OF JUSTICE AND DEMOCRACY

In 1985, the US authorities were preparing a military attack on Rajneeshpuram to arrest Osho 'for immigration violations'. Somewhat similar to what happened at Waco, Texas, the National Guards were assembled and kept ready in a nearby town. Osho revealed the secret plans hatched behind the doors:

'Before the last election in America, the governor of Oregon held a secret meeting with all the top officials of his government. The Attorney General was there, Norma Paulus (a republican politician from the state of Oregon) was there, and everybody who means anything in the government. They did not allow the journalists inside...And still you go on calling this a democratic country?

'They were deciding about my people, but they did not allow any of my

people to be present there. And the governor came out and gave a press conference in which he lied completely. What happened inside and what he said outside are completely contradictory. In the press conference he said, "Things are normal. There is no need to be afraid, everything is in control. We are trying to calm down the Rajneeshes."

'I don't know how he was trying to calm us down. He never came here, he never sent a message to us, but he was calming us down. Does he think he is a magician? And he said he was trying to keep the opposing people from getting too hot.

'Inside, everything was different. Now the confidential record of the meeting has been found—he thought it had been burnt. But in this world impossible things also happen. Now we know what happened inside the meeting; there was no question of calming anyone down, no question of creating peace. On the contrary, they were deciding how much time it would take their army to reach Rajneeshpuram to destroy it completely. They had decided to put the army on alert so that at any moment, within three hours, they could destroy my people.'

Ever since the bombing of the Hotel Rajneesh in Portland in 1983, Rajneeshpuram had its own armed guards. It was common for every pick-up truck in Oregon to have a gun, so it was natural to be prepared.

Suddenly, as the hostility against the city and its residents increased and the threat of some kind of violent invasion seemed imminent, Osho defused the situation in one stroke by deciding to leave. He saw that the issue at stake was not the legality of the city or just a few misguided individuals running the city, but he himself. So out of compassion and his deep concern for the lives and safety of the sannyasins living in the city, Osho left Rajneeshpuram.

Sadly, however, that is not the end of the story. On 29 October 1985, Osho and his caretakers were arrested as soon as they landed in Charlotte, North Carolina for a stay. A group of heavily armed men of the US government jumped out of the darkness and surrounded the chartered plane Osho was travelling in and bound him, his caretaker, his cook and his doctor, in chains placed around the wrists, the waist and the legs. Everyone was arrested without any warrant, taken to jail, and spent the next three days in a ludicrous court scene where no one seemed to know why these people had been arrested, let alone why they should be held! In one discourse, Osho describes the ordeal:

'When I was arrested in America, I was handcuffed, a heavy chain wrapped around my waist and chains on my feet, as well. I could not even walk. And they were afraid that people would be all over the street, and I may raise my hands, so they put another chain that connected my handcuffs to the chain around my waist so I could not move my hands. And they rushed so madly in their car…and the reason was that people were all around and they were waving and giving me the sign of victory. Then I understood why they were in such a hurry. Photographers were all around, press people were all around, and if they see that people are greeting me and they have arrested me without any arrest warrant, it will look like the whole talk about democracy is simply nonsense.'

All except Osho were released on bail. According to rumour, judge was unable to do anything but keep Osho imprisoned. The story is, that the judge was about to get a promotion and the government had made it clear to her what they wanted. The choice was between her career or Osho. There are no prizes for guessing which came first!

The next twelve days were the most bizarre in Osho's life. This peace-loving, gentle mystic was dragged across the country, from one jail to another, for what should have been a six-hour plane journey to Portland. Osho narrates how inhumanly he was treated:

'For twelve days my attorneys had been running from one jail to another— because they were taking me from one jail to another every day, changing the jails, trying to find some indirect way to kill me.

'They put me in a cell with a man who was going to die of herpes and AIDS. The cell was meant for two, but for six months nobody had shared it because the doctor had ordered that he should remain alone. They put me in that cell. And while the doctor was present, the jailer was present, the US marshal was present, as they moved me, the man, who was counting

his last breaths, told me, "Bhagwan, you don't know me, but I have been watching you on television, and I have fallen in love with you. Don't come close to me. Just stand near the door, because I am suffering from herpes and AIDS and I am dying. And they have put you here purposely, because for six months they have not put anybody else in here. Everything in the cell is contaminated. You just remain by the door, and knock on the door, because it will take hours of knocking, for anybody to turn up."

'It took almost one hour before the jailer came. I asked him, "For six months this cell has not been given to another person. You know perfectly well this man is dying…why have you put me in here?"

'Immediately, my cell was changed. They had no answer. I asked the doctor, "You must have taken the Hippocratic Oath to save people's lives. You were present, you have been preventing even murderers from being put in this cell and you did not say anything."

'He said to me, "We cannot do anything. Orders came from the top that every indirect method should be used—so if the person dies, we are not responsible."'

At one point Osho was even forced to put himself into a jail in Oklahoma under a false name, David Washington, while his attorneys were prevented from knowing his whereabouts.

Finally, Osho was brought to Portland, Oregon, and granted bail. Amongst other charges, he was being accused of 'arranging sham marriages'. It was almost an ultimate irony of the whole Rajneeshpuram story. Osho had been saying for decades that all marriages are in a way a sham! But, most importantly, during the period in question, he never spoke to anyone. He remained in his room in silence seeing only his secretary, his caretaker and his physician and that too when needed. For such allegation twelve days in jail and a city destroyed? The US Attorney's agenda was loud and clear: get rid of Osho and thus destroy the commune.

The utter disregard for justice and for human rights was evident in the treatment given to Osho. All the inhumanities have been clearly documented in a court declaration made by his personal attorney Philip J. Toelkes. Here are some relevant excerpts from a court document dated 7 May 1995:

'Osho was never charged with any violent act. The goal of the United States government was to get him out of the United States...The weakness of the charges finally brought against Osho is compelling evidence of the government's inability to prove real criminal activity by Osho. Shortly after Osho arrived in June 1981, and before any steps could be taken to permit him to remain, the United States government began an open-ended investigation with the avowed intention to get Osho out of the United States. That investigation continued for five years and involved the Federal Bureau of Investigation (FBI), the Immigration and Naturalization Service (INS), the Customs Service, the State Department, the Justice Department in Washington DC, the United States Attorney for the State of Oregon and other agencies.

'The State of Oregon, Wasco and Jefferson County officials, and private citizens also did their best assist the effort to find a way to get rid of the "Red People". By 1983, all levels of government were participating in a task force focussed on the Rajneesh Community. Local citizens tried to dis-incorporate their city rather than co-operate with Osho's people and permit them basic services. Local public officials disregarded their clear legal obligation to issue building permits in an effort to deny Osho's people their right to build on land they had recently purchased from those same local residents. The 1000 Friends of Oregon and agencies of the state brought many land use cases to prevent Osho's people from living together upon, and healing, what had been, and is again today, an arid waste land, out of sight and mind of neighbours...Governor Victor Atiyeh displayed an attitude underlying the State Government's unrelenting hostility to this religious minority when he said that if their neighbours don't like them, they should move out. All this presents a fascinating interpretation of the obligation of public officials to protect the civil rights of all citizens. How would the same statements and actions look if applied to blacks, or Jews or the forebears of Mr Atiyeh himself?

'Charles Turner, the then United States Attorney for the State of Oregon, and the man responsible for the prosecution of the indictment, held a press conference after arresting Osho without warrant. In that press conference, Mr Turner…stated…that the goal of the prosecution of Osho was to get Osho out of the United States, and acknowledged that the legal process had been used to serve political ends…The goal was not punishment, but destruction of the community and the deportation of Osho. That goal obtained, punishment was not a priority.

'The only allegation in any indictment of wrongful acts by Osho himself was that he intended to remain permanently in the United States…In fact, there is ample evidence that Osho had no intention to remain (in the United States) but was simply visiting for medical reasons and was prepared to leave. Osho relied on his disciples to handle these details, as with all worldly matters. Under the law today applicable, a hope to remain, coupled with a willingness to comply with the law, is not even a technical violation.'

These hyper-technical criminal charges had never been prosecuted in the US as was done against Osho. They were usually raised in the administrative process. The reason they were prosecuted criminally was that the criminal process afforded the government an opportunity to use force against Osho without having to prove its case. The Immigration and Naturalization Service initially tried, in the administrative process, to deny that Osho was a valid religious leader and entitled to the visa requested, stating that Osho's teaching was 'the anti-thesis of religion'. This position was constitutionally impermissible as a content based evaluation of religious doctrine, but was relevant to show the religious animosity of the decision makers. Because the decision was against the law and ignored the fact that Osho was a world renowned religious teacher, the authorities had to reverse themselves, admitting that he did qualify and admit that Osho was a religious teacher and entitled to the visa.

But the Immigration authorities continued to refuse to grant permanent residence because they were under unrelenting pressure from powerful politicians in Washington DC to find a way to get Osho out of the US. Because the Immigration service could find no basis to deny, after three years of worldwide investigations, they finally turned the matter over to the US Attorney's office, hoping that they could do better. Because there was a total political hostility to Osho, and directions from the highest levels of government, up to and including the White House, to somehow get rid of this man, the US Department of Justice filed an indictment based on their speculation as to Osho's state of mind.

Many days after the indictment was issued, the US Attorney refused to even admit to Osho's attorneys that an indictment existed and refused to negotiate with them to permit the matter to be properly resolved in court. Instead, at the same time that the US Attorney refused to admit the existence of the indictment, they arrested Osho as a fugitive from the indictment they themselves would not acknowledge existed. After trying for five years to prevent Osho from remaining in the US, they arrested him when he appeared to be leaving! The US government had misused the legal process to attain purely political goals.

When Osho was finally released, it transpired that there was an attempted bombing of the room where he was sitting, waiting to leave. The message was already clear, but was later implicitly reinforced to Osho's attorneys: it would be better for his own safety to plead guilty and leave the country, meaning, 'or else…'

His disciples were in a fix. If they did as he wished and help him fight and prove his innocence, it was made amply clear to them that they should not expect him to survive, *especially* if he suceeded. Moreover, they were deeply concerned about damaging his already fragile health in all this vicious political drama. Obviously, they could not put him at risk any further.

'It was made so clear by the government attorneys to my attorneys, that they had to come up to me and tell me, "We have never seen such a thing happening. It is absolutely insane, absolutely illegal, criminal. Now they want you to accept any two crimes, the smallest crimes, but accept that you are guilty of two crimes so that they can save the face of America and American democracy and American justice. And once you have accepted two crimes then there will be no trial and you will be freed."

'I was very stubborn. I told my attorney, it is better to fight the case because *they don't have any evidence and they cannot have any evidence. But the attorney said, "The question is of blackmail. They are threatening us that they will withdraw the bail and they will put you in jail. And they can go on postponing the case for ten years, fifteen years, and in these ten or fifteen years they will harass you, torture you. And we are afraid they may even take your life, because they have made one thing clear, that the government is not ready to be defeated by a single individual."*

'…And what happened? As I accepted two crimes, the judge immediately ruled that I am punished with $4,00,000—that is near about Rs 60,00,000, for two crimes which I have not committed, which they have forced in a blackmail way threatening my attorneys that my life is at risk, "just to save my life!" But they never mentioned that once I accepted, then Rs 60,00,000 will be the fine. They did not mention that. This was the second trick.

'As I was going to the airport, I received the news that they had put a bomb under my chair. They were waiting that if I didn't accept, and I wanted to go with the trial, then they would just explode the bomb and finish the whole thing, so there would be no person and no question of any trial.'

In mid-November his lawyers agreed to a 'deal' proposed by the government attorneys whereby Osho maintained his innocence on the charges through an 'Alford plea', but was sentenced on two of them. He was fined $4,00,000 and ordered to leave the US, not to return for five years. He was to leave the country immediately after the court hearing. According to Osho the government had planned, this would also be the end of Rajneeshpuram.

The fact, however, remains that the US government was determined to deport Osho from the US by any means. US Attorney General, Edwin Meese, left no doubt on this point when he declared to drive him 'right back in India, never to be seen or heard of again'. Nevertheless, as far as the law and human rights are concerned, many questions remain unanswered. City Attorney for the city of Rajneeshpuram, Sangeet Duchane, JD, has raised following questions:

'Why had the US Attorney failed to inform Osho's attorneys about

the indictment? Why were they prevented from reaching Osho to inform him of a possible indictment and advise him to return to Oregon, thereby avoiding any arrest? Why was Osho refused bail in North Carolina, and then released immediately when he reached Oregon? Why did it take the government twelve days to transport Osho the distance of a six-hour flight? Why was the government suddenly no longer interested in prosecuting Osho once he had reached Oregon, when they had claimed in North Carolina that he was a dangerous man?

'...Then, as time passed and Osho's body gradually weakened, his health worsening in unexplainable ways, a horrible story unfolded. It suddenly became clear why the government was satisfied to have Osho in custody for twelve days...Osho reveals that he was poisoned by the United States government during his twelve days in custody...That was the government's plan—to force Osho back to India, keep him out of the press for a few years and then let him die a slow, quiet death that would be difficult to trace to them.'

After Osho's sentencing in federal court, one of his lawyers, Robert McCrae, said, 'They have done it again. They have crucified Jesus again.'

Excerpts from:

From the False to the Truth
The Messiah vol. 1
The Rebellious Spirit
The Invitation
Jesus Crucified Again: This Time in Ronald Reagan's America

10

TROUBLE AT HOME

Osho climbed the steps of the jet hired for his personal use, slowly, with the engines loud in the darkness of the night. His disciples stood nearby with tears rolling down their faces. It was hard for them to believe that the most incredible adventure of their lives was ending so abruptly, so rudely, so painfully. Their hearts ached with the thought that they could not make their so precious guest spend more time with them. He turned, his beard swirling in the wind, and smiled broadly as he waved a final goodbye to his friends, disciples and admirers.

Flying via Ireland and Cyprus, Osho finally arrived in Delhi on 17 November 1985. The two ends of the journey could not have been more contrasting: from the dark, cold Portland night of tearful disciples to the bright sunshine of Delhi, thronging with a sea of ochre-clad Indian *sannyasins* who swamped the airport in their delight at seeing their beloved master again.

Back in the US, the famous author Tom Robbins was the only

member of the intelligentsia to publicly support Osho. According to Robbins:

'…Osho is a great man and his persecution makes a liar and hypocrite out of anyone who claims there is religious freedom in the United States. He is obviously a very effective man; otherwise he wouldn't be such a threat. He is saying the same things that nobody else has the courage to say…A man who has all those kinds of ideas—they are not only inflammatory, they also have a resonance of truth that scares the pants off the control freaks…If crucifixion were still in vogue, of course, he would've been nailed up. But since we're civilised, they had to force him into exile instead. I am sure they would have much preferred to crucify him on the White House lawn.'

Regardless of the inhuman treatment given in the US, Osho remained appreciative and loving towards the land and the people of America. In answer to a question, his following words testify to this fact:

'I will still say, "Bravo, America!" for the simple reason that America has not mistreated me. The small group of bureaucrats who mistreated me are not America…America has not much knowledge about me. It was the American government's behaviour, mistreatment, that made me known to every American. And wherever I went in those twelve days—I passed almost all over America—I was greeted with love and respect by strangers. Everybody could see that the American government was behaving like a fascist government; everybody could see that this was religious persecution, that this was not democracy. Even amongst the bureaucrats who came in contact with me—the jailers, the doctors, the nurses, the other attendants in the jail, the inmates—there was not even a single exception…I was being persecuted by the Christian fanatics and by the bureaucracy; that the government was afraid for some reasons and the church was afraid for some reasons…But from the American people I experienced great love.'

In India it was a different story. Well wishers, friends and lovers from all over India, including members of parliament and the intelligentsia, had sent messages of welcome and support. Upon arrival, Osho gave a press conference and described the abusive treatment he had received at the hands of a prejudiced and corrupt government in the US. The next day he left for Kulu-Manali, in the Himalayas. The small team of disciples who had been travelling with him had arranged a house for him and other facilities so that he could be looked after properly.

He moved into this new environment as if he had been living there all his life. From his calm demeanour, it seemed that nothing could unsettle him. He simply flowed with the existence; he had no vested interest whatever the outcome. He was the epitome of what he had been talking about for decades—simply being a witness. There was not a trace of resentment. 'What is, is, and what ain't, ain't', as the title of one of his 650 books has it. It was simply impossible to grasp that this man had just watched the destruction of one of the most significant experiments of all times, based on his vision, without even a trace of regret.

During this time Osho referred to the dispersal of his disciples to all the corners of the earth, following the incident at Rajneeshpuram, as a fire test. Reflecting on Rajneeshpuram, Osho says:

'I feel it is good that they destroyed the commune. It helped my people spread all over the world. And wherever my one sannyasin is, he will create the right atmosphere...Now I'm not interested in creating a big commune, because any big commune is going to be destroyed by the power that is any government. It does not matter whether it is the Indian government or the American government...The moment you have a power, although your power is of love and peace and silence, the powerful people in New Delhi will start getting disturbed. I don't want to repeat history. Only idiots repeat history.'

And so the disciples were once again thrown back to their own resources as never before. This gap claimed many casualties. Those who continued to be with him, would really be Osho's people.

Meanwhile, he continued with his usual isolated existence, eating simple meals, sitting in his chair, seeing his secretary, and giving discourses. His health had been extremely affected by his time in prison in the US. When released from the prison he suffered from terrible stomach upsets, pain and nausea. But as days went by, it seemed that he was not recovering at all. It was assumed that this was the result of a very sensitive individual facing the ugliness of prison life.

His eyesight became poorer, his walking less steady, and strangely, his hair kept falling out. As with everything else, his body was yet another part of existence to witness. So, while the physical effects were obvious, they lacked any of the usual 'psychological' components people generally experience. Since he was beyond psychology, it became very difficult to gauge the pain and discomfort he was in. There was little outward sign of it. The physical signs, however, were there for all to see. Kulu-Manali was not the place to receive expert medical attention, although, he implied that the pain and discomfort would pass and there was nothing to worry over. However the unease regarding his health just grew. His doctor and caretaker watched with increasing fear.

On most days, both national and international media came and Osho held conferences with them. On other days, he talked to his disciples and answered their questions. There was also a plan to buy the hotel resort as a place for Osho's work to continue.

But another setback awaited them. In December 1985, it was made clear by the Government of India that Osho's foreign disciples will not be allowed to visit him in the Himalayas. It was the beginning of a worldwide witch-hunt, the enormity of which only later generations may truly appreciate. Meanwhile, Osho's disciples invited him to visit Nepal. He accepted the invitation. In Kathmandu, he stayed in the Soaltee Oberoi Hotel and soon drew huge crowds for his morning walk and for his evening discourse. Osho liked Nepal and felt that it was a good place to stay. Contacts were made with the king and friends were asked to look for possible places.

Osho's health though still was poor, at least seemed to have stopped deteriorating further. He barely managed to keep his weight steady but lost a lot of hair. Despite all this he stuck to his normal routine:

eating his simple meals, taking a nap in the afternoon, sitting in his chair, seeing his secretary and giving discourses in the evening.

Then the first foreign *sannyasin*'s visa for Nepal was refused. Information was received, through the political grapevine indicating that a re-run of the recent events in India was imminent. No matter how much the Nepali people wanted Osho to stay, the common view was that India called shots in Nepal. Osho's secretary heard disconcerting rumours of his possible arrest. Behind the smoke screens of freedom, democracy, human rights, and all the rest, the reality was simple: might is right. Here is what Osho says:

'I left the country (India) and went to Nepal, because that is the only country where I can go without a visa; otherwise the Indian government had informed all the embassies that no visa should be issued to me so that I cannot leave India. They have a treaty with Nepal; no visa is needed.

'But Nepal is a small and a very poor country, the poorest—and under tremendous pressure from India…India can take over any moment. It has no army worth the name.

'When it became clear from reliable sources; absolutely certain that they would compel the Nepalese government either to arrest me or to send me back to India, I had to leave Nepal.'

The King of Nepal too turned his back on Osho, but for a different reason. Osho explains: 'The King of Nepal was ready for me to have my residence and commune there, but the condition was that I should not speak against Hinduism. Nepal is a Hindu kingdom, the only Hindu kingdom in the world. I refused. I said, "I never plan what to speak and what not to speak. I cannot promise. And if I see anything wrong, then it does not matter whether it is Hinduism or Christianity or Mohammedanism, I am going to speak against it."'

By chance a disciple arrived with a promise from the Greek prime minister's son, a cabinet member in his own right, that Osho would be welcomed in Greece. It was just in time. However, his chartered jet was refused permission to land in Kathmandu because the Queen of England was visiting the country! Time was of essence; there was growing discomfort among Osho's friends that the Nepalese government might well prevent Osho from leaving.

Excerpts from:

Jesus Crucified Again: This Time in Ronald Reagan's America
The Invitation
Beyond Psychology
Socrates Poisoned Again After 25 Centuries

11

THE WORLD TOUR

For the next two years, Osho again travelled extensively. He left Kathmandu for Thailand. Once in Bangkok, it became impossible to book Osho on a connecting flight. In Germany, his *sannyasins* were frantically making calls around the world, trying to book him a seat. Whenever his name came up on the computer, the airlines simply refused the request. They finally managed to find a booking clerk on the other side of the world, and juggled the spelling of his name sufficiently for it to go through. Thailand was not a pleasant wait for those travelling with Osho. His routine, however, remained unchanged: sleeping happily, eating a simple meal, and just sitting in the waiting room. The active intercontinental calls eventually confirmed a flight to Abu Dhabi, the nearest spot for him to reconnect with his private jet.

Abu Dhabi was not a happy situation, though. The time needed for refuelling was spent in the first-class lounge at the airport.

Osho's disciples were conspicuous by the *malas* around their necks and their clothes. The Arabs, in contrast, wore traditional *dishdashas* (white robes), with worry beads, and keffiyehs on their heads. One could feel a palpable hositlity towards the *mala*, a 'religious symbol'— first the Christians, then the Hindus, now the Muslims.

Osho left once more with his motley group, this time to the island of Crete where permission had been granted to land. Everybody was very helpful; the luggage was specially processed through customs before being taken off to the house on the south of the island where Osho had been invited. It was owned by Michael Cacoyannis, the director of the movie, *Zorba the Greek*. The place couldn't have been more appropriate and beautiful.

Osho had permission to stay there for one month. The *sannyasins* had completely repainted the house and made it ready for Osho to move in. As usual, Osho walked around, saw the house, looked for a good spot for the discourse.

But problems were already starting. Every Athens paper was bombarded with a well-orchestrated smear campaign against Osho. Scandalous fabricated stories were published to malign him and his people. Nothing that he said was ever published, only what was said about him.

Osho took no notice of this and gave a series of incredibly beautiful discourses, interspersed with questions from the press from all over Europe. He discussed the problems of youth, of old people, of every aspect of modern society. He talked about Socrates, and how that tradition of an enlightened man is exactly what he is talking about.

'Socrates is one of the persons I love the most. And coming here I feel tremendously joyous, because it is the same air Socrates must have breathed, the same land he must have walked, the same people whom he must have talked to, communicated with.

'To me, without Socrates, Greece is nothing. With Socrates, it is everything. The day Athens chose to poison Socrates, it poisoned the whole Greek spirit.

It has never again been to the same heights. Twenty-five centuries have passed, but not a single man has been able to reach the same glory, the same light, the same insight. In killing Socrates, Greece committed suicide.

'And it can be seen easily. If they had listened to Socrates rather than poisoning him, and dropped their conditionings, which he was asking them to do, Greece would have been at the very top of the world today in intelligence, in consciousness, in the search for truth. But people are ignorant.

'They have to be forgiven, but they should not be forgotten. If you forget them, you are bound to commit the same mistake again. Forgive those people who poisoned Socrates, but don't forget, so that it never happens again…

'What Socrates was doing twenty-five centuries ago, I am doing now.

'Twenty-five centuries have gone by without any change as far as humanity is concerned. Three times they have tried to kill me…three attempts on my life. In every possible way the same people whom I am trying to make free, trying to take their chains away, are ready to kill me. Humanity has not changed. It will still do the same.

'But what Socrates was not capable of doing, I am capable of doing.

'He remained in the very small area of Athens, not even the whole of Greece. Athens was a city-state, and he remained an Athenian for his whole life. I belong to the whole world.'

Trouble was brewing, rapidly. The bishop of the local church started to create a furor against Osho, saying that he should not be allowed to speak. Amazingly, the church issued exactly the same complaints that were levelled to justify the execution of Socrates in Athens twenty-five centuries ago: corrupting the youth. The bishop even threatened to dynamite Osho's house! Osho, in his discourses, humorously exposed hypocritical claims to morality by the bishop and others, describing what the reality was just beneath the veneer of respectability.

Here is the story in Osho's words about what happened on 5 March 1986:

'In Greece they allowed me a four-week visa, but the archbishop of Greece started making a great noise, sending telegrams to the president and to the prime minister, and writing threatening letters to the owners of the house in which I was staying, saying that if he wants to save his house, I should be thrown out. Because, if I am not thrown out within thirty-six hours, he is going to burn down the whole house with all the people in it; burn them alive. And this is the archbishop of the most ancient Christian church. He represents Jesus Christ!

'The government got scared. They had no reason…because I had not even left the house in two weeks. I was asleep in the afternoon when the police came. My legal secretary, Anando, was telling the officers, "Sit down, have some tea, and I will wake him up." But they threw her from a four-foot porch down onto the gravel, and dragged her over the gravel to the jeep, and took her away to the police station: she was trying to prevent government action.

'And as I was awakened by John, I heard noises as if dynamite was being exploded. The police started throwing rocks at the house from all sides destroying the beautiful ancient windows and doors…and they also had dynamite. They said, "You have to wake him up this very moment, otherwise we will dynamite the house."

'No arrest warrant…no reason to be so furious…just because the archbishop had told the government that if I was allowed to stay in Greece, the morality, the religion, the culture, everything would be in danger. In just two weeks I would corrupt the minds of the young people…

'But I wonder: they have built up this morality and this religion and this culture over 2,000 years…what kind of culture and what kind of morality is this which can be destroyed in two weeks by an individual man? It does not deserve to exist if it is so week, so impotent.'

Osho calmly put on his clothes and was taken out to a waiting police car. The police agreed to let his physician accompany him. Osho sat in the back, silently. Some miles on, suddenly the car pulled off the road and stopped. The policemen thrust a piece of paper at Osho and said, 'Here, sign this'. But he threw it back at them. Meanwhile, some *sannyasins* on motorbike, one with a video camera, arrived on the spot and started filming the activities of the police. This complicated the situation for the police who initially tried to chase off the cameras, but later gave up and drove on.

Osho was taken to the tourist police station where he was held for several hours. It appeared that the Christians had given the politicians an ultimatum. The original idea of the authorities was to put Osho on a ship standing in Heraklion harbour bound for India. Hours of negotiation took place. The usual large sums of money changed hands and Osho was permitted to fly to Athens.

Osho's Greek *sannyasin* who helped him come to Greece recalls his deportation from there in the following words:

'It was the first time in history that all the Greek newspapers agreed on one thing: they were against Osho. The local bishop of the Greek Orthodox Church also voiced strong opposition to Osho's presence. I went to see him, hoping to reason with him, but it was futile. Trembling with anger, the bishop told me he would burn the house where Osho was living, and threatened that "blood will flow" unless Osho left the island. In his eyes I saw the same fear, the same hypocrisy, the same attitude with which the same Christian priests had abused (Nikos) Kazantzakis, the creator of (the novel) Zorba the Greek.

'When he arrived in Crete, Osho had warned me that it would be very difficult for him to stay in Greece after fifteen days. At the time it seemed very strange, because I had a guarantee from the Greek government that he could stay for at least one month. But Osho was right. On 5 March 1986, police broke into the villa and arrested Osho without a warrant and drove him to the port of Heraklion, where only an immediate payment of $25,000 persuaded the authorities not to put him on a boat for India...

'I did my best to reach the Greek prime minister, hoping to halt the deportation, but although I was promised an interview, it was never given. I later learned from my personal friends inside the government that the decision to deport Osho was in response to pressure from the Reagan administration, via the US Embassy in Athens.'

In Athens, once again, Osho was met by a phalanx of armed, uniformed men. The sight of guns around this man who, didn't even own a paper knife, brought a hint of surrealism to the whole scene. He walked over to a hall where there were some press people. He entered a concrete building and immediately was surrounded by cameras, television and the press reporters.

Osho gave a press conference. It was a very powerful moment. Suddenly that fiery radical from his young days surfaced and lashed out at the government of fascism, of having learnt nothing from the murder of Socrates, of being grossly uncivilised, all the absolutely true things about politicians that every intelligent person knows but hardly ever has the guts to say.

Suddenly, the police chief, with his cap pushed down, East German style, stepped in and demanded Osho to put a stop to his criticism against the authorities. Osho turned, his eyes became large. In a voice full of power and authority, Osho said: 'You be quiet. This is my press conference. Do not interrupt!' The large, aggressive man could not endure the fury and disappeared into the crowd as if hit by a thunderbolt.

There were no further interruptions as Osho spoke on his theme of how Greece as the home of democracy should be ashamed of its decline into fascism. Meanwhile, Osho's jet was waiting. There was just one problem: there was nowhere to go.

After finishing his press conference in Athens, Osho walked back across the tarmac to his jet. He then noticed that the Greek authorities had written 'deported' on his passport. 'On what grounds?', he demanded of a customs agent present there. 'For speaking? For being a tourist who has never even left his residence?' Osho's energy was ferocious. He simply took hold of a pen and scratched out the deportation order and then demanded that the agent stamp it. Osho knew that this customs agent would not move from his bureaucratic mode unless something shook his core. That something in this case was Osho's energy: the eyes, the intensity, the authoritative voice. The agent hurriedly stamped the passport and disappeared. It was a strange situation. The whole team travelling with Osho had been taken aback by the crudeness of the Greek government's capitulation to the archaic Orthodox Christian campaign against Osho. It was now late in the night and eventually Osho's jet took off again into the dark sky with nowhere to go.

The plane headed towards Nice and landed there in the middle of the night. Negotiations were already on with the French government to secure a place for Osho. However, there was a general apprehension that this was not the place to stop. But where to go? The plane sat quietly on the tarmac while phone calls were made to find out where Osho could next be taken to.

On 6 March 1986, it was decided to take Osho to Switzerland. On reaching there and clearing the customs, Osho's team was granted permission to stay for a week, when suddenly a word reached the custom officers on duty, that the man is persona non grata. So where to now? The German government had already denied Osho the right to land on German soil even to refuel his plane, so Sweden was the next destination. Again, the group barely managed to clear the customs, when all of a sudden armed police arrived. Again the same story. It was communicated that he was 'a danger to national security', and was ordered to leave immediately.

Where to next? London. There weren't too many options at that hour because legally a plane can only fly so many hours without an obligatory rest period. People were already waiting in London to help with any possible problems. So once again this strange band of outcasts was on the move—a mystic, his secretary, his cook, his caretaker, his doctor...a dangerous group indeed!

London seemed prepared for his arrival. As soon as Osho was wheeled to the customs in his wheelchair, it became obvious the reception was not going to be friendly. Those holding British passports were allowed through, but the rest were treated like terrorists. An American physician on the flight with Osho was refused permission to enter the country. An Australian lawyer was cross-examined like a criminal. Another American was also refused permission to stay. Osho was denied entry. Instead he was told that he must spend the night in prison with his two travelling companions.

But, the team argued, they didn't even *want* to stay there. They were in transit and were just waiting for the pilots to have their obligatory rest and that they would stay in the lounge. But they were denied even this because the authorities stated that the lounge was only for paid passengers. Osho's groups showed their first class ticket and asked why they could not access and rest in the first class lounge? Incredibly, without any logic, they were told, curtly, that it was against the bylaws and that he must go to jail.

Finally, Osho and the two American *sannyasins* were locked up in a small, dirty cell crowded with refugees. The rest of the group went to hotels. Everyone was waiting for the pilots to finish their rest so that they could move away. Here is what Osho said about the ridiculous ways of the British airport authority:

'I had asked only to stay for six hours in the night in the international airport lounge, because my pilot's time for running the jet was finished. He had to take a rest by law.

'From the lounge, in the middle of the night, within six hours, how could I manage to destroy the British character, morality, religion? I had no idea, otherwise I would not have asked about staying even though it was my right—that the British morality, character, religion all live in the lounge of the international airport.'

The next day the group was prepared to leave again, this time for the Caribbean where it seemed as if Osho would be welcome. Meanwhile at Heathrow, the authorities clearly wanted to put Osho on a regular flight to India that was to depart in the afternoon. With the Indian government denying access to his Western disciples on the one hand, and the rest of the world, on the other hand, willingly or under pressure, refusing Osho himself access to their countries, it seemed a foolproof plan to curtail his voice. There were endless delays with luggage, with the paperwork required to leave, while the British tried to create a flimsy excuse that since Osho had not left the UK, within stipulated time, he must forcibly be repatriated on the afternoon flight to India.

For the group of disciples travelling with Osho, the idea of getting separated from their master was not only painful but also a crippling blow to his work. The extent of the emotional trauma that those people went through perhaps is difficult for an outsider to comprehend fully. For them, it was their life's purpose to devote themselves to the growth of their own consciousness, and to be with an enlightened mystic who can help with this, a rarity in any age, any time. Perhaps the last such master was Gautam the Buddha, twenty-five centuries ago. This was not going to be any ordinary separation.

Finally, on 7 March 1986, with everything worked out, the jet took off, this time for the Caribbean. The first stop was Ireland, and the sleepy airport of Shannon. At the airport, Osho with his group managed to sail through customs with a three-week visa in their hands. They went to a nearby hotel and were settling there when the police arrived and wanted to revoke their visas. It was the same drama all over again. The time was enough for the Irish authorities to catch up with the latest events. The *sannyasins*, thoroughly acquainted with the ugliness of politics by now, decided to contest the legality of this action in court. Finally an agreement was reached whereby the group would not be forcibly removed. The British in the meantime were busy in using Commonwealth 'diplomacy' to ensure that whatever welcome the island of Antigua in the Caribbean had in mind for Osho, would be rapidly withdrawn.

This gave valuable time needed to the people who were working around the world trying to find one spot on this planet where Osho would be allowed to sit and talk to his friends. It was amazing to see, a world most of it boasting of freedom and equality seemed to have run out of free space. Indeed, the ancient insult of 'there being no room in the inn' appeared to be replaying itself in the modern era, although on a much larger scale.

The Spanish government seemed willing to allow Osho to stay in the country. In the meantime, fervent activity to welcome him was taking place in Madrid against a backdrop of political pressure.

At the same time, the Uruguayan government was being helpful. Anxious for the possible benefits of an international attraction like Osho, they were ready to consider having him in their country. For people around Osho, however, this whole saga was an opportunity to open their eyes to the reality that we live in a totally hypocritical world.

Sannyasins in various parts of the world, at that time, were working hard to find a place for Osho, each labouring under the illusion that at least *their* country would not be as rotten as others, that *their* politicians are not as corrupt as the others. The Italian *sannyasins* had been campaigning, the Spanish were trying, the Dutch and the Swedes were also trying. It was a glorious lesson for all the lovers and friends of Osho around the world. Each in turn reached the same point of discovery: there is so much ugliness and corruption in the world of today. It was a living experience for them of everything that Osho had been trying to show for decades. Now they had a first-hand knowledge of it.

As politician after politician stuck out their palms for pay-offs against persuasion to use their influence to smooth Osho's admission here or there, the mood in the group around Osho started to become both hopeless and at the same time more mature. With the chances of success becoming slimmer with each new twist of the political game, it equally strengthened their understanding of Osho's vision for a better world, for a better humanity of the future.

Canada had by then refused permission for Osho's plane to land at Gander for refuelling on the intended flight to Antigua in the Caribbean. This extraordinary denial of the right to refuel was made despite a bond from Lloyds of London against the guarantee that Osho would not step outside the plane. So, on the condition that there should be no publicity that might embarrass the authorities, he was allowed to remain in Ireland until other arrangements could be made. During the wait, Antigua withdrew permission for Osho to go there. Holland, when asked, also refused Osho. Germany had already passed a 'preventive decree' that denied Osho an entry to their country. In Italy, his tourist visa application remained stalled.

On 19 March 1986, a tenuous departure to Spain was worked out and the party prepared to leave Ireland. But the doubt whether they would be allowed to stay there hovered over them. It was not certain till the last moment. As they were ready to depart, an official from the Uruguayan embassy came on board and provided Osho an entry visa to that country. A brief stop in Dakar, Senegal, only added to the sense of universal isolation and alienation from a world Osho's travelling companions would never otherwise experience. Bribes had to be paid to get through customs, and then on to nearby hotel.

Throughout this whole period, Osho was like a young man on an adventure holiday. He continued to eat his simple meals, sleep each afternoon, talk to his secretary, and sit in his chair. While everyone around him was going crazy trying to save what was clearly a desperate situation, Osho sent off people to find out more about a beautiful castle in Ireland that might be for sale.

All over the world, his people were deeply anxious and worried, not knowing where he was, how he was, or whether they would ever get to see him again. Like the silence at the centre of the cyclone, he was the essence of calm, seeming to enjoy the whole escapade, at the same time, giving enough energy to push everyone to ever greater efforts. Even as he was leaving Rajneeshpuram for what was certainly to be the last time, he wished more trees to be planted there. That was his incredible intensity for the present—ignoring a past that is gone, and will never come back, and not preparing for a tomorrow, that never comes. It is always today, he pointed out repeatedly. His total attention was given to this moment, out of which the next will come.

His health, however, was not good, but as usual he gave little indication of his suffering. His hair had stopped falling out but his gait was affected and it seemed as if his eyes were permanently damaged, which made reading very difficult. He had stopped reading books years ago; now he could barely read the headlines of the endless newspaper clippings about him that his secretary used to bring for him to look at. He simply glanced at them as if they were about somebody else.

After the long haul across the Atlantic, Osho's plane landed at Recife, a seaport in North East Brazil. The authorities immediately wanted to spray the plane, which meant exposing Osho to chemical fumes. With his sensitivity to asthma and his current poor health, the group tried to prevent the spraying.

'Shall I play dead?' he asked. He happily joined a game of wearing an oxygen mask and a blood pressure machine which was enough to deter the man with the spray machine. As he said in one of his discourses in Kathmandu: 'I am no goody-goody saint.' With a twinkle in his eye, he always seemed ready for some fun, a joke, and used every available opportunity to create as many situations as possible for everyone to experience something new.

Finally, he arrived in Montevideo, Uruguay. A friend was already present to help everyone through customs. Soon Osho was moved into a beautiful house in Punta del Este, a famous beach resort town for rich Argentineans. Almost immediately he started giving discourses. For next three months, he talked twice daily to about twenty people. These discourses hold an extraordinary reflection of the whole situation.

Meanwhile, the US government was trying to pressurise Uruguay to deny Osho residency, while his people were struggling against all odds, playing a serious game of influence and intrigue to find their master a home in this big world.

The US officials apparently told President Sanguinetti of Uruguay that Osho was an anarchist; he was highly intelligent and had the power to change men's minds. If their country (the US) was not able to handle him what chance did he have?

But as the Uruguay round of the General Agreement on Tariffs and Trade (GATT) talks were getting under way in the same town of Punta del Este, the US pulled out all the stops: either Osho goes or the country's loans would be revoked. During those final days in Uruguay, the police kept watch from a discreet distance. By now the group travelling with him was used to the life of ultimate outcasts.

A small blue Volkswagen was always ready there, except when it was doing one of its regular patrols around the house. It was a constant reminder that the promise of Osho being allowed to stay in the country was very unreliable. Finally the word came through: he had to go. A plane was waiting for just this eventuality and gained permission to land at the local airport, avoiding Montevideo. The police were also on their way. He and his team left immediately. When the police arrived, they were told that everybody had left for Montevideo. It gave Osho enough time to stand with his companions on the tarmac, dancing to the songs of the musicians who were always with him. One 18 June 1986, the jet took off once more into a dark sky with nowhere to go. The day after he was forced to leave, new American loans for Uruguay were announced. Somehow the whole odyssey had become a way for Osho to teach his people exactly what was wrong with the world and why a new vision was needed.

Osho described the unfair means adopted to force him out of Uruguay:

'The American government has been telling all the governments of the world that I should not be allowed, even as a tourist, in their countries. One small country, Uruguay, in South America, was very happy that I had come there, because the president had been reading my books, and he had not dreamt that I would ever come to Uruguay. So he said, "We will make every effort to give you land, so that you can create a community. Because not only will we be enriched by your presence and your disciples, but thousands of pilgrims will start coming; and we are a poor country, it will be a financial gain too." And he immediately managed a one-year residence visa for me.

'But when the President, Ronald Reagan, became aware of it, he threatened the president of Uruguay: "Within thirty-six hours Osho should leave the country. Otherwise you will have to return all the loans that we have given you in the past, and all the loans—billions of dollars—which we were going to give you in the coming two years will not be given. So you can choose."

'Now, Uruguay cannot manage to return the money and cannot afford not to take billions of dollars in the coming two years, because its whole planning is based on those billions of dollars. The whole economy of the country would collapse. The president had tears in his eyes when he told me, "Your coming to our country has at least made me aware of one thing: that we are not independent. We have been living under a delusion. You will have to leave. It is illegal—because you have a valid residence visa for one year; and you have not committed any heinous crime—that is the only reason that a residence visa can be cancelled." And I had only been there one month. And he said, "It is unfortunate that I have to do it. I am doing it against my own conscience."

'Even this much the American president was not willing to concede: that I should simply leave the country. My plane was standing at the airport...I said, "There is no problem; I can leave the country. I will not put your country into such jeopardy."

'He said, "The American president insists that you should be deported; you should not leave the country without being deported. I am forced to commit crimes: first, to tell you for no reason to leave the country, you have done nothing. Second, to deport you. But I am absolutely helpless. Still, I want one thing: that on your passport there should be no stamp of deportation from Uruguay. We have a small airport—so move your airplane to that airport, and in the evening leave without informing us; so we can say, He left without informing us. There was no time to deport him."

'But he was wrong. As my jet moved to the small airport—the American embassy must have been watching—the American ambassador was there with all the stamps and the official whose business it is to deport people. I was delayed there, because they had to fill in all the forms, and as I left the country, I said, "It doesn't matter..." In fact, my passport has become a historical document: I have been deported from so many countries without any reason.

'When I left Uruguay, the president was invited to America immediately, *and President Reagan gave him thirty-six million dollars as a "gesture of friendship". That was a reward because I was thrown out within thirty-six hours: exactly thirty-six million dollars, one million dollars per hour! In fact, I should start asking these governments for my percentage: You are getting billions of dollars because of me, I should get at least 2 per cent.'*

But Osho's heart remained full of compassion and goodwill for the US. Answering a question on the evening of 6 June 1986, at Uruguay, he declared: 'Although America has misbehaved with me and my people, I still insist on Gurdjieff's statement, "Bravo America!" because the American government is not America. These are the few elected fools. The whole of America has a different flavour to it. It is more innocent than any other country, because it is younger than any other country. And it is innocence that is needed as a base for somebody to become enlightened…The people of America are the most innocent, fresh, young, and are capable of giving birth to the new man.'

Shortly before his departure from Uruguay, the island of Mauritius informed that Osho was welcome there. Two people flew to this little country in the Indian Ocean only to discover that what the government meant was really that the prime minister would consider allowing Osho to come there in return for a sum of two billion dollars!

Osho finally went to Jamaica's resort city, Montego Bay. Without any trouble visas were given to the group. Contacts had already been made and there seemed to be no problem. However, a US naval jet had landed almost at the same time, its non-uniformed officers sweeping into the administration building with loaded briefcases. A wave of nervousness spread through the group and with fingers crossed they waited and hoped that it may have nothing to do with them.

Soon, everyone was installed in a beautiful house overlooking the ocean. Osho went off to take his afternoon nap; and for the first time in days, the group with Osho began to settle down. But it was only a matter of hours before there was knock on the door. It was the police. All visas were withdrawn 'for reasons of national security' and everybody was asked to get out of the country within twenty-four hours.

The last possibility was Portugal. Efforts were being made to allow Osho a respite in that country. Generally, the only way to make it across the Atlantic is to fly up to Canada and then back across to Portugal. But Canada had already refused permission for any plane carrying Osho to stop even to refuel, as Germany had. Finally things were sorted out, and after refuelling in Canada the plane headed back across the Atlantic. Osho's way of travelling remained the same. He ate his food, took his nap, and relaxed. There was never a trace of concern about what was happening, he always seemed totally at rest.

Since the situation in Uruguay, Osho had been insisting to be taken back to India. But his group still hung on to the hope of finding him a home elsewhere. They knew that once Osho returned to India, they may never see him again. As the plane crossed the Atlantic for Europe again, everyone in the group had a feeling that perhaps Osho's world tour was coming to an end.

On 20 June, the plane with its precious passenger landed in Madrid, but strangely nobody was there to meet them. A rapid phone call added a touch of comedy to the unfolding tragedy: 'What are you doing in Madrid? We are waiting for you in Lisbon!' The group entered Portugal and tried to hide Osho in the Ritz Hotel. The plan was to sneak him off later to another, quieter location. Like a stage farce they got him to the elevator unseen and then into a waiting car in the basement car park. But Osho, wearing a long white robe, his round hat and beard down to his waist, was unmistakable. Even in his just crossing the hall of the hotel, one could see raised eyebrows.

Unfortunately, the new location was dusty and almost immediately Osho got an asthma attack. Consequently, the whole plan was abandoned. The team returned the way it had gone, only now they were trying to sneak Osho back into the hotel. No one knew whether to laugh or cry, except for Osho who just enjoyed the whole episode, and particularly the idea that people thought it possible to hide him. A house outside Lisbon was the next planned stop. Osho and the group moved to Sintra, but soon the police appeared. Any attempt to secure a longer stay in Portugal was denied.

It was finally time for India again. On 28 July 1986, after weeks of political circus, those who had travelled half way around the world trying to find him a home where he could speak to his people, stood on the observation roof at Lisbon airport as their beloved master, Osho waved farewell to them from the plane for the last time. And then he was gone. For those left behind, it was a farewell of tears and deep sadness. In all, twenty-one countries had either deported Osho or denied him entry.

Dr Amrito, Osho's personal physician who had accompanied him throughout the tour, recaps the experience as follows:

'Somewhere in this strange journey is a message for his Western disciples, who have been brought up to believe that the whole cold war, the battles that have left millions dead, was about freedom, democracy, and a supposed respect for human rights that characterised these Western countries. They don't see Osho as a threat to society or as a terrorist. They find that all he does is speak. They know that all he wants to do is help anyone who is interested to understand oneself, to be blissful, to be joyful, to simply relax into the beautiful mystery that is life. The idea that this is grounds for being the most unwelcome man on the planet just doesn't fit with their conditioning. These disciples and lovers of Osho spent their youth hearing how the Western world is really about helping people have better, freer, happier lives. In fact for the Americans, the pursuit of happiness is a right enshrined in their constitution…But somehow this journey is a lesson in how the real world works, once the propaganda is put aside. The group with Osho is now in a covert world of intrigue and deals, of bribe and political expediency.

'Osho's group was naïve; it is simply not possible for the whole Western world to ban a man on the basis of bizarre allegations of immigration violations—the judicial equivalent of a parking offence. They just could not see the fact that behind the scenes of this Christian democratic façade, lies an ugly reality of which they have never been aware of, despite living in these societies all their lives. Each place that prevented Osho from even staying for a few days was somehow seen as an aberration. They ran straight to the next option, full of hope and expectation. It was as if Osho was de-conditioning his people by allowing them to rub their noses into a whole new reality... To experience the hypocrisy first-hand, though—that is a lesson sannyasins on Osho's world tour will never forget.'

Another disciple, Prem Maneesha, who was in the group that had travelled with Osho, expressed her sentiments.

'One feature of this time, this experience, was seeing that we as disciples wanted to protect Osho—understandably, as is only natural and human. But it created a dilemma—the wish to protect him, out of our love and concern, and the possibility of interfering in his work by doing so.

'He has said he is his work, he is only here for his work, so for his body to be preserved but he is unable to work (perhaps same dilemma Socrates foresaw when he was presented with that option) was meaningless. And he has always said never to act out of fear; and that would include, I expect, even fear on his behalf, for his welfare. On the other hand, who of us would promote or instigate any act or say anything that might expose him to danger?

'Hasya (Osho's secretary for international work) in Kathmandu had actually asked Osho not to talk on cow-slaughter or to attack Hinduism, for fear there would be repercussions. Her concern was that there was no country available for Osho to go to as an alternative should he upset the Nepalese authorities. Osho didn't say anything on that occasion ("Was I good?" he asked Hasya, mischievously afterwards) but did speak while we were in Kathmandu. He simply disregarded the consequences. It was more important to him to articulate his truth—whatever the cost.

'Then, and throughout the world tour, we were seeing in action a man who has nothing to lose. This was what struck me forcibly. He needed no one's favours, no one's support; he "needs" nothing because he has realised the ultimate. Even life, after his Enlightenment, ceased to have intrinsic meaning, it seems, because he was willing to risk that life to say what he knew to be true. This is hard for us to grasp—certainly difficult for people who are not lovers of, or in sympathy with someone like Osho. Because, all of us are always in need of each other for support, definition, validation.

'To understand that someone exists free of these needs is to first understand that one doesn't, and secondly that one can. So we actually have a certain resistance to understanding the phenomenon called Osho because even to understand him is to acknowledge our own psychological and spiritual poverty, and not too many of us want to do that.'

Excerpts from:

The Rebellious Spirit
Zen: The Quantum Leap From Mind to No-Mind
The Transmission of the Lamp

12

HE'S BACK

On 29 July 1986, after the whirlwind trip around the world, Osho reached Mumbai and put up in the house of a *sannyasin* as a personal guest. He appointed Ma Yoga Neelam as his secretary for India. Indian *sannyasins* soon got into motion and began looking for a house for him to stay. He did not want a commune anymore, but just a house where people could come and listen to him. Within a few days, his friends and lovers, from all over the world started thronging him again. While the search for a suitable place for him went on, the numbers swelled. But no house was good enough for him.

Due to family pressure, the host *sannyasin*, expressed his inability in keeping Osho as his guest any longer. It was time to move, again. The obvious choice was Pune where Osho had first gone in March 1974. Plans were made and the place was prepared to receive Osho. The authorities were also informed to avoid any problems in the journey, to be undertaken by car, and a police escort arranged for a Sunday morning. Suddenly, in the middle of the night Osho decided to leave.

Immediately preparations were made and the convoy set out in the dead of night, arriving in Pune just before dawn on 4 January 1987.

Osho had seen through the reality behind the authorities and their offer of safe passage. They were planning no such thing. In fact, when the police arrived at the house, in Mumbai, the next morning, they were furious to see that their man had already reached Pune. The Pune authorities were also furious: Their plan was to prevent Osho from entering the city. The police behaved in an un-called for manner. They barged into Osho's bedroom, forcibly, without any warrant and delivered an order which forbade him from entering the city or staying in it. Apparently, the cat-and-mouse game was still on. The Indian government refused visas to anyone who, they thought, wanted to visit Osho, while blatantly denying in the parliament their actions. And yet, thousands of visitors kept pouring in from India and abroad. The authorities in Pune did their best to curtail the inevitable expansion of the commune.

Regardless, the commune started to flower again. The whole area was cleaned up, a new Buddha Hall was built, expansion rolling— and Osho was talking again. As the front cover of *Asia Week* put it: He's Back!

Osho's work continued to grow with a great momentum. The Rajneesh International Meditation University now became the Osho Multiversity with ten faculties. It turned into the largest school of transformation, in the world, where thousands of people can scientifically and simultaneously be affected and touched. Through a number of innovative programs and training courses, each experience leads towards the same inner silence and peace that Osho calls meditation. And meditation *is* the means and the end for one's transformation.

Osho Multiversity is the gateway—an entire multiverse of gateways— Osho has devoted his life and teachings in making it available to humanity. Acoording to Osho, in the Mulitversity all kinds of spiritual dimensions that man has taken should be allowed. The function is to bring all climates and all flavours together, even if they are contradictory. It should be made clear that the Multiversity is not in any competition with any educational system. Hence it needs no recognition by any government. It is exploring that which no university is exploring. It explores all that which ordinary universities and educational systems don't provide.

The ten faculties of Osho Multiversity include: Centre for Transformation; School for Centering and Zen Martial Arts; School of Creative Arts; International Academy of Healing Arts; Institute for Love and Consciousness; Meditation Academy; School of Mysticism; Institute of Tibetan Pulsing Healing; Club Meditation; and Creative Leisure. The Institute for Consciousness in Organisations is a newly developed faculty.

Soon after its inception the commune became a Mecca for the arts. Leading musicians, poets, painters and dancers presented their art delighting thousands of visitors to the commune. World renowned artists included Shivkumar Sharma, Hari Prasad Chaurasia, Zakir Hussain, L. Subramaniam, Qiu Zheng Ping of Shanghai, Sonal Mansingh, Mallika Sarabhai, poet Neeraj and many others. These events recall an earlier era in Indian history when music, art and meditation were one.

Other changes were being implemented in the commune campus. Osho enigmatically asked for all the buildings on the campus be painted black with blue windows. When several huge pyramidal buildings are built of these colours, the effect is striking. Additional restaurants opened, supplied by food organically grown nearby. Osho Basho, a health facility, was planned for meditators to swim, play tennis, or volley ball or simply spend some relaxing time in a Jacuzzi.

A beautiful bookshop opened, full of Osho's books, audio and video cassettes on a wide a range of topics. But, perhaps the most touching was the plan Osho laid for the creation of a Zen garden, specifically for meditation, adjacent to the campus. Osho gave his vision of how he would like it to be landscaped—separate areas where people can sit and enjoy being alone, but which includes waves of earth so that at the same time meditators can get a sense of oneness to the whole creation.

That autumn, Osho added some final touches to this new phase of his work. He specified that maroon robes should be worn for all daytime activities in the commune. He explained that the maroon colour is helpful in keeping the working energy in the commune harmonious; that it is about an energy experience and has no religious implications. He stated clearly that robes are to be worn only inside the commune. He also introduced the 'White Robe Brotherhood'. At last, the silent communion between master and disciple that he had been talking about for so long could happen. It involved an initial period of intense dancing, followed by sitting silently while Osho conducted periods of Indian music interspersed with silence. After some time, Osho would stand, *namaste* everyone, and leave, being driven slowly around the periphery of Buddha Hall. This was followed by one of his discourses on video.

Osho was quite insistent about the importance of this evening event. He describes these moments as the peak of his disciples' day, often describing how the silence is now so deep and so tangible that anyone can enter and immediately be drawn to that depth. It is as if he is trying to ensure that his people realise that this is the key to their transformation. He says he would like his people all over the world to sit in meditation each evening at seven o'clock local time—a global White Robe Brotherhood.

In a sense, his whole life's work and experimentation was coming to a completion. His work on the individual has materialised through scores of meditation techniques he has designed so scientifically, including the Dynamic and Kundalini meditations. His work on making the meditative experience available to all is complete, with the thousands of hours of video discourses where that same combination of sound and silence is anyone's for the turn of a switch; for helping the transition from non-meditator to meditator. Osho also had given the world the meditative therapies, which create the ultimate bridge between therapy and meditation. The most famous, the Mystic Rose, he describes it as the most important meditation since Vipassana.

Osho was gently bringing about changes in his way of working on the people too. Whereas in the past he had talked of the path of love and the path of meditation, especially of active meditation, now he simply talked of witnessing. He devoted himself to Zen, and to demonstrating existentially that the Buddha is the witnessing consciousness. At one point he describes why Zen has so little to offer for so many centuries of effort. It is indeed the greatest effort to date as Osho describes it, but it failed. It failed because the Zen masters were saying the right thing in the wrong way.

Zen masters of the past were insisting that the disciple totally relax, and stay alert with no effort. But as Osho points out in his inimitable way, 'If it were possible for you to be alert with no effort you would already be alert with no effort.' It was this contradiction that brought about the collapse of Zen. Osho described how he was using his words and the gaps between the words—coming as they do from his silence—to create a milieu in which meditators *can* experience alertness with no effort. And this indeed is the very basis of Osho's vision of meditation in the marketplace, of Zorba the Buddha, of the enlightened man being the ordinary man.

In this period Osho created three new 'meditative therapies': Mystic Rose, No Mind, and Who Is In. These were aimed at helping the ordinary person move directly into meditation without the need of therapy. In fact, at one point back in Kathmandu he suddenly looked up and asked:

'How long are we going to go on doing therapy?...I have talked about the meditation, and a group of people have done it for twenty-one days, but all of you have not been participants...be a participant in this meditation called Mystic Rose. It has four steps. All are designed for a particular purpose: to bring out all the poison from your being that has been injected by every generation for centuries. Laughter is the first step. One of the great writers, Norman Cousins, has just now written of his life-long experiment: that if he laughs for twenty minutes without any reason, all his tensions disappear. His consciousness grows, the dust disappears.

'You will see it yourself; if you can laugh without any reason, you will

see something repressed within you...From your very childhood you have been told not to laugh, but to "Be serious!" You have to come out of that repressive conditioning.

'The second step is tears. Tears have been repressed even more deeply. It has been told to us that tears are a symptom of weakness—they are not. Tears can cleanse not only your eyes, but your heart too. They soften you. It is a biological strategy to keep you clean, to keep you unburdened. It is now a well known fact that less women go mad than men. And the reason has been found to be that women can cry and weep more easily than men. Even to the small child it is said, "Be a man, don't cry like a woman!"

'But if you look at the physiology of your body, you have the same glands full of tears whether you are man or woman. It has been found that less women commit suicide than men. And of course, no woman in history has been the cause of founding violent religions, wars, massacres. If the whole world can learn to cry and weep again it will be a tremendous transformation, a metamorphosis.

'The third step is silence. I have called it "The Watcher on the Hills". Become as silent as if you are alone on the top of a Himalayan peak, utterly silent and alone, just watching, listening...sensitive, but still. And the fourth step is let-go.'

His routine continued to remain almost the same. He ate his simple food, took his nap in the afternoon, gave discourses when his health permitted, and saw his secretary in the evening. He was always interested in looking at new books, magazines and newspapers that his disciples were now producing in greater numbers than ever before. He gave suggestions for the cover designs and titles reflecting his life-long love for beauty and aesthetics.

But soon Osho's failing health became an issue of great concern, amongst his people. To make him comfortable and feel better, an air-conditioned walkway was built so that he could spend some time in the greenery, he so loved, without the city air aggravating his asthma. While the original symptoms abated, a more sinister picture started to emerge. Immediately after being released from the jails in the

US, the main symptoms had been of hair loss, deep bone pain and gastroenterological problems. Now a more chronic problem started to bother him. He seemed much weaker than before and often complained of bone and joint pains, particularly in the right side of his body.

His absences from the evening discourses gradually increased as time passed by. Then, he was inflicted with a simple ear infection that resisted all the usual treatments and finally required surgery. At this point, his medical staff sent all the available information to London for diagnostic help. The opinion by experts in London confirmed that his symptoms were entirely consistent with thallium poisoning, although by this time all the traces will have gone, if indeed, as Osho maintained, it was administered during his stay in US custody.

The problems on the right side continued nagging him, with recurring eye symptoms, pains in the shoulder and down that arm. It had now spread to his jaw. In order to alleviate this pain, Osho had all the teeth on the lower, right side removed. His thyroid had stopped functioning for some time. This created a suspicion that perhaps the continued right-sided disability may have been due to radiation poisoning. Osho described how, during one strange night in a jail in Oklahoma, he was put in a cold cell without blanket or pillow and made to lie on a particular mattress, different from the other inmates. He had curled the end of the mattress over to make a pillow, perhaps placing the radioactive material between his right jaw and shoulder instead of on the right side of his head as may have been expected.

He continued to lose health, still he managed to proceed with his work and gave discourses on two of his favourite subjects, Khalil Gibran and Nietzsche. In addition, he answered questions from his listeners, gradually alerting them to the dire state of the world and the urgent need for personal transformation.

Although Osho had stopped meeting with the press, the press continued to be interested in his views on various issues—particularly, issues facing India. The editor of *The Illustrated Weekly of India*, called to see if he could send some questions for a cover story on Osho: *If*

I Ran India. The cover story appeared in the issue of 8-14 October 1989. The story was introduced in the following words:

'Some see him as one of our greatest living thinkers. Others, as a spiritual conman, offering the quick fix to his gullible flock. What no one can deny, however, is the magic of his appeal. The Pied Piper of Koregaon Park still attracts people from all over the world. Thousands who come all the way to listen to a man many of us in India dismiss offhand as just another religious prankster. For Rajneesh looks at life differently. He persuades you to look at life differently. To see things you have never seen them before.*

'…But what are Osho Rajneesh's thoughts on the issues that matter? Not to discuss matters of the spirit, but to find out what he felt about Indian politics.'*

Pritish Nandy elicited the seer's views on the key issues concerning the country today: corruption, communalism, education policy, Ram Janmabhoomi, the status of women, socialism, and of course, Doordarshan and the freedom of the press.

But Osho was more concerned with the growth of his people. He wanted to expose to them the weaknesses of it and remind them again how important personal growth has become. He primarily focussed on the following issues: disintegration of the world; environmental destruction as a further symptom of a sick world dominated by greed and utter abuse of power. Also, he saw Mikhail Gorbachev as a complete disaster who, was being manipulated by the US government and the media to destroy the USSR, without realising what was he destroying. Osho correctly predicted that Gorbachev would be given a Nobel Prize for the break up of the USSR, which would eventually invite hugely disruptive elements back into the Soviet Union with appalling results.

While the world was applauding Gorbachev, Osho's seemed to be the only voice of caution. He foresaw the return of all the old diseases, of religious manipulation and rivalry, of national and ethnic conflicts, of the end of Yugoslavia. He says he himself is no longer interested in the world, only in his people. Unless, what he calls a 'new man' is born, planet earth is headed for destruction, and only this new man can save it. It is from his people that this new man can come.

'We just have to make it clear to the world what the alternatives are, that these are the two alternatives. Your old world, your old ideologies have brought you to the climax where life cannot continue any more. We are not at all rooted in the past. We have only future, no past. You have only past and no future.

'We have to make it clear to them that what we are doing is creating a new man, because the old man has failed, utterly failed. All his efforts have led nowhere. And at least when you are dying, let us, give us a chance. At the most we may also be failures: that's the worst that can happen. But you will not be a loser anyway—you were going to die.

'So we have to make the whole world aware that we are proposing an alternative to the old rotten structure which is dying, every day dying, and coming closer to final death. Before it dies we can save the intelligent group of young people from this dying structure. If the old people are too old and cannot change, nothing to be worried about—they were going to die anyway—but the whole humanity should not die with them.

'If we can save only the youth around the world, that's enough. Just Adam and Eve created the whole world. If we can save the youth, we can re-populate the world with new beings, higher in every possible way, better in every possible way. And we will not commit the same mistakes that have been committed in the past.'

Just a year before he left his body, he suffered a series of severe chest pains which were diagnosed as a heart attack by a Pune cardiologist. It was the first indication that the effects of his incarceration in the US may be life threatening.

On 10 April 1989, he ended his discourse saying gently, but with powerful authority, 'Remember, you are a Buddha. *Sammasati.*' And as he stood up to leave, he felt a disconnection happening in his body which almost caused him to stumble. He slowly left the hall, hands folded in a humble *namaste*. No one realised the significance of these words. He would never speak publicly again.

A new larger bedroom that had been in process for two years was completed and he moved into it. But within two weeks, he suddenly wanted to move back to his earlier small bedroom. The new room was then used as a group room for the Mystic Rose. It later became clear that actually he saw the new bedroom as his *samadhi* all along. His health continued to deteriorate. He spent more and more time simply in his bed, seeing almost no one, getting up only for the evening discourse. When asked by a local news reporter how he is, he said he has only 'six months to go'. The reporter, however, didn't register the import of this comment.

I recall very vividly having his *darshan*, long after leaving Rajneeshpuram, late in 1985, meeting him alone in his breakfast room on 25 June 1989. Ma Deva Anando, ushered me to his room. I bowed down to him. I saw him sitting on a chair smiling very lovingly, very beautifully. His body looked fragile but luminous. I heard him say in a low voice: 'They destroyed my dream! They tried to destroy my body. I feel pain in my bones. My whole body is on fire! It will take nine years for the effect of poison to go away.'

He explained further that because *sannyasins* were harassed and denied visas, he had asked them not to wear orange clothes and to keep the *mala* inside. My heart ached hearing him talk about his tortured body. He inquired lovingly about myself and said: 'Good you came. There is no need to go anywhere. This is your home. You have much work to do of mine...' Overwhelmed with his love and compassion, I touched his feet in deep gratitude.

By October 1989, Osho was no longer strong enough to dance with his people. For years he had invited people to dance in joy and celebration, and had danced along with them. Now, he sent a message: his people will have to dance on their own, that they follow the music, not him. His body was becoming weaker day by day. He entered the White Robe Brotherhood, stood with his hands folded in *namaste*, while his lovers and friends gathered in the Buddha Hall joyfully waving their arms and swaying to the music. As the musicians brought the music to a crescendo, the hall exploded with the shout of 'Osho!' Then he turned a little further round the podium, to face more of his people, and the shout of 'Osho!' exploded again.

As Osho explains, 'Osho' is not even his name; it is just a healing sound. Some months before, he amazed everyone by the humorous way in which he disposed of all his old names. The first to go was Bhagwan. 'The joke is over', he declared. Then he dropped 'Shree Rajneesh'. He explained that his name, Osho, was derived from William James' word 'oceanic', meaning that which dissolves into the ocean. Oceanic describes the experience, he says, but what about the experiencer? For that the word Osho is used. Later, he came to find out that 'Osho' has also been used historically in the Far East meaning 'The Blessed One, on Whom the Sky Showers Flowers'. Thus, Osho had all his former names removed from everything. Just the healing sound of Osho remains, as if he is doing his best to write himself out of the incredible script that has been his time on earth.

Excerpts from:

This, This, A Thousand Times This
The Last Testament vol. 2

13

I LEAVE YOU MY DREAM

On 16 January 1990, Osho came out to sit with disciples, friends and lovers, for the entire duration of the evening meditation, for what was to be the last time. The following night, Amrito made an announcement in the Buddha Hall: 'From today, Osho is not going to be sitting with us. He will, however, come and *namaste* us as usual but will then leave immediately. He said to tell you that he will be continuing to meditate with us after he has left the hall. In addition, everyone is requested to stay for the entire evening.'

The next day, Osho was not even able to sit for the fifteen minutes of meditation music and silence. He entered the Buddha Hall; his *namaste* that evening was slow and deliberate but he tried to cover every inch of the hall. His body was obviously in a very fragile condition. He reached out to the wall for support as he left the podium. He stepped to one side and looked at the musicians with his hands folded in *namaste*, as if to say thank you and goodbye. As Osho was being guided gently back to his room, the meditation music and silence continued as usual.

The next morning, Osho's body was in such pain that it became very difficult for him to walk, and he was unable to come out to see his people that evening. However, he was in his room meditating with them, beginning at seven o'clock as usual. So the evening *darshan* took place without him.

By the morning of 19 January, Osho got up in the morning in even more pain, with his pulse weaker and irregular. A simple pace-making device would have had the remedy to the heart problem but he declined any specialised medical help. 'Existence decides its timing', he informed his staff.

Slowly, during the course of that day, his body weakened further. He talked of the work that was to be done. He said that he would like the commune to continue functioning the way it is, and expressed his satisfaction over the work going so well. And finally, he declared: 'I leave you my dream.' At five o'clock in the evening on 19 January 1990, Osho left his body.

His *sannyasins*, Osho's lovers and friends were gathered in the Buddha Hall, in the evening, for meditation and to see their beloved master. Amrito entered the hall, took the microphone, and in a voice cracked with tears shared the news.

The shock wave rippled amongst everyone waiting in Buddha Hall. The news spread like a wild fire via news media in India and around the world. It was announced that his people would gather in the hall while his body was placed for *darshan*, and then it will be taken to the cremation ground along the ghats of River Mula-Mutha.

Osho's body, draped in black velvet and flowers was brought to the Buddha Hall to rest on the podium for ten minutes. Then the body was carried to the ghats in a long procession of *sannyasins* singing and dancing. The route from the ashram to the ghat swelled with people. The police was there to control the traffic and help in managing the crowd. At ten o'clock in the night, Osho's younger brother, Vijay Bharti, put a torch to the funeral pyre. Many people remained at the ghats, singing, humming, in celebration and in silence, until the early hours of the morning

As Osho's funeral pyre continued to burn throughout the next day, preparations were made in Chuang Tzu Auditorium for his *samadhi*. There were tears, of course, but also a very strong realisation, a beautiful reminder that Osho was still with us. On Sunday morning, 21 January, his ashes were brought to the commune as *sannyasins* lined the way, showering rose petals, singing and celebrating. The ashes are now placed in the new *samadhi* in Chuang Tzu Auditorium, with a plaque that reads:

Osho—Never Born, Never Died. Only Visited This Planet Earth Between December 11, 1931 to January 19, 1990.

What happens when a Buddha, an enlightened master leaves the body? Does he die like every other being? How can we understand the phenomenon of death of an enlightened being such as Osho? He has already given us an insight into it.

'If you have come to know that, "I come alone, and I go alone," then there is no coming and going, because the soul is never born, never dies. Life is an eternal continuum. It continues. It never comes, never goes. This body may have been born, this body may die—but that life, the energy, the self, the soul, or whatsoever you call the consciousness that exists in this body, has never been born and will not die. That consciousness is continuous. There has never been any break in it.

'...A Buddha does not live in time, does not live in space. His body moves, we can see his body, but the body is not the Buddha. The Buddha is the consciousness that we cannot see. His body is born and dies; his consciousness is never born, never dies. But we cannot see that consciousness, and that consciousness is Buddha. This enlightened consciousness is the very root of our whole existence—and not only the root, but the flowering of it also. Time and space both exist in this consciousness, and this consciousness does not exist in time and space.

'If death was a reality, existence would be utterly absurd, existence would be mad. If Buddha dies, that means such beautiful music, such splendour, such grace, such beauty, such poetry, disappears from existence. Then the existence is very stupid. Then what is the point? Then how is growth possible? Then how is evolution possible?

'...No, Buddha cannot die. He is absorbed; he is absorbed by the whole. He continues. Now the continuity is bodiless, because he has become so expanded that no body can contain him except the body of the universe itself. He has become so oceanic that it is not possible to have small manifestations. Now he can exist only in essence. He can exist only as a fragrance, not as a flower. He cannot have a form, he can only exist as a formless intelligence of existence.'

A leading scholar of Sikh religion and history and renowned author and journalist, Khushwant Singh, expressed his sentiments, on Osho leaving his body, in these words:

'I was truly grieved to hear of the passing of Acharya Rajneesh. In my opinion...he was the most original thinker that India has produced: the most erudite, the most clear-headed and the most innovative. And, in addition, he had an inborn gift for words, spoken and written. We will not see the like of him for decades to come...It is impossible to do justice to this great man in a few words. I would exhort my readers to read his sermons now printed in hundreds of books. With the going of Rajneesh, India has lost one of the greatest sons. India's loss will be shared by all who have an open mind throughout the world.'[1]

Mentioning Osho as one of the 'ten people who have changed the destiny of India', Khushwant Singh added, 'Acharya Rajneesh: for liberating the minds of future generations from the shackles of religiosity and conformism. He was a deeply spiritual man who denounced all religions.'[2]

The former President of India, Gyani Zail Singh, paid his tribute to Osho as well.

'I consider Rajneesh to be a very learned person. I respect Rajneesh who *is one of the few Indian philosophers who has taken the world by storm. Other so-called gurus and swamis enjoy political patronage, they are embroiled in so many controversies like tax evasion and land grabbing, etc. Rajneesh was the only person who always paid his income tax and ran his ashram adhering to existing laws...Rajneesh was a class apart because he was a learned man.'[3]*

On January 11 1991, former Prime Minister of India, Chandra Shekhar, said in a public function in Delhi, 'Osho gave a vision, to this country and to the world, of which any people can be proud of. Osho has given us great strength. I bow down to his memory for giving us that strength.'

Well known columnist, M.V. Kamath, former editor of *Illustrated Weekly* said, 'I once said...that Osho was a *yuga purush*. *Yuga* should not be taken literally...What I meant to say was that Osho has contributed substantially to the wisdom and philosophical content of our times. Certainly, he stands out as one among the most outstanding thinkers of the century that is now slowly petering out...With Osho, words flow endlessly. Provocatively. Challengingly. In a hundred years more copies of Osho's works will have been printed than the *Bible* itself, till now the outstanding best-seller.'

The famous poetess of India, Amrita Pritam paid her tribute in the following words, 'There are some who happen to be geniuses in the fields of thought, art or science, and occasionally, the world honours them. But Rajneesh (Osho) is unique, totally exceptional. He is one whose very existence has honoured this world, has honoured this country.' Addressing the fellow members of Rajya Sabha (Upper House of India's Parliament), she said, 'He (Osho) has the best interests of India and of mankind at heart...He is one of the greatest men India has ever produced.'

Many in India now feel distressed when we recognise the fact that, in the context of what happened to Osho in the West, at no level— political, intellectual, or institutional—did anyone see the absurdity of remaining unassertive, apathetic and privy to what certainly was the most indefensible exhibition of taking the whole country and its age-old contribution to human consciousness for granted.

There is a growing realisation that India must show an independent understanding of its own people, its own place in the comity of nations, and the primary source of its values. Only through such an honest attempt will it be possible to recognise what an enormous contribution Osho has made in furthering the values of *Satyam, Shivam, Sunderam*—truth, goodness and beauty. The following words coming from Osho speak for themselves:

'Truth is not something that can become collective; it remains individual. The collective masses are not without reason so much afraid of a man of truth, because truth can never become collective; only lies can become collective. Even a single man of truth is enough to put fire to the whole forest of lies, because even thousands of lies cannot face a single statement of truth...

'I have said that I started my journey in the majority of one, and today I have to say to you that I will end my journey in the majority of one—for the simple reason that I cannot give you the truth. If through my devices you discover it, you also become a majority of one. But truth itself is so powerful that it is enough to give one man courage to stand against the whole world.'

It seems as if it is the beginning of something new. Suddenly, it is apparent how long he has been preparing his people. He said back in 1974 that he would be gradually withdrawing from them. Now, although not in the body, his presence is still very much there for anyone to experience. His refusal to have any medical intervention to allow him to stay in his body longer means that as far he was concerned, his work was done.

His people have all they will ever need to continue the search for truth. Osho, the ultimately contemporary man, is the first person in history to use modern technology to provide a taste of meditation, a taste of enlightenment without the physical presence of a master. No longer do the thirsty need to seek out those who may help them only to discover that they are being deceived. No longer do the thirsty need to seek outside at all. The final answer, the ultimate destination is, as it has always been, inside—within the individual. And now, for anyone who is interested, the door is permanently open!

Excerpts from:

No Water No Moon
Hsin Hsin Ming: The Book of Nothing
The Book of Wisdom vol. 1
Path of the Mystic

End notes:

1. *Sunday*, Calcutta, 28 January 1990
2. *Mid-Day*, Bombay, 14 July 1991
3. *The Daily*, 22 November 1992

POST SCRIPT

A Gathering of Friends*

We have gathered here to consider a few very significant matters.

I had no idea that what I am saying to individual people would some day also need to be made public. I had never thought about it. I talk to people according to my capacity and capability, about whatever feels blissful to me and whatever it seems may help them. But slowly, slowly on getting the opportunity to come into contact with hundreds and hundreds of people, I came to realise, I began to see, that I have my limitations; and no matter how much I may wish to, I cannot bring my words to all the people who are in need of them. And many people have a tremendous need of them. The whole country, the whole earth is extremely thirsty and in distress.

Even if we leave the rest of the planet aside, this country itself is in a spiritual crisis. All the old values have been shattered, respect and regard for all the old values have disappeared and no new values have been given birth to. Man is simply standing with no idea where to go or what to do. In such a situation it is natural that man's mind should become very restless very distressed and very unhappy.

---

* A discourse given by Osho on 23 December 1967, Lonavala

Each individual is carrying so much misery within himself, that if we were able to open his heart and look into it, we would be at a loss. The more people I have come in contact with, the more puzzled I have become to see that man is carrying within him exactly the opposite of what he appears to be from the outside. His smiles are false, his happiness is false and all his so-called rejoicings are also false. And an enormous hell, a deep darkness, much unhappiness and misery have accumulated in him.

There are ways to destroy this anguish, this pain. It is possible to be free of them. Man's life can become a life of heavenly peace and melody. And since I started to perceive this, I also felt that if we don't bring that which can take man's life towards peace, to those who are in need of it, we are in a way committing a crime. Knowingly or unknowingly we are committing sins of omission.

So I started to feel that it is necessary to take anything that can transform people's lives to the maximum number of people. But I have my limitations, my capabilities and capacities have limitations. Alone, no matter how much I run, no matter how many people I reach, no matter how extensive it may be, seeing the vastness of life all around, and this society with its deep anguishes, there is no way to deal with it all. If we drop some colour on the seashore, a small wave may become coloured, but it does not make any difference to the vast ocean. And the interesting thing is that the small wave which may become coloured, is in no time going to get lost in that great ocean and the colour too will disappear.

So we have gathered here to discuss how the colour of peace can be spread far and wide in this vast ocean of life. But along with this, I am also aware that a person who becomes interested in his own peace alone, can never become peaceful in the true sense, because to be interested only in oneself is one of the causes of disease. To be only self-centred is one of the fundamental reasons for disease. A person who becomes self-centred and is interested only in himself and is oblivious of everything else around him, is like someone who builds a beautiful house and does not want to bother with the piles of garbage surrounding the house. He may create a beautiful garden in his property without bothering that the garbage around the house is creating a stink all around his house. If the whole neighbourhood is dirty, his garden, his flowers and their fragrance will not mean much. That stink will enter into his house, and drown the fragrance of his flowers.

Man should not only be interested in himself, but also in his environment. A religious person is not only interested in himself, but also takes an interest in everything around him. I also feel that it is not enough to be only concerned with one's own peace: it is necessary to be concerned that the breeze of peace reaches all sentient beings to whom we are inter-related, with whom we are connected. This should also be of interest to us. And a person who becomes eager and thirsty to bring all of life around himself towards peace, will discover that he may or may not succeed in making others peaceful. but in the very effort he himself certainly becomes peaceful.

There is an anecdote in the life story of Buddha, perhaps it is a fictitious story but it is very beautiful. When Buddha attained nirvana, the ultimate liberation, he reached the door of *moksha*, salvation, and the gatekeeper opened the gate. But Buddha stood with his back towards it. So the gatekeeper asked, 'Why are you standing with your back towards *moksha*?' Buddha said, 'There are many people behind me, and until they all attain *moksha*, I will stop here and wait. I am not so hard, so cruel and violent that I can enter salvation alone. All the peace I have attained is simply saying to me, that I should be the last person to enter *moksha*, first all others should enter.'

It is a very beautiful story: the story goes that Buddha is still waiting at the gate of *moksha*, so that all others may enter first; he himself wants to enter last of all.

The heart of someone in whom such a feeling has risen, has already attained *moksha*, he need not enter any gate of *moksha*. For him, all notions of *moksha* become irrelevant. Only those people become peaceful in whose life a strong inspiration to spread peace all around starts functioning.

I feel that those friends who have become interested in this direction, should not remain only interested in themselves, but they should become interested in other people and their environment too. Because this interest may benefit others, and even if it does not, it will still be very meaningful for their ownselves; it will be helpful for them to enter deeply into great peace, and into great blissfulness, because one of the reasons for disease lies in becoming self-centred. And someone who spreads out from his centre to all those around him starts moving towards becoming peaceful. We have gathered here so that I can discuss with you in what ways the message of love, peace and compassion can be spread to as many people as possible. What methods can we find to make sure that the message reaches them? Is it possible? It is not to be propaganda, it is not to create a cult, it is not to create an organisation, or a group. We are not to create a centre which becomes powerful in itself, but we are to spread the message as widely as possible, without becoming a group, without becoming a cult, without becoming an organisation, without creating any centralised power. And this needs a great deal of contemplation.

If one wants to create a cult then there is not much need to think about it; if one is to create an organisation, there is not much need to think about it—everyone in the world knows how to create groups and organisations. Thousands of cults have already been created. We are not going to create another cult among all those cults. That is why it has to be thought through thoroughly, so that we do not create a cult or an organisation and yet we are able to share with everybody what we love and what feels blissful to us. We don't want to become propagandists and at the same time it may be possible to disseminate. Hence, it is a very delicate issue and it needs to be thought through very carefully and with great sensitivity. It is like walking on a tight rope. One option is not to disseminate at all, because there is the danger of becoming a cult. This means we simply do not spread the message at all to anybody. And the second alternative is that we spread the message, but end up creating a cult. That danger also exists.

We have to spread the message, but it is absolutely necessary to take care that a cult is not created. So it is a question of making the dissemination possible without propagandising, without becoming a cult, or an organisation; so that the necessary transmission, the vital message reaches maximum number of people. This is what you have been invited here to discuss. In the coming sessions, I will gradually tell you about the things I can see. And I will also expect you to think along these lines. I will say a few basic things to you so that you can think them over. The first thing is that our gathering of friends today is not as big as the message is. An organisation is not needed, only a gathering is needed. And the difference between an organisation and a gathering must be clearly understood. A gathering means that everybody is free, has come out of his own freedom and can leave of his own freedom. The meaning of a gathering is that everybody is equal, nobody is higher or lower, nobody is in any hierarchy, nobody is a follower, nobody is a leader. This is the meaning of a gathering. We have to create a gathering of friends, not an organisation in which there are authorities, hierarchies, higher and lower people. And an organisation has its own infrastructure, there is a hierarchy from the bottom to the top, there are rungs and positions, and along with it all comes politics. Because politics is bound to enter wherever there is status and position. Those who hold a position become scared that somebody may replace them. Those who do not hold a position become eager to reach a position. So the organisation has its own hazards.

In a gathering, each person has only come there out of his love. Except for love there are no other commandments which he has to follow; nor are there any oaths and pledges which he has to fulfill; nor are there any vows and precepts to which he commits himself. He has joined it only out of his love and individual freedom, and he can leave the moment he wants to do so. And even when he is part of the gathering, he is not bound by any dogma or ideology; even then he is free to have different opinions, to have his own thought, to follow his own thought, to follow his own wisdom. He is not there to be somebody's follower. So a gathering of friends, Jeevan Jagruti Kendra, may come into existence; we have to think along these lines.

Certainly, the rules by which a gathering of friends is formed, are different from the rules by which an organisation is formed.

The gathering of friends is totally what we may call an anarchic institution. An organisation is a well planned system bound by rules, principles and laws. I do not intend to bind people by laws, rules or principles, because I am fighting against these very things. Such organisations already exist all over the world; what is the point in creating one more of them. Certainly in an organisation, there is more efficiency, there cannot be that much efficiency in a gathering. But to have efficiency at the cost of freedom is an expensive bargain. Democracy is not as efficient as a dictatorship, but efficiency can be sacrificed, freedom cannot be sacrificed. A gathering of friends means that it is a voluntary get-together of free individuals. If there are to be some minor laws and systems within it, they will be below the individuals not above them. They will be functional, they cannot be the goal. We will be free to disrupt them at any moment. They should never be capable of disrupting us. The laws will be for us, not the other way around. It is important to keep this in mind.

Now, some friends think that there should be a charter. Certainly there should be a charter but not the way it would be for an organisation. It should be formed keeping in mind that it is for a gathering of friends. It will be very much functional; it will be utilitarian, and it will be outlined for this purpose, but there will be no insistence on clinging to it. It can be thrown and burnt at any moment. And it is important to bear in mind that howsoever valuable the charter may be, our individual friends are more valuable than it, because this charter has been formed for the sake of these friends; they have not gathered here for the sake of the charter. So, we have to create a gathering of friends where the value and dignity of each and every individual is preserved. Obviously, the greater the number of individuals, the more varied their way of thinking and understanding will be. The bigger the gathering of friends, naturally, the more dissimilarities there will be among them.

So, we should not attempt to create uniformity, otherwise an organisation starts coming into existence. And the more we try to create a uniformity, the more the individuality of the person, his dignity and his freedom begin to be destroyed. The concern is not for uniformity, but for the respect for all friends, even for their differing opinions. Because my whole vision is that free thinking may be born all over the country. So if the people who want to give birth to free thinking are themselves trapped within controlled thinking, then there will be danger. So, even towards me this gathering of friends should not show any special reverence. Towards me too, there should not be any feeling of reverence. Towards me too, there should be a rational approach and an intelligent approach. If what I say seems right to you, if it is to your liking, if it appears useful, only then you should communicate it to people. Do not commit the mistake of communicating to people what I say just because I have said it.

The gathering of friends is not to be centred around an individual either, because that person, I or anyone else, may become the centre of worship. We will neither have any worship, nor will we be anybody's followers, nor will we have any leader. Collectively, we are in love with a vision, a message, and it feels that if it reaches more people they will be benefitted; that is why we friends have gathered, wishing to bring this vision to people.

So first of all we will talk a little about organisations. We don't want to create an organisation, only a gathering of friends. And we will try to understand the subtle difference between the two. It will be the responsibility of every individual that he tries to save the gathering of friends from becoming an organisation. It is not in my hands alone. I can only say it, but it is not in my hands alone. And if we are not very alert then there is a danger that it may become an organisation. So it is necessary to be very alert. And it has to be a very conscious experiment, so that it does not become an organisation.

There are certain unknown ways in which a cult is formed; before we even become aware of it, a cult starts forming. So we have to be careful about that. And if we are aware beforehand then maybe we can manage things in such a way that this does not happen. This is one alternative. And the other possibility is that if we are afraid that it may become an organisation, or a cult, we don't do anything at all. That is the other danger, that if nothing is done, then the message that has to be spread, cannot be spread. Then it is left on my shoulders alone to run as much as I can to bring this message to the people. I will continue to do that anyway; it makes no difference to me. But the same message could reach many more people. The more friends cooperate, the farther it can reach, the more easily it can reach. And today science has developed so much technology that is modernising society, that we would be foolish not to make use of it. We would be making a mistake if we did not make use of it. For instance here, if I spoke without the use of a microphone it would be adequate. Then even if my voice did not reach you very clearly, it would still be adequate. When there are fewer people they can hear me, but if there were more people then my voice would not carry far enough. When we use a microphone, my voice can reach a long way. Today so much technology is available that if it is all made use of, one person can do more work in his lifetime than Buddha and Mahavira could have managed in twenty lives, had they wanted to.

Buddha and Mahavira were at a disadvantage. Making use of whatever means were available to them, the work they did was more than enough. But if someone was asked to work in the same way in present times, it would be sheer foolishness. Today a lot of technology is available, that can be made use of. And one person can do so much more work in one life, than he could manage even if he were to live for 400 years without modern technology. So we must make use of all of this technology. That too is important to think about. It is not possible for me to do it alone. For that many more friends are needed, many types of friends are needed. Someone can do manual labour, someone can use his intellect, someone can take care of the money, someone can help in some other way; whatever one's understanding, whatever one's disposition, one can help accordingly. It is also important to remember that the wider the variety of friends the better it is, because the more different types of people come, contributing in different ways, doing different types of work, offering different types of help, the richer the work becomes.

It often happens that friends within their own circles are afraid of strangers. They are afraid that once the stranger comes in he will cause all kinds of trouble. So it generally happens that whenever a group of friends gathers together somewhere, they make their circle and are then afraid of new friends joining them. The fear is that the newcomer may create a disturbance. And this fear is natural too. This protective feeling is not altogether bad. But twenty-five year old friends fearing one newcomer is a sign of great weakness. Instead their thinking should be that we twenty-five people will transform the newcomer, not that the newcomer will change us twenty-five people! And if we twenty-five are so weak that one newcomer can change us, then we should be changed; what harm is there in it? What is so bad about it?

It always happens that whenever any group gathers, it starts forming a circle. Then a distance is created between it and the people outside that circle. It happens unknowingly, no one does it consciously. These are natural traits of the mind.

If you go to some unknown village and you have a few friends with you, then perhaps you will not make any friends in that village. You will remain surrounded by the circle of those few friends and will not come out of it. In a situation where you found yourself unavoidably alone then it would be a different matter, you might have to make a friend. Otherwise you would not make a new friend.

So every group has the tendency to remain confined to itself; there is a tendency to become confined. And in being confined there is a sort of security; all is known, all is good, whatever we like the others like too; some stranger coming in might say new things and might disturb everything. We need to drop this fear. If the work is to become widespread and vast then this fear must be dropped. The emphasis should be on remaining so accommodating, keeping our hearts so spacious and open, our arms extended so far that we are able to assimilate even people of the most opposite nature. Not a single one must be left out. We must make space within ourselves even for one who is totally different from us and we must find out what skills he has that can be useful to us.

Connected with this, in the recent past in India, Mahatma Gandhi did a great experiment. He gathered together many people of different and even antagonistic views. Totally dissimilar people, people between whom no consensus of opinion could ever be achieved, came under the same umbrella and became instrumental in an epic undertaking.

Whenever someone thinks that people of different views, ideas and personalities should not included in a particular endeavour, then that endeavour cannot become great; it will remain very limited. It will remain like a small river thinking that, 'Not every river and rivulet coming from other distant places should join me; who knows what sort of mud and rubbish, what sort of substances and minerals they may bring with them, and how good or bad their water is?' If a river starts thinking along these lines then it will remain only a rivulet; it cannot become a great river, a Ganga. And if it is to become a Ganga, it will have to receive them all. So this capacity to receive everything needs to be there.

It is necessary to reflect on how to assimilate as many people as possible. We will have to create space. Slowly, slowly, we will have to see how we can provide people with the opportunity to join in, how we can find work for them and how to help them also to participate.

So many people all over the country come and say to me that they want to help in the work; so many people write me letters asking me what they can do to help in the work. It is your responsibility to make room for all these friends to contribute. And you completely drop and let go of the notion that there could be anyone who might not be useful for something. Such a person does not exist on the earth. What to say about people, even animals and birds become a help. Even their help becomes…

There is absolutely no one who is of no use—no person on this earth is useless.

So we need to look at how best to employ someone who is interested. If we concern ourselves with ideas about this man being like this and that man being like that, then it will be very difficult, you cannot imagine how much the work will be set back.

A man used to come to Gandhi's ashram. People complained that he was really immoral, that he was a drunkard, that he did this and he did that, Gandhi simply went on listening to all this. All the friends became very disturbed that Gandhi was not banning this man from coming to the ashram, on the contrary he went on bringing him closer, until finally once his fears had vanished, the man began to enter the ashram rather arrogantly.

One day some of Gandhi's closest people told him that the situation had gone too far; that day they had seen this man with their own eyes sitting in a bar; and it was absolutely disgraceful and defamatory that this man should be drinking wine there dressed in khadi, Gandhi style clothes, and that it was very unfortunate that such a man should come to the ashram; and that it would be a disgrace to the ashram.

And Gandhi said, 'For whom have I opened this ashram? For good people? Where will the bad people go, then? And those who are good, what need is there for them to come to the ashram? For what and for whom am I here in the first place? And the second thing is that you say that he is sitting there in the bar wearing khadi clothes, so what will people think? If I were to see him there I would hold him close to my heart. Because the first thought that would arise in my mind is, that it is amazing, it seems my words have started reaching the masses; even drinkers have started wearing khadi. You are seeing that someone wearing khadi is drinking wine; I would have seen that someone who drinks wine has started wearing khadi. And in such a case, the day is not too far away when this man may drop drinking wine. Transformation has begun in this man. He has shown courage; at least he wears khadi. Love has taken birth in his heart, transformation has begun in him.

'So, this man can be looked at from either side: that he is drinking wine while dressed in khadi; then your mind will want to throw him out of the ashram. But it can also be seen from the other side, that a man who is a drunkard is wearing khadi. Then you will feel like welcoming him into the ashram with a celebration.

'If this ashram is to expand and if it is to reach out to the masses, then you will have to take the second perspective not the first. Then whosoever comes close to us, will only be seen for the good in him and for the way in which he can be helpful. And I would also like to say to you that we are giving a great deal of incalculable and priceless energy and impetus towards being good to the man whom we start looking upon with love.'

If twenty good people start to accept a bad man as good, it becomes difficult for him to continue being bad. But when the whole world starts calling someone bad, it becomes easy for him to become or continue being bad. If someone is a thief and another man shows trust in him, as though he were not a thief, his ability to steal and the likelihood that he will steal weaken. Because there is no one anywhere who does not respect the good feelings of another heart.

If a thief were to come amongst us here and we were all able to just trust him, as though he were a good man, then he would not be able to steal here. It sounds against all common laws, but it becomes impossible. Because so many people placing respect and trust in him, would be so much more precious than to steal, that he could not reject it.

Each and every individual has the feeling to be good, but the problem is that nobody is ready to accept them. And when they meet someone who is ready to accept them as good, you can't imagine what wakes up and rises in them.

You may have heard the name of an American actress Greta Garbo. She was born in a poor family in a small country in Europe. And until the age of nineteen, she was working as an assistant in a barber's shop, for next to nothing. An American tourist whose beard she was lathering saw her face in the mirror and said, 'Very beautiful, your face is very beautiful.' Greta said to him, 'What are you talking about? I have been doing this job for six years, and no one has ever told me that I am beautiful. What are you talking about?! Am I really beautiful?!'

The American said, 'You are very beautiful. I have rarely seen so beautiful a woman.' And Greta Garbo has written in her autobiography, 'On that very day I became beautiful for the first time. One man called me beautiful. I myself was unaware of it. That day when I came back home and stood in front of the mirror, I realised that I had become an altogether different woman.'

This girl who was an assistant in a barber's shop until the age of nineteen, later proved to be America's greatest film actress. And she only had that American who for the first time had told her that she was beautiful to thank for it. She said that, 'If this man had not said those few words to me that day, I would probably have remained a barber's assistant my whole life. I had no idea at all that I am beautiful.' It is possible that he just said it very casually. It is possible that he was simply being polite. And it is possible that this man had not even been aware of what he was saying; it may just have been a passing comment. And he may not have even felt that a simple statement from him had given birth to an image of beauty in a woman, that something that had been asleep had somehow awakened in her.

It is necessary to awaken what is asleep in the people for whom you want to do something. Hence it is necessary to focus less on what they are and more on what they could be. If you have a big job to be done and without help you couldn't get any work done, and I told you to get so and so to help, you might say, but this man is bad, he is dishonest, he cannot be trusted.

It is okay that this man is bad or dishonest—who is not? And it is not a question of what he is, but rather of what he could be. If you are to get him to do any great work, you will have to give a call to that within him which he could become.

Kripalani used to work as a cook in Gandhi's ashram. An American journalist was staying in the ashram and he asked, 'This man who cooks your food seems to be J.B. Kripalani.' Kripalani was washing dishes, he said, 'This old man is amazing! In fact, I was only fit to be a cook and this man awakened in me something that is beyond description.'

The awakening can happen even in the most insignificant person. Once we give him a call, once we draw what is asleep in his soul nearer and we trust in him, once we give a call and create a challenge to what is asleep in him, much can come out of him. And you can demoralise even the greatest man. Even if you tell the greatest man that he is nothing, and if this is what he hears several times coming from everywhere, rest assured he will become nothing.

So if a spiritual revolution is to be carried out on a vast scale in this country—and it is absolutely necessary that it should happen—and if we can do no more than pave the way for it, that too is enough, because someone else will complete it. What difference does it make through whom it happens? The point is not that it has to happen only through us. No, if we can even pave the way for it so that later, some day, a revolution could pass down it, that is more than enough; the matter is already taken care of. So if it is to be done, a very comprehensive group has to be formed. An organisation can never be comprehensive. A group of friends can be very comprehensive, very extensive. Because within it there is an acceptance of diversity. No one is forced or controlled. Within the group everybody is free and nobody is being controlled. Because whenever an intelligent person starts to feel that he is being controlled, he becomes troubled by it. No intelligent person enjoys being in bondage.

People with an inferiority complex want to be controlled; only those who are full of inferiority would rather be in fetters; no one else is going to care for that. Hence the group has to be kept so open that when someone comes in he doesn't even feel that he came in somewhere, that he got tied down somewhere. He should feel free. Whether he comes in or goes out, it should not feel different to him, or that it has created any difference.

I would like such a group to happen, such a comprehensive group of friends to happen. Because the people who initially gather for a revolution are not aware of how big a revolution it is going to be. The companions of Lenin had no idea that what happened in 1917 would become such a universal phenomenon. Voltaire and his friends also had no idea what the French Revolution would bring. Gandhi and his friends also had no idea what would happen or would not happen. Christ couldn't have known at all what was beginning there...Christ just had eight friends and they too were not very educated people, just rustics; someone was a carpenter, someone was a cobbler, someone was a fisherman—not educated people. Christ had no way to even imagine that it would become such a widespread revolution, that one day half the world would recognise his message. He couldn't have even imagined it.

No one who first sows the seeds has ever imagined how big the trees will be. Had it been so, the work would have become inconceivably beautiful.

Meeting with more and more people across the country, I have begun to feel that this work could become an enormous banyan tree. Thousands of people could find shade under this tree. It could become such a huge spring that it could quench the thirst of millions. But this is not yet clear to those friends who are the first to gather here. If they can be aware of it, then perhaps they may begin to work in an organised fashion. Recently, I was reading a book on science. In Russia when they are building roads, they project how many people will be using these roads in 100 years time, and then build them accordingly. And then here we are, we also build roads in our country, but we don't even take into consideration how many people will be travelling on them in two years time. So, every two years the roads have to be dug up again to make them wider. And every five years we realise that the traffic has increased and that the roads are no longer adequate. Are we blind or what, that we can't even estimate how many people will be using the roads! These are amazing people who can project how many people there will be in a certain town after 100 years, and how many people will be using the roads after 100 years, and how wide the roads will need to be after 100 years, and then decide that it is better to build them accordingly now.

The work of those who have foresight becomes easy, and there are less recurring difficulties.

Right now the group of friends is small but in ten years time it could be bigger than you might possibly imagine. And we have to work with that in mind—the road has to be made wide enough to accommodate that possibility. In ten years time, unknown strangers will be walking down this road; you may not be here, I may not be here, none of us may be here, but someone will be walking on this road. So we must keep that in mind while we are working. And we should remember too that we are not precious, it is the path which we are creating and to which we dedicate our lives, that is precious. If it is large and wide enough, many people will be able to walk on it.

We need to consider these points in detail. I have just mentioned a few things around the issue which we will consider during the next days. And it is necessary to contemplate each of these points in detail to see what can be done about them. My understanding of the details is very limited. You have more understanding than I do about those things.

I can tell you some of the central points around which some thinking needs to be done. But I have almost no understanding of the details; how things are to be done, how many people will be required to do them, how much money will be needed, how much labour will be needed. All of this you probably know more than I do. How to give it a practical form and how far to take it, you certainly know about all that more than I do. I don't know even the ABC of it. That is why I thought that I would tell you my ideas and would also listen to your ideas. And between the two sets of ideas, in their merger, perhaps something will be possible. I can tell you some things about the sky but I don't know much about the things of the earth. And talks about the sky alone do not have much value. The roots have to go into the earth. They have to take water and nourishment from the earth. So I will talk about how a tree can spread across the sky, and how can it flower, but you will have to think a little about the roots. And remember, flowers are not as important as the roots are. Flowers depend on the roots.

So what roots can we provide this work with, so that this tree can grow? I will give my whole effort and energy to it whether it grows bigger or not—I am giving it. It is not work for me, it is my joy, my bliss. It doesn't make any difference whether I have companions or not, it will continue in the same way. But if there were companions, this work could become vast, and reach out to many people.

I have said some things to you about these few points. Now you give it some thought; to the details; what can be done; how can it be done? Give some thought to it with a very open mind and then we will discuss it here. All your opinions are invited tomorrow morning; express them, consider them, and then come to a decision.

The camp that I am doing here is a small camp. But then the idea will be to arrange a camp for all my friends from all over the country who have become interested in this work. This one is experimental, because fewer people will be able to come to a conclusion more easily. It may perhaps not be as easy with a large number of people.

So we should reflect and then we should again have a camp in which people from all over the country can gather. It is also necessary for them all to meet each other, it is necessary that they become acquainted with each other. They are doing the work in their areas. Your cooperation and encouragement are necessary for their work. They shouldn't feel alone there. They should feel that there are also more friends all over the country, that they are not standing all alone somewhere, that they have fellow travellers, and that if there was ever a need they would all be with them, to give advice, or if there was work to be done, they would come and help.

Recently, friends in Rajkot told me that they want to take my message to those cities and places where I have not yet been. And they want to create a base there so that I can go there.

It has become necessary. When I go to a new city, a few hundred or a few thousand people get to hear me. If some preparatory work could be done before-hand, 10,000 people, 50,000 people will be able to hear me.

Friends at different places come up with different suggestions. Their suggestions are very significant, very useful. All these friends can meet to consider the situation. This meeting will become the basis for that to happen. So right now I will not say anything more. From tomorrow morning we will begin to discuss the details. And bear in mind that you have not come here to listen to me. This is not a gathering for my discourses. I have talked as much as I have, so that you can also speak. I have not been giving a speech; it has been just to encourage you to think and discuss.

And the idea is that in these two days we come to some conclusions thinking and contemplating collectively, so that we can move ahead based on firm decisions, which will in turn get some work done.

THE DYNAMICS OF GURU-
SHISHYA RELATIONSHIP

Historically and sociologically, a guru has always held a very prominent
and an exalted place in the Hindu society. He is identified with the
Divine: *acharya devo bhava*. Almost every Hindu family has a family
guru who functions as a guide, a counsellor and a motivator. In the
eyes of the family, his status in the society is very high.

Broadly, we can see a guru in three different roles:

- **As a family guru:** He is also a scriptural authority, a head of a
  religious sect. One who conducts rituals, presides at auspicious
  occasions such as birth of a baby in the family, marriage and other
  celebrations.

- **As a formal teacher and an educator:** He teaches and imparts
  education in a school environment.

- **As a self-realised being who has seen:** A *seer*—one who *sees*
  the inter-interconnection between various things. He is the
  one who has *seen*, or *known* the truth. One who has resolved all
  contradictions of life and has attained equanimity, the supreme

state of consciousness—*samadhi*. Once having realised, he may become a recluse and disappear from the society enjoying freedom in a state of bliss. Or, if he chooses, he may remain in the society and help seekers in their spiritual growth. His very presence has a divinity, a charisma, which manifests compassion, love and benediction.

We shall look at the dynamics of guru-*shishya* relationship keeping in view the guru of this stature and a disciple as a seeker. First (although it is not possible to do justice to the description of a guru), we may look at its presence as follows:

- A guru is a phenomenon, not a person. He has no personality. A guru is an authentic being with his own individuality.

- A guru is beyond duality.

- He is not a thinker or a philosopher—he is a seer, *drashta*. He sees through an exalted state of consciousness.

- He does not teach; he shows as one can show the path to a traveller by sitting on a hill-top.

- He is neither a teacher nor a leader but a catalytic agent whose very presence, words and gestures can bring a transformation in an individual's life.

- He does not expect nor does fulfill anyone's expectation.

- A guru functions more as a physician—a healer *par excellence*. Buddha called himself a *vaidya*, a physician. A guru makes the diagnosis of our inner illness, gives a prognosis, and also a medicine (read meditation) to heal and regain the seeker's health.

- A guru is not a reformer, he is a transformer. A reformed person may again go back to one's weakness or commit sin, but a transformation is irreversible.

- If a guru chooses to remain in society then he treats the collective illness—the illness and insanity prevalent in society. In this respect, he functions as a rebel—non-compromising, unmasking, often shocking and seemingly crazy.

- Such a guru can be loved or hated but cannot be ignored. He cannot be comprehended through mind; mind cannot see the one who has transcended mind.

- An authentic guru—a *sadguru*, does not do miracles, though miracles happen around him.

- People come to him with all kinds of questions; a guru answers, but not to really give an 'answer', but rather to dissolve the whole question altogether. Thus he brings the questioner to a point where the person can begin the real quest, seeking, searching and not depend on a given or a readymade answer.

In their search for truth, guru engages seekers, disciples into a creative dialogue. Through the earnest and energetic process of a verbal and non-verbal exchange, a guru unravels the deepest mysteries of life and the universe around us. Remarkable examples of such dialogues are seen in the Upanishads between a guru and a disciple; in the dialogue between Lord Krishna and the great warrior Arjuna in the *Bhagavad Gita*; exchanges with Socrates by Plato and others; conversations between Gautam the Buddha and disciples; the famous dialogue between sage Ashtavakra and the King Janaka. In modern times, similar dialogues and conversations are seen with Swami Ramakrishna Paramhamsa, Maharshi Ramana, J. Krishnamurti, and Osho.

The contemporary enlightened mystic, Osho, gives the following perspective for understanding the place and role of a guru:

'The role of the guru is to give you a glimpse of the real—not a teaching, but an awakening. The guru is not a teacher: the guru is an awakener. He has not to give you doctrines. If he gives you doctrines, he is a philosopher. If he talks about the world as illusory and argues and proves that the world is illusory, if he discusses, debates, if he intellectually gives you a doctrine, he is not a guru, he is not a master.

He may be a teacher, a teacher of a particular doctrine, but he is not a master, not a guru.

'A guru is not a giver of doctrines. He is a giver of methods—of methods which can help you to come out of your sleep. That is why a guru is always a disturber of your dreams, and it is difficult to live with a guru. It is very easy to live with a teacher because he never disturbs you. Rather, he goes on increasing your accumulation of knowledge. He helps you to be more egoist, he makes you more knowledgeable. Your ego is more fulfilled. Now you know more, you can argue more. You can teach yourself, but a guru is always a disturber. He will disturb your dream and your sleep…'.

There is a Sufi saying: 'When the disciple is ready, the master arrives.' An earnest desire to grow and a sense of deep commitment are the hallmarks of one who aspires to be a disciple. When at the core of one's being a person comes to realise that he needs to seek a path for coming out of his unconscious and conditioned life, mysteriously a person appears to guide and show the way. There is a progressive evolution from the point when one begins to ask and enquire. There are three stages: the first is of a student, the second is of a disciple, the third is of a devotee. The student learns only intellectually, he relates only on the plane of intellect—but that is the beginning. If he can relate intellectually, he may find trust in the guru. Then he can relate emotionally; that makes him a disciple. And when he is able to relate emotionally, trusting the guru, the person turns into a devotee. A deep communion is established between the disciple and guru.

When he is a student, he sees guru as a teacher. When he becomes a disciple, he recognises guru as a master. Now a communion begins to take place; now at the emotional level a contact, a unique kind of love arises. The seeker is now on the path. The student is not aware that he is a student. He may think he is a disciple, he may think he is a devotee; but his functioning is absolutely unconscious. The student acts through logic. The disciple operates through love. The devotee moves through trust. Trust is the culmination of love. Osho explains: 'And the third and the highest state is that of a devotee. In that state the master and the disciple are no more separate: union happens—not only communion but union, a kind of unity. That has been our way in the East. The seeker comes as a student, falls in love with the master, becomes a disciple; and one day the love has matured, the master and the disciple have met, really met. In that meeting, the devotee is born. Then the master is no more a human being: the master is thought to be a God. That's why we have called Buddha 'Bhagwan'. It is not in the Christian sense of the word 'God'. It is in the sense that the devotee has come to a point where he can see that his master only lives in the body but is not the body. Now he can see the transcendental energy of the master. The master represents God on the earth. The master is a penetration of the beyond, of the unknown, into the known.'

Discipleship is basically that of attitude and gratitude. Guru shows the unconscious and the wounded state of a disciple; he unmasks the disciple so that the person may see the true, the original face as how the Zen Masters put it. Disciple's attitude is that of total receptivity and a deep gratitude towards the guru for showing the way, unraveling the mystery, and pointing at the truth.

There is actually no guru-disciple 'relationship' as it is between two individuals. One may say, it is a relationship of no relation; because, it is based on total freedom. The guru is, of course, a free person, but he keeps the disciple also free to be—to grow, to find, to seek. A relationship implies dependency. An authentic guru would never wish a disciple to be dependent on him. A guru's greatest joy is to see the disciple find his own path and move on—all alone. It is a path of the alone to the alone. There is only love from the disciple and grace from the guru.

Excerpts from:

Vigyan Bhairav Tantra vol. 1
Philosophia Perennis vol. 2

A Conversation with Ma Yoga Neelam

It was a bright sunny morning when I had an enjoyable free flowing conversation with Ma Yoga Neelam at the Osho Nisarga Foundation, Dharamshala, in the lap of the Himalayas. I have known her closely since 1988 and have immensely enjoyed working with her since then.

Ma Neelam is a founder member of Osho Nisarga Foundation. Since its inception, her inspirational, energetic and caring presence has made this place a paradise for Osho lovers and seekers from India and around the world. She presents meditation camps at Osho Nisarga and is also invited regularly to present meditation camps around the country.

Ma Neelam was initiated into *sannyas* by Osho on 17 October 1972 at a meditation camp in Mount Abu, Rajasthan. In December 1985, when Osho returned from the US and was in Manali, Himachal Pradesh, he said to her, 'You will be my personal secretary.' Later, after he came back to India from the world tour and stayed in Juhu, Mumbai, Neelam was also his caretaker for some time. She began working as his personal secretary in Pune since January 1987.

The following is an account of what Ma Neelam said during our conversation in which she, very lovingly and joyfully, shares the experiences of being with Osho and being an integral part of his work. I have placed his words in quotes as closely recalled by Ma Neelam.

The Conversation

During my work related meetings with Osho, I would ask how I should bring his message to what he called 'my people'. And he replied: 'You don't need to worry about how to take me to them. You just look after how to welcome them once they arrive here. Take care of the buildings and their renovation; make sure rooms and other facilities are available for the visitors.' He also added a significant observation by saying, 'Existence has some mysterious way. You should always take care of the roots the flowers will grow on their own.' So his guidance in essence was: 'Just look after the commune at the basic level, at the ground level. Invite friends to offer their programmes, therapy groups, presentations.' In all, I could see Osho's practical approach to the growth and expansion of his work.

He welcomed new ideas. For example, I had a vision of having a School of Creative Arts in one of the new buildings added to the campus. Osho liked the idea and made me Director of the School of Creative Arts.

I never had any experience whatsoever in any property expansion projects. But Osho gave clarity and direction to my thinking and ideas. He never bothered about the details. He just gave me general guidance and left it up to me to work out the details. Once the guidance was given he would never interfere. He trusted fully and gave a free hand to do the work. He gave a vast space for one to be creative and innovative. He was always happy with whatever work I did.

Osho was extremely particular about the upkeep and maintenance of the commune. He immensely emphasised that the kitchen be kept neat and clean, the quality of drinking water be checked regularly, and a high standard of hygienic conditions are maintained so that the visitors and seekers remain healthy and disease free. This way, I was made responsible for an overall commune care. Occasionally, I would say to him that, 'Sometimes I don't know exactly how to do and manage this work.' And he would say: 'Good! I will guide you. You need not worry.' The overall approach was not of making a uniform facility available to one and all. Rather, my entire effort was in making available whatever was required according to need and comfort for the individual.

As Osho's secretary, one of the areas of my work was public relations. Explaining nature of this work, he says: 'Present your self as my secretary. And do this work as a play, don't take it too seriously. Just relax and do the work playfully. Connect with local citizens of Pune and invite them to our festivals and cultural programmes. My doors are open to artists, the press, and local friends of the commune.'

It was an enjoyable experience inviting world renowned artists and having them perform in the Buddha Hall. The artists came very happily though they were not paid any money for their performance. As Osho explained, the artists carry a dream to find a place where they come across a wonderful diversity of a receptive national and international audience. This is that place. They share their art we share our meditation, silence, love, peace and appreciation.

At one point Osho said, 'Remove the "sex guru" label, it has served its purpose.' The way to do this was to invite the press, invite poets, writers, artists so that they may see our meditations, our creativity, the peace and love that surround this commune. Osho appointed Swami Anand Tathagat as the ashram in charge. He was of immense help in managing graceful public relations meetings, visits, and programmes effectively. I was equally supported by you (Swami Satya Vedant), Chancellor, Osho Multiversity and Swami Chaitanya Keerti, the Osho Commune Press in charge.

As a personal secretary to Osho, I also received significant guidance from him in the areas of publication, distribution and promotion.

I was to promote *Rajneesh Times Fortnightly Newsletter* which carried

Osho's discourses and the news of commune activities. Publishing his books was a great creative challenge which I enjoyed immensely. He himself took a personal interest in looking into all its details—the cover, the design, the paper and the layout. He did not allow any tempering with his words; no changes were to be made to the content which was transcribed from the audio discourses. He explained to me that his words were not meant to give any information; rather, they were for the purpose of our inner growth and transformation.

Much attention was paid to his photographs on the cover of the book. I worked intensely to make sure that his selected photographs were clear and with clear expression. His eyes, in particular, were a powerful means to connect the seeker deep in the heart—the emptiness and the luminous power coming through his eyes made an immediate impact. Once he said, 'My picture on published books will do its own work.'

Osho's guidance on the distribution and promotion of his books was equally helpful; it was entirely a new experience for me. Osho's book exhibitions were presented in different cities around India. Osho Meditation Centres would plan and organise the exhibition. One or two *sannyasins* were sent to represent the Osho commune and provide necessary help to make the exhibition a success. Public relations was again an integral part of such exhibitions. Prominent individuals outstanding in their respective fields were invited to either inaugurate the exhibition or as chief guests.

Osho believed that besides meditation centres, information centres be created in various cities. Such centres would provide information about the commune and its activities, meditation, Osho's books and audio-video discourses. As for Osho meditation centres are concerned, Osho encouraged to start such a centre even in one's home—even if just about ten people could be accommodated if not more. He encouraged having more than one meditation centre in a city. He didn't mind if such centres came up even within a distance of five to ten kilometres. The basic purpose of these centres, of course, was to make Dynamic Meditation available in the morning before one leaves for work. And then later in the evening after returning from work one may be in Kundalini Meditation, listen to Osho's discourse, and then go home.

The work started growing in India and more and more meditation camps were needed in various cities. So I helped organise Osho Meditation Camps. Swami Anand Swavbhav was appointed by Osho as his *Dharmadoot* (ambassador) for leading these camps. Osho's guidance was to organise these meditation camps not too distant from their homes or at remote places so that people could travel easily and attend these camps.

Sometimes it was brought to my attention that some people would not use his name in association with the meditation conducted by them. When I would make this known to him he would discourage me from making it an issue. He would ask me to send the right information to such people based on his guidance and leave it at that. For him the very fact a meditation was being presented held more importance. But he was very particular that a *sannyasin* must use his name with the meditation. For him that meant the individual is courageous enough to stand by him and his name. The name worked more as a device for the *sannyasin* to stay firm in his commitment.

I would also like to mention here that he never discouraged anyone from making use of his name—even if it were used in connection with naming a shop or a business. I find this of much significance because such a big copyright issue has been made in the last few years as regards using 'Osho' and the meditations designed by him. I find this issue totally contrary to Osho's vision, his work and his guidance.

It raises several questions, such as: should there be copyrights of Osho's words? Is it not better for over six billion people of this earth to have direct access to his discourses and meditation techniques without fetters or any restrictions or permission from any authority anywhere? What can be the risks if all his books are in the free domain? Are his books protected against editing and distortion if there are copyrights owned by some Foundation? Will there be then more publication of his books? Does knowledge of any kind flourish and grow more when it is controlled?

For me, it raises a fundamental issues of significance of freedom over control. One needs to know, what is Osho's insight on control of his movement and how did he want his movement to grow? What is his message to his *sannyasins*? Let me quote here excerpts from one of my recent letters made available to *sannyasins* and the public at large dealing with this issue. As I have mentioned in this letter:

'Osho devised many meditation techniques in late sixties and early seventies. Never in his lifetime did he express his wish to trademark the meditations, as he always felt that the meditations are a gift of the Awakened Ones and are meant to raise the consciousness of humanity. He openly proclaimed this in one of his discourses in the Buddha Hall: "Things can be copyrighted, thoughts cannot be copyrighted, and certainly meditation cannot be copyrighted. They are not things of the marketplace. Nobody can monopolise anything. But perhaps the West cannot understand the difference between an objective commodity and an inner experience."'

When asked how to protect the purity of his meditations, he gave a very simple solution: 'Make my meditations as widely available as possible so that millions of people come to know them directly. That's the only positive way; otherwise you will be wasting time and money in fighting with people.' This was a very clear guideline and this was his wish.

As for sharing what changes came in my life being with Osho and working under his guidance I would say many instances and situations contributed to change. But here, just for example, while at the Ranch (Rajneeshpuram), we worked almost twelve hours a day and often I would get tired. While doing my work my mind would wander around, missing family, people I was with and would feel divided, split inside me. I brought this to Osho's attention. Very gently and lovingly, he says, 'When you work totally you get energy from the work itself. But when you get divided or split you feel tired. For example, when moping, be with the mop totally. Be total, be one with the work and you will feel energised.' This insight, this guidance, completely changed my life. I simply crossed over my habits, my limitations, my patterns. He says: 'Be total with work.' And this has become a sutra for me ever since.

While listening to his discourse, for example, often ideas would come to my mind or I would suddenly remember certain details in the work I had missed, or anything that had nothing to do with my being present in the discourse. So I thought in my mind, wouldn't it be a good idea if I kept a little notebook with me and start jotting down all that while being in the discourse. Because otherwise by the time the discourse was over I would forget what I remembered. So I asked Osho if I could scribble notes while listening to his discourse. Again, in his gentle and loving voice he said: 'When with me be relaxed. Only a relaxed mind will bring back all those things you want to scribble as notes.' And then he gave me an incredible insight, I would say a kind of meditation. He said: 'When such ideas come to you, just tell the idea to come back for example at ten o'clock at night. The idea will certainly come at that time and then you write it down.' This insight worked like a magic! In all these years since then, in different situations, I have followed the trick and it has worked without fail.

With a grateful heart, I concluded our conversation and with a loving hug we departed for lunch.

THE INNER CIRCLE AND THE PRESIDIUM

Having returned from his world tour and after having spent six months in Mumbai, Osho settled down in Pune. However, being a pragmatist and fully aware of how the work needs to grow, he created a totally new set up, in December 1989, where no one person would have a total control of the operational side of management. He eliminated the very possibility of monopolising authority and power in one hand. Also, he clearly applied the concept of Meritocracy to make sure the management gets contribution from individuals of merit, expertise and background.

Osho created two functional entities: first, the Inner Circle of twenty-one *sannyasins* for looking after the day-to-day operation of the Osho Commune International; secondly, the Presidium, a small group of *sannyasins* to look after the expansion and growth of his work internationally. He made it clear though that in both cases, the function was important and not the person. Each person was responsible to simply make a meaningful contribution and the decision arrived at needed to be unanimous. It needed to be a collective decision with a collective responsibility. The two bodies were not supposed to go into any philosophical discussion; that, Osho said, he had already done it sufficiently. They were required to see only the practical application and management of Osho's vision and work.

The twenty-one original members of the Inner Circle appointed by Osho:

- Swami Amrito
- Swami Amitabh
- Ma Anasha
- Ma Anando
- Ma Avirbhava
- Swami Chiten
- Ma Garimo
- Ma Hasya
- Jayantibhai(Swami Satya Bodhisatva)
- Swami Jayesh
- Ma Kavisha
- Ma Mukta
- Ma Neelam
- Ma Nirvano
- Swami Plotinus
- Swami Prasad
- Swami Satya Vedant
- Swami Tathagat
- Ma Turiya
- Swami Yogi
- Ma Zareen

OSHO'S LIFE AT A GLANCE

1931-53 Early Years

December 11,1931: Osho is born in Kuchwada, a small village in the state of Madhya Pradesh, central India.

March 21, 1953: Osho becomes enlightened at the age of twenty-one, while majoring in philosophy at D.N. Jain College in Jabalpur.

1953-56 Education

1956: Osho receives his MA from the University of Saugar with first class honours in philosophy.

He is the All-India Debating Champion and Gold Medal winner in his graduating class.

1957-66: University professor and public speaker

1957: Osho is appointed as a professor at the Sanskrit College in Raipur.

1958: He is appointed professor of philosophy at the University of Jabalpur, where he taught till 1966.

A powerful and passionate debater, he also travels widely in India, speaking to large audiences and challenging orthodox religious leaders in public debates.

1966: After nine years of teaching, he leaves the university to devote himself entirely to the raising of human consciousness. Four times a year he conducts intense ten-day meditation camps.

1969-74 Mumbai

Late 1960s: His Hindi talks become available in English translations.

1970: On 14 April he introduces his revolutionary meditation technique, Dynamic Meditation.

In July, he moves to Mumbai, where he lives until 1974.

Osho—at this time called Bhagwan Shree Rajneesh—begins to initiate seekers into Neo-*Sannyas* or discipleship, a path of commitment to self-exploration and meditation which does not involve renouncing the world or anything else. He continues to conduct meditation camps at Mount Abu in Rajasthan but stops accepting invitations to speak throughout the country. He devotes his energies entirely to the rapidly expanding group of *sannyasins* around him.

At this time, the first Westerners begin to arrive and are initiated into Neo-*Sannyas*. Among them are leading psychotherapists from the human potential movement in Europe and the US, seeking the next step in their own inner growth. With Osho they experience new, original meditation techniques for contemporary man, synthesising the wisdom of the East with the science of the West.

1974-81 Shree Rajneesh Ashram Pune

During these seven years he gives a ninety-minutes discourse nearly every morning, alternating every month between Hindi and English. His discourses offer insights into all the major spiritual paths, including Yoga, Zen, Taoism, Tantra and Sufism. He also speaks on Gautam Buddha, Jesus, Lao Tzu, and other mystics. These discourses have been collected into over 600 volumes and translated into fifty languages.

In the evenings, during these years, he answers questions on personal matters such as love, jealousy, meditation. These *darshans* are compiled in sixty-four *Darshan Diaries* of which forty are published.

The commune that arose around Osho at this time offers a wide variety of therapy groups which combine Eastern meditation techniques with Western psychotherapy. Therapists from all over the world are attracted and by 1980 amongst the international community gains a reputation as 'the world's finest growth and therapy center.' Almost 1,00,000 people pass through its gates each year.

1981: He develops a degenerative back condition. In March 1981, after giving daily discourses for nearly fifteen years, Osho begins a three-year period of self-imposed public silence. In view of the possible need for emergency surgery, and on the recommendation of his personal doctors, he travels to the US. The same year, his American disciples purchase a 64,000 acre ranch in Oregon and invite him to visit. He eventually agrees to stay in the US.

1981-85 Rajneeshpuram

A model agricultural commune rises from the ruins of the central Oregonian high desert. Thousands of overgrazed and economically unviable acres are reclaimed. The city of Rajneeshpuram is incorporated and eventually provides services to 5,000 residents. Annual summer festivals are held which draw 15,000 visitors from all over the world. Very quickly, Rajneeshpuram becomes the largest spiritual community ever pioneered in the US.

October 1984: Osho ends three and one half years of self-imposed silence.

July 1985: He resumes his public discourses each morning to thousands of seekers gathered in a two-acre meditation hall.

September-October 1985: The end of Rajneeshpuram in Oregon.

September 14: Osho's personal secretary Ma Anand Sheela and several members of the commune's management suddenly leave. Osho invites law enforcement officials to investigate Sheela's crimes. The authorities, however, see the investigation as a golden opportunity to destroy the commune entirely.

October 28: Without warrants, federal and local officials arrest at gun point Osho and others in Charlotte, North Carolina. While the others are released, he is held without bail for twelve days. A five-hour return plane trip to Oregon takes four days. Subsequent events indicate that he was poisoned with thallium while in jail.

November: Fearing for his life and the well-being of *sannyasins* in volatile Oregon, attorneys agree to an Alford Plea on two out of thirty-five of the original charges against him. According to the rules of the plea, the defendant maintains innocence while saying that the prosecution could have convicted him. Osho and his attorneys maintain his innocence in the court. He is fined $400,000 and is deported from the US.

It becomes apparent that the federal and state governments were intent on destroying Rajneeshpuram.

1985-86 World Tour

January-February: He travels to Kathmandu, Nepal and speaks twice daily for the next two months. In February, the Nepalese government refuses visas for his visitors and closest attendants. He leaves Nepal and embarks on a world tour.

February-March: At his first stop, Greece, he is granted a thirty-day tourist visa. But after only eighteen days, on March 5, Greek police forcibly break into the house where he is staying, arrest him at gun point, and deport him. Greek media reports indicate government and church pressure provoked the police intervention.

During the following two weeks he visits or asks permission to visit seventeen countries in Europe and the Americas. All of these countries either refuse to grant him a visitor's visa, or revoke his visa upon his arrival and force him to leave. Some refuse even landing permission for his plane.

March-June: On March 19 he travels to Uruguay. Osho is ordered to leave Uruguay on June 18.

June-July: During the next month he is deported from both Jamaica and Portugal. In all, twenty-one countries denied him entry or deported him after arrival. On July 29 1986, he returns to Mumbai, India.

1987-89 Osho Commune International

January 1987: He returns to the ashram in Pune, India.

July 1988: Osho begins, for the first time in fourteen years, to personally lead the meditation at the end of each evening's discourse. He also introduces a revolutionary new meditation technique called Mystic Rose.

January-February 1989: He stops using the name Bhagwan, retaining only the name Rajneesh. However, his disciples ask to call him 'Osho' and he accepts this form of address. Osho explains that his name is derived from William James' word 'oceanic' which means dissolving into the ocean. Oceanic describes the experience, he says, but what about the experiencer? For that we use the word 'Osho'. At the same time, he came to find out that 'Osho' has also been used historically in the Far East, meaning 'The Blessed One, on Whom the Sky Showers Flowers'.

March-June 1989: Osho is recovering from the effects of the poisoning, which by now are strongly influencing his health.

July 1989: His health is getting better and he makes two appearances for silent *darshans* during the Festival, now renamed Osho Full Moon Celebration.

August 1989: Osho begins to make daily appearances in the Buddha

Hall for evening *darshan*. He inaugurates a special group of white-robed *sannyasins* called the White Robe Brotherhood. All *sannyasins* and non-*sannyasins* attending the evening *darshans* are asked to wear white robes.

September 1989: Osho drops the name Rajneesh, signifying his complete discontinuity from the past. He is known simply as 'Osho', and the ashram is renamed 'Osho Commune International'.

1990 Osho Leaves his Body

January 1990: During the second week in January, Osho's body becomes noticeably weaker. On January 18, he is so physically weak that he is unable to come to the Buddha Hall. On January 19, his pulse becomes irregular. When his doctor inquires whether they should prepare for cardiac resuscitation, Osho says, 'No, just let me go. Existence decides its timing.' He leaves his body at five o'clock in the evening. Two days later, his ashes are brought to Osho Commune International and placed in his *samadhi* in Chuang Tzu Auditorium with the inscription:

OSHO: Never Born Never Died Only Visited This Planet Earth Between 11 December 1931 - 19 January 1990.

Recommended Reading*

Appleton, Sue. *Was Bhagwan Shree Rajneesh Poisoned by Ronald Reagan's America?* The Rebel Publishing House. 1986.

Appleton, Sue. *Bhagwan Shree Rajneesh: The Most Dangerous Man Since Jesus Christ.* The Rebel Publishing House. 1987.

Braun, Kirk. *Rajneeshpuram: The Unwelcome Society.* Scout Creek Press. 1984.

Forman, Juliet. *Bhagwan: The Buddha For The Future.* The Rebel Publishing House. 1987.

Forman, Juliet. *Bhagwan: Twelve Days That Shook The World.* The Rebel Publishing House. 1989.

Jyoti, Ma Dharm. *One Hundred Tales from Ten Thousand Buddhas.* Diamond Pocket Books. 1988.

Meredith, George (Dr). *Bhagwan: The Most Godless Yet The Most Godly Man.* The Rebel Publishing House. 1988.

Murphy, Dell. *The Rajneesh Story: The Bhagwan's Garden.* Linwood Press. 1993.

Shay, Ted. *Rajneeshpuram and the Abuse of Power.* Scout Creek Press. 1985.

Shunyo, Ma Prem. *My Diamond Days With Osho: The New Diamond Sutra.* Full Circle Publishing Ltd. Publishing House. 2000.

Thompson, Judith and Paul Heelas. *The Way of the Heart: The Rajneesh Movement.* Aquarian Press. 1986.

---

* For a comprehensive list of Osho's works, please visit www.osho.com